SKELMERSD

D0298285

FICTION RESERVE STOCK

LL 60

TELEMPATH

Spider Robinson

MACDONALD and JANE'S · LONDON

02678056

ISBN 0 354 04257 2

First published in Great Britain in 1978 by
Macdonald and Jane's Publishers Limited
Paulton House, 8 Shepherdess Walk, London N.1.

Printed and bound in Great Britain by
REDWOOD BURN LIMITED
Trowbridge & Esher

This book is dedicated
to CHARLES and EVELYN for the
heredity and environment,
to JEANNE and LUANNA for the patience,
and to the BEARDEN BULLDOGS for the sawbuck.

Winds out on the ocean
Blowin' wherever they choose.
The winds ain't got no emotion, babe:
They don't know the blues.
                    —*James Taylor*

Telempath

Chapter One

Excerpt from the Journal of Isham Stone

I hadn't meant to shoot the cat.

I hadn't meant to shoot anything, for that matter—the pistol at my hip was strictly defensive armament at the moment. But my adrenals were on overtime and my peripheral vision was straining to meet itself behind my head—when something appeared before me with no warning at all my subconscious sentries opted for the Best Defense. I was down and rolling before I knew I'd fired, through a doorway I hadn't known was there.

I fetched up with a heart-stopping crash against the foot of a staircase just inside the door. The impact dislodged something on the first-floor landing; it rolled heavily down the steps and sprawled across me: the upper portion of a skeleton, largely intact from the sixth vertebra up. As I lurched in horror to my feet, long-dead muscle and cartilage crumbled at last, and random bones skittered across the dusty floor. Three inches above my left elbow, someone was playing a drum-roll with knives.

Cautiously I hooked an eye around the doorframe, at about knee-level. The smashed remains of what had recently been a grey and white Persian tom lay against a shattered fire hydrant whose faded red surface was spattered with brighter red and less appealing colors. Overworked imagination produced the odor of singed meat.

I'm as much cat-people as the One-Sleeved Mandarin, and three shocks in quick succession, in the condition I was in, were enough to override all the iron discipline of Collaci's training. Eyes stinging, I stumbled out onto the sidewalk, uttered an unspellable sound, and pumped three slugs into a wrecked '82 Buick lying on its right side across the street.

I was pretty badly rattled—only the third slug hit the exposed gas tank. But it was magnesium, not lead: the car went up with a very satisfactory roar and the prettiest fireball you ever saw. The left rear wheel was blown high in the air; it soared gracefully over my head, bounced off a fourth-floor fire escape and came down flat and hard an inch behind me. Concrete buckled.

When my ears had stopped ringing and my eyes uncrossed, I became aware that I was rigid as a statue. *So much for catharsis,* I thought vaguely, and relaxed with an effort that hurt all over.

The cat was still dead.

I saw almost at once why he startled me so badly. The tobacconist's display window from which he had leaped was completely shattered, so my subconscious sentries had incorrectly tagged it as one of the rare unbroken ones. Therefore, they reasoned, the hurtling object must be in fact emerging from the open door just beyond the window. Anything coming out a doorway that high from the ground just had to be a Musky, and my hand is *much* quicker than my eye.

Now that my eye had caught up, of course, I realized that I couldn't possibly track a Musky by eye. Which was exactly why I'd been keyed up enough to waste irreplaceable ammo and give away my position in the first place. Carlson had certainly made life complicated for me. I hoped I could manage to kill him slowly.

This was no consolation to the cat. I looked down at my Musky-gun, and found myself thinking of the day I got it, just three months past. The first Musky-gun I had ever owned myself, *mine* for as long as it took me to kill Carlson. After my father had presented it to me publicly, and formally charged me with the avenging of the human race, the friends and neighbors—and dark-eyed Alia—had scurried safely inside for the ceremonial banquet. But my father took me aside. We walked in silence past fields of growing corn to Mama's grave, and in the distance the setting sun over the

Mountain looked like a knothole in the wall of Hell. Dad turned to me at last, pride and paternal concern fighting for control of his ebony features, and said, "Isham . . . Isham, I wasn't much older than you when I got my first gun. That was long ago and far away, in a place called Montgomery—things were different then. But some things never change." He tugged an earlobe reflectively, and continued, "Phil Collaci has taught you well, but sometimes he'd rather shoot first and ask directions later. Isham, you just can't go blazing away indiscriminately. Not *ever*. You hear me?"

The crackling of the fire around the ruined Buick brought me back to the present. Damn, you called it again, Dad, I thought as I shivered there on the sidewalk. You *can't* go blazing away indiscriminately.

Not even here in New York City.

It was getting late, and my left arm ached abominably where Grey Brother had marked me—I reminded myself sharply that I was here on business. I had no wish to pass a night in any city, let alone this one, so I continued on up the street, examining every building I passed with extreme care. If Carlson had ears, he now knew someone was in New York, and he might figure out why. I was on his home territory—every alleyway and manhole was a potential ambush.

There were stores and shops of every conceivable kind, commerce more fragmented and specialized than I had ever seen before. Some shops dealt only in a *single item.* Some I could make no sense of at all. What the hell is an "rko"?

I kept to the sidewalk where I could. I told myself I was being foolish, that I was no less conspicuous to Carlson or a Musky than if I'd stood on second base at the legendary Shea Stadium, and that the street held no surprise tomcats. But I kept to the sidewalk where I could. I remember Mama—a *long* time ago—telling me not to go in the street or the monsters would get me.

They got her.

Twice I was forced off the curb, once by a subway entrance and once by a supermarket. Dad had seen to it that I had the best plugs Fresh Start had to offer, but they weren't *that* good. Both times I hurried back to the sidewalk and was thoroughly disgusted with my pulse rate. But I never looked over my shoulder. Collaci says there's no sense being scared when it can't help you—and the fiasco with the cat proved him right.

It was early afternoon, and the same sunshine that was warming the forests and dorms and work-zones of Fresh Start my home seemed to chill the air here, accentuating the barren emptiness of the ruined city. Silence and desolation were all around me as I walked, bleached bones and crumbling brick. Carlson had been efficient, all right; nearly as efficient as the atomic bomb folks used to be so scared of once. It seemed as though I were in some immense devil's autoclave, that ignored filth and grime but grimly scrubbed out life of any kind.

Wishful thinking, I decided, and shook my head to banish the fantasy. If the city had been truly lifeless, I'd be approaching Carlson from uptown—I would never have had to detour as far south as the Lincoln Tunnel, and my left arm would not have ached so terribly. Grey Brother is extremely touchy about his territorial rights.

I decided to replace the makeshift dressing over the torn biceps. I didn't like the drumming insistence of the pain: it kept me awake but interfered with my concentration. I ducked into the nearest store that looked defensible and found myself sprawled on the floor behind an overturned table, wishing mightily that it weren't so flimsy.

Something had moved.

Then I rose sheepishly to my feet, holstering my heater and rapping my subconscious sentries sharply across the knuckles for the second time in half an hour. My own face looked back at me from the grimy mirror that ran along one whole wall, curly black hair in tangles, wide lips stretched back in what looked just like a grin. It wasn't a grin. I hadn't realized how bad I looked.

Dad has told me a lot about Civilization, before the Exodus, but I don't suppose I'll ever understand it. A glance around this room raised more questions than it answered. On my left, opposite the long mirror, were a series of smaller mirrors that paralleled it for three-quarters of its length, with odd-looking chairs before them. Something like armchairs made of metal, padded where necessary, with levers to raise and lower them. On my right, below the longer mirror, were a lot of smaller, much plainer wooden chairs, in a tight row broken occasionally by strange frameworks from which lengths of rotting fabric dangled. I could only surmise that this was some sort of arcane narcissist's paradise, where men of large ego would come, remove their clothing, recline in luxuriously upholstered seats, and contemplate their own magnificence. The smaller, shabbier seats, too low to afford a decent view, no doubt represented the cut-rate or second-class accommodations.

But what was the significance of the cabinets between the larger chairs and the wall, laden with bottles and plastic containers and heathen appliances? And why were all the skeletons in the room huddled together in the middle of the floor, as though their last seconds of life had been spent frantically fighting over something?

Something gleamed in the bone heap, and I saw what the poor bastards had died fighting for, and knew what kind of place this had been. The contested prize was a straight razor.

My father had spent eighteen of my twenty years telling me why I ought to hate Wendell Carlson, and in the past few days I'd acquired nearly as many reasons of my own. I intended to put them in Carlson's obituary.

A wave of weariness passed over me. I moved to one of the big chairs, pressed gingerly down on the seat to make sure no cunning mechanism awaited my mass to trigger it (Collaci's training again—if Teach' ever gets to Heaven, he'll check it for booby traps), took off my rucksack and sat down. As I unrolled the bandage around my arm I glanced at myself in the mirror and froze, struck with wonder. An infinite series of *me*s stretched out into eternity, endless thousands of Isham Stones caught in that frozen second of time that holds endless thousands of possible futures, on the point of some unimaginable cusp. I knew it was simply the opposed mirrors, the one before me slightly askew, and could have predicted the phenomenon had I thought about it—but I was not expecting it and had never seen anything like it in my life. All at once I was enormously tempted to sit back, light a joint from the first-aid kit in my rucksack, and meditate awhile. I wondered what Alia was doing right now, right at this moment.

Hell, I could kill Carlson at twilight, and sleep in his bed—or hole up here and get him tomorrow, or the next day. When I was feeling better.

Then I saw the first image in line. Me. A black man just doesn't bruise spectacularly, as a rule, but there was something colorful over my right eye that would do until a bruise came along. I was filthy, I needed a shave, and the long slash running from my left eye to my upper lip looked angry. My black turtleneck was torn in three places that I could see, dirty where it wasn't torn, and blood-stained where it wasn't dirty. It might be a long time before I felt any better than I did right now.

Then I looked down at what was underneath the gauze I'd just peeled off, saw the black streaks on the chocolate brown of my arm, and the temptation to set a spell vanished like an overheated Musky.

I looked closer, and began whistling "Good Morning, Heartache" very softly through my teeth. I had no more neo-sulfa, damned little bandage for that matter, and it looked like I should save what analgesics I had to smoke on the way home. The best thing I could do for myself was to finish up in the city and get gone, find a Healer before my arm rotted.

And all at once that was fine with me. I remembered the two sacred duties that had brought me to New York; one to my father and my people, and one to myself. I had nearly died proving to my satisfaction that the latter was impossible; the other would keep me no great long time. New York and I were, as Bierce would say, incompossible.

One way or another, it would all be over soon.

I carefully rebandaged the gangrenous arm, hoisted the rucksack and went back outside, popping a foodtab and a very small dosage of speed as I walked. There's no point in bringing real food to New York—you can't taste it anyway and it masses so damned much.

The sun was perceptibly lower in the sky—the day was in catabolism. I shifted my shoulders to settle the pack and continued on up the street, my eyes straining to decipher faded signs.

Two blocks up I found a shop that had specialized in psychedelics. A '79 Ford shared the display window with several smashed hookahs and a narghile or two. I paused there, sorely tempted again. A load of pipes and papers would be worth a good bit at home; Techno and Argo alike would pay dearly for fine-tooled smoking goods—more evidence that, as Dad is always saying, technology's usefulness has outlasted it.

But that reminded me of my mission again, and I shook my head savagely to drive away the daydreaming that sought to delay me. I was—what was that phrase Dad had used at my arming ceremony?—"The Hand of Man Incarnate," that was it, the product of two years' personal combat training and eighteen years of racial hatred. After I finished the job I could rummage around in crumbling deathtraps for hash pipes and roach clips—my last detour had nearly killed me, miles to the north.

But I'd *had* to try. I was only two at the time of the Exodus, too young to retain much but a confused impression of universal terror, of random horror and awful revulsion everywhere. But I remember one incident very clearly. I remember my brother Israfel, all of eight years old, kneeling down in the middle of 116th Street and methodically smashing his head against the pavement. Long after Izzy's eight-year-old brains had splashed the concrete, his little body continued to slam the shattered skull down again and again in a literally mindless spasm of escape. I saw this over my mother's shoulder as she ran, screaming her fear, through the chaotically twisting nightmare that for as long as she could remember had been only a quietly throbbing nightmare; as she ran through Harlem.

Once when I was twelve I watched a farmer slaughter a chicken, and when the headless carcass got up and ran about I heard my mother's scream again. It was coming from my throat. Dad tells me I was unconscious for four days and woke up screaming.

Even here, even downtown, where the bones sprawled everywhere were those of strangers, I was wound up tight enough to burst, and ancient reflex fought with modern wisdom as I felt the irrational impulse to lift my head and cast about for an enemy's scent. I had failed to recover Izzy's small bones; Grey Brother, who had always lived in Harlem, now ruled it, and sharp indeed were his teeth. I had managed to hold off the chittering pack with incendiaries until I reached the Hudson, and they would not cross the bridge to pursue me. And so I lived—at least until gangrene got me.

And the only thing between me and Fresh Start was Carlson. I saw again in my mind's eye the familiar Carlson Poster, the first thing my father ran off when he got access to a mimeograph machine: a remarkably detailed sketch of thin, academic features surrounded by a mass of greying hair, with the legend, "WANTED: FOR THE MURDER OF HUMAN CIVILIZATION—WENDELL MORGAN CARLSON. An unlimited lifetime supply of hot-shot shells will be given to anyone bringing the above head to the Council of Fresh Start."

No one ever took Dad up on it—at least, no one who survived to collect. And so it looked like it was up to me to settle the score for a shattered era and a planetful of corpses. The speed was taking hold now; I felt an exalted sense of density, and a fever to be about it. I was the duly chosen instrument for mankind's revenge, and that reckoning was long overdue.

I unclipped one of the remaining incendiary grenades from my belt—it comforted me to hold that much raw power in my hand—and kept on walking uptown, feeling infinitely more than twenty years old. And as I stalked my prey through concrete canyons and brownstone foothills, I found myself thinking of his crime, of the twisted motives that had produced this barren jungle and countless hundreds like it. I remembered my father's eyewitness account of Carlson's actions, repeated so many times during my youth that I could almost recite it verbatim, heard again the Genesis of the world I knew from its first historian—my father, Jacob Stone. Yes, *that* Stone, the one man Carlson never expected to survive, to shout across a smashed planet the name of its unknown assassin. Jacob Stone, who first cried the name that became a curse, a blasphemy and a scream of rage in the throats of all humankind. Jacob Stone, who named our betrayer: Wendell Morgan Carlson!

And as I reviewed that grim story, I kept my hand near the rifle with which I hoped to write its happy ending. . . .

Chapter Two

Excerpts from I Worked with Carlson, *by Jacob Stone, Ph.D., authorized version: Fresh Start Press 1986 (mimeo)*

. . . The sense of smell is a curious phenomenon, oddly resistant to measurement or rigorous analysis. Each life form on Earth appears to have as much of it as they need to survive, plus a little. The natural human sense of smell, for instance, was always more efficient than most people realized, so much so that in the 1880s the delightfully eccentric Sir Francis Galton had actually succeeded, by associating numbers with certain scents, in *training himself to add and subtract by smell,* apparently just for the intellectual exercise.

But through a sort of neurological suppressor circuit of which next to nothing is known, most people contrived to ignore all but the most pleasing or disturbing of the messages their noses brought them, perhaps by way of reaction to a changing world in which a finely tuned olfactory apparatus became a nuisance rather than a survival aid. The level of sensitivity which a wolf requires to find food would be a hindrance to a civilized human packed into a city of his fellows.

By 1982, Professor Wendell Morgan Carlson had raised olfactometry to the level of a precise science. In the course of testing the theories of Beck and Miles, Carlson almost absentmindedly perfected the classic "blast-injection" technique of measuring differential sensitivity in olfaction, *without regard for the subjective impressions of the test subject.* This not only refined his data, but also enabled him to work with lifeforms other than human, a singular advantage when one considers how much of the human brain is terra incognita.

His first subsequent experiments indicated that the average wolf utilized his sense of smell on the order of a thousand times more efficiently than a human. Carlson perceived that wolves lived in a world of scents, as rich and intricate as our human worlds of sight and word. To his surprise, however, he discovered that the *potential* sensitivity of the human olfactory apparatus far outstripped that of any known species.

This intrigued him. . . .

. . . Wendell Morgan Carlson, the greatest biochemist Columbia—and perhaps the world—had ever seen, was living proof of the truism that a genius can be a damned fool outside his own specialty.

Genius he unquestionably was; it was *not* serendipity that brought him the Nobel Prize for isolating a cure for the entire spectrum of virus infections called "the common cold." Rather it was the sort of inspired accident that comes only to those brilliant enough to perceive it, fanatic seekers like Pasteur.

But Pasteur was a boor and a braggart who frittered away valuable time in childish feuds with men unfit to wash out his test tubes. Genius is seldom a good character reference.

Carlson was a left-wing radical.

Worse, he was the type of radical who dreams of romantic exploits in a celluloid underground: grim-eyed rebels planting homemade bombs, assassinating the bloated oppressors in their very strongholds and (although he certainly knew what hydrogen sulfide was) escaping through the city sewers.

It never occurred to him that it takes a very special kind of man to be a guerrilla. He was convinced that the moral indignation he had acquired at Washington in '71 (during his undergraduate days) would see him through hardship and privation, and he would have been horrified if someone had pointed out to him that Che Guevara seldom had access to toilet paper. Never having experienced hunger, he thought it a glamorous state. He lived a compartmentalized life, and his wild talent for biochemistry had the thickest walls: only within them was he capable of logic or true intuition. He had spent a disastrous adolescent year in a seminary, enlisted as a "storm trooper of Mary," and had come out of it apostate but still saddled with a relentless need to Serve A Cause—and it chanced that the cry in 1982 was, once again, "Revolution Now!"

He left the cloistered halls of Columbia in July of that year, and applied to the smaller branch—the so-called "Action-Faction"—of the New Weathermen for a position as assassin. Fortunately he was taken for crazy and thrown out. The African Liberation Front were somewhat less discerning—they broke his leg in three places. In the Emergency Room of Jacobi Hospital, Carlson came to the conclusion that the trouble with Serving A Cause was that it involved associating with unperceptive and dangerously unpredictable people. What he needed was a One-Man Cause.

And then, at the age of thirty-two, his emotions noticed his intellect for the first time.

When the two parts of him came together, they achieved critical mass—and that was a sad day for the world. I myself bear part of the blame for that coming together—unwittingly I provided one of the final sparks, put forward an idea which sent Carlson on the most dangerous intuitive leap of his life. My own feelings of guilt for this will plague me to my dying day—and yet it might have been anyone. Or no one.

Fresh from a three-year stint doing biowar research for the Defense Department, I was a very minor colleague of Carlson's, but quickly found myself becoming a close friend. Frankly I was flattered that a man of his stature would speak to me, and I suspect Carlson was overjoyed to find a black man who would treat him as an equal.

But for reasons which are very difficult to explain to anyone who did not live through that period—and which need no explanation for those who did—I was reluctant to discuss the A.L.F. with a honky, however "enlightened." And so when I went to visit Carlson in Jacobi Hospital and the conversation turned to the self-defeating nature of uncontrollable rage, I attempted to distract the patient with a hasty change of subject.

"The Movement's turning rancid, Jake," Carlson had just muttered, and an excellent digression occurred to me.

"Wendell," I said heedlessly, "do you realize that you personally are in a position to make this a better world?"

His eyes lit up. "How's that?"

"You are probably the world's greatest authority on olfactometry and the human olfactory apparatus—among other things—right?"

"As far as there is one, I suppose so. What of it?" He shifted uneasily within his traction-gear: wearing his radical *persona*, he was made uncomfortable by reference to his scientist mode. He felt it had little to do with the Realities of Life—like nightsticks and grand juries.

"Has it ever occurred to you," I persisted to my everlasting regret, "that nearly all the undesirable by-products of twentieth-century living—Technological Man's most unlovable aspects—quite literally *stink?* The whole *world's* going rancid, Wendell, not just the Movement: automobiles, factory pollution, crowded cities—Wendell, why couldn't you develop a selective suppressant for the sense of smell—controlled anosmia? Oh, I know a snort of formaldehyde will do the trick, and having your adenoids removed sometimes works. But a man oughtn't to have to give up the smell of frying bacon just to survive in New York. And you know we're reaching that pass—in the past few years it hasn't been necessary to leave the city and return to be aware of how evil it smells. The natural suppressor-mechanism in the brain—whatever it is—has gone about as far as it can go. Why don't you devise a small-spectrum filter to aid it? It would be welcomed by sanitation workers, engineers—why, it would be a godsend to the man on the street!"

Carlson was mildly interested. Such an anosmic filter would be both a mordant political statement and a genuine boon to mankind. He had been vaguely pleased by the success of his cold cure, and I believe he sincerely wished to make the world a happier place—however perverted his methods tended to be. We discussed the idea at some length, and I left.

Had Carlson not been bored silly in the hospital, he would never have rented a television set. It was extremely unfortunate that the "Late Show" (ed. note: a television show of the period) that evening featured the film version of Alistair Maclean's *The Satan Bug.* Watching this absurd production, Carlson was intellectually repelled by the notion that a virus could be isolated so hellishly virulent that "a teaspoon of it would sweep the earth of life in a few days."

But it gave him a wild idea—a fancy, a fantasy, and a tasty one.

He checked with me by phone the next day, very casually, and I assured him from my experiences with advances in virus-vectoring that Maclean had *not* been whistling in the dark. In fact, I told him, modern so-called "bacterial warfare" made the Satan Bug look like child's play. Carlson thanked me and changed the subject.

On his release from the hospital, he came to my office and asked me to work with him for a full year, to the exclusion of all else, on a project whose nature he was reluctant to discuss. "Why do you need me?" I asked, puzzled.

"Because," he finally told me, "you know how to make a Satan Bug. I intend to make a God Bug. And you can help me."

"Huh?"

"Listen, Jake," he said with that delightful informality of his, "I've licked the common cold—and there are still herds of people with the sniffles. All I could think of to do with the cure was to turn it over to the pharmaceuticals people, and I did all I could to make sure they didn't milk it, but there are still suffering folks who can't afford the damned stuff. Well, there's no need for that. Jake, a cold will kill someone sufficiently weakened by hunger—I can't help the hunger, but I could eliminate colds from the planet in forty-eight hours . . . with your help."

"A benevolent virus-vector. . . ." I was flabbergasted, as much by the notion of decommercializing medicine as by the specific nostrum involved.

"It'd be a lot of work," Carlson went on. "In its present form, my stuff isn't compatible with such a delivery system—I simply wasn't thinking along those lines. But I'll bet it could be made so, with your help. Those pharmaceuticals goniffs have made me rich enough to pay you twice what Columbia does, and we're both due for sabbatical anyway. What do you say?"

I thought it over, but not enough. The notion of collaborating with a Nobel Prize winner was simply too tempting. "All right, Wendell."

. . . We set up operations in Carlson's laboratory-home on Long Island, he in the basement and myself on the main floor. There we worked like men possessed for the better part of a year, cherishing private dreams and slaughtering guinea pigs by the tens of thousands. Carlson was a stern if somewhat slapdash taskmaster, and as our work progressed he began looking over my shoulder, learning my field while discouraging inquiries about his own progress. I assumed that he simply knew his field too well to converse intelligently about it with anyone but himself. And yet he absorbed all my own expertise with fluid rapidity, until eventually it seemed that he knew as much about virology as I did myself. One day he disappeared with no explanation, and returned a week or two later with what seemed to me a more nasal voice.

And near the end of the year there came a day when he called me on the telephone. I was spending the weekend, as always, with my wife and two sons in Harlem. Christmas was approaching, and Barbara and I were discussing the relative merits of plastic and natural trees when the phone rang. I was not at all surprised to hear Carlson's reedy voice, so reminiscent of an oboe lately—the only wonder was that he called during conventional waking hours.

"Jake," he began without preamble, "I haven't the time or inclination to argue, so shut up and listen, right? Right. I advise and strongly urge you to take your family and leave New York *at once*—steal a car if you have to, or hijack a Greyhound (ed. note: a public transportation conveyance) for all of me, but be at least twenty miles away by midnight."

"But—"

". . . head north if you want my advice, and for God's sake stay away from all cities, towns, and people in any number. If you possibly can, get upwind of all nearby industry, and bring along all the formaldehyde you can—a gun too, if you own one. Good-bye, my friend, and remember I do this for the greater good of mankind. I don't know if you'll understand that, but I hope so."

24

"Wendell, what in the name of *God* are you—?" I was talking to a dead phone.

Barbara was beside me, a worried look on her face, my son Isham in her arms. "What is it, Jacob?"

"I'm not sure," I said unsteadily, "but I think Wendell has come unhinged. I must go to him. Stay with the children; I'll be back as quickly as I can. And Barbara—"

"Yes?"

"I know this sounds insane, but pack a bag and be ready to leave town *at once* if I call and tell you to."

"Leave town? Without you?"

"Yes, just that. Leave New York and never return. I'm virtually certain you won't have to, but it's just possible that Wendell knows what he's talking about. If he does, I'll meet you at the cabin by the lake, as soon as I can." I put off her questions then and left, heading for Long Island.

When I reached Carlson's home in Old Westbury I let myself in with my key and made my way toward his laboratory. But I found him upstairs in mine, perched on a stool, gazing intently at a flask in his right hand. Its interior swirled, changing color as I watched.

Carlson looked up. "You're a damned fool, Jake," he said quietly before I could speak. "I gave you a chance."

"Wendell, what on earth is this all about? My wife is scared half to—"

"Remember that controlled-anosmia you told me about when I was in the hospital?" he went on conversationally. "You said the trouble with the world is that it stinks, right?"

I stared at him, vaguely recalling my words.

"Well," he said, "I've got a solution."

And Carlson told me what he held in his hand. A single word.

I snapped, just completely snapped. I charged him, clawing wildly for his throat, and he struck me with his left hand, his faceted ring giving me the scar I bear to this day, knocking me unconscious. When I came to my senses I was alone, alone with a helpless guilt that careened yammering through the halls of my reason and a terror that clutched at my bowels. A note lay on the floor beside me, in Wendell's sprawling hand, telling me that I had—by my watch—another hour's grace. At once I ran to the phone and wasted ten minutes trying to call Barbara. I could not get through—trunk failure, the operator said. Gibbering, I took all the formaldehyde I could find in both labs and a self-contained breathing rig from Carlson's, stepped out into the streetlit night and set about stealing a car.

It took me twenty minutes—not bad for a first attempt but still cutting it fine. I barely made it to Manhattan, with superb traffic conditions to help me, before the highway became a butcher shop.

At precisely nine o'clock, Wendell Morgan Carlson stood on the roof of Columbia's enormous Butler Library, held high in the air by fake Greek columns and centuries of human thought, gazing north across a quadrangle within which grass and trees had nearly given up trying to grow, toward the vast domed Lowe Library and beyond toward the ghetto in which my wife and children were waiting, oblivious. In his hands he held the flask I had failed to wrest from him, and within it were approximately two teaspoons of an infinitely refined and concentrated virus culture. It was the end result of our year's work, and it duplicated what the military had spent years and billions to obtain: a strain of virus that could blanket the globe in about forty-eight hours. There was no antidote for it, no vaccine, no defense of any kind for virtually all of humanity. It was diabolical, immoral and quite efficient. On the other hand, it was not lethal.

Not, that is, in and of itself. But Carlson had concluded, like so many before him, that a few million lives was an acceptable price for saving the world, and so at 9:00 P.M. on December 17, 1984, he leaned over the parapet of Butler Hall and dropped his flask six long stories to the concrete below. It shattered on impact and sprayed its contents into what dismal breeze still blew through the campus.

Carlson had said one word to me that afternoon, and the word was "Hyperosmia."

Within forty-eight hours every man, woman and child left alive on earth possessed a sense of smell approximately a hundred times more efficient than that of any wolf that ever howled.

During those forty-eight hours, a little less than a fifth of

26

the planet's population perished, by whatever means they could devise, and every city in the world spilled its remaining life into the surrounding countryside. The ancient smell-suppressing system of the human brain collapsed under unbearable demand, overloaded and burned out in an instant.

The great complex behemoth called Modern Civilization ground to a halt in a little less than two days. In the last hours, those pitiably few city-dwellers on the far side of the globe who were rigorous enough of thought to heed and believe the brief bewildered death-cries of the great mass media strove valiantly—and hopelessly—to effect emergency measures. The wiser attempted, as I had, to deaden their senses of smell with things like formaldehyde, but there is a limit to the amount of formaldehyde that even desperate men can lay hands on in a day or less, and its effects are generally temporary. Others with less vision opted for airtight environments if they could get them, and there they soon died, either by asphyxiation when their air supply ran out, or by suicide when, fervently hoping they had outlived the virus, they cracked their airlocks at last. It was discovered that human technology had produced no commonly available nose-plug worth a damn, nor any air-purification system capable of filtering out Carlson's virus. Mankind failed utterly to check the effects of the ghastly Hyperosmic Plague, and the Exodus began. . . .

. . . I don't believe Carlson rejoiced over the carnage that ensued, though a strict Malthusian might have considered it as a long-overdue pruning. But it is easy to understand why he thought it was necessary, to visualize the "better world" for which he spent so many lives: Cities fallen to ruin. Automobiles rotting where they stood. Heavy industry gone to join the dinosaurs. The synthetic-food industry utterly undone. Perfume what it had always been best—a memory—as well as tobacco. A wave of cleanliness sweeping the globe, and public flatulence at last a criminal offense, punishable by death. Secaucus, New Jersey abandoned to the buzzards. The back-to-nature communalists achieving their apotheosis, helping to feed and instruct bewildered urban survivors (projected catch-phrase: "If you don't like hippies, next time you're hungry, call a cop."). The impetus of desperation forcing new developments in production of power by sun, wind and water rather than inefficient combustion of more precious resources. The long-delayed perfection of plumbing. And a profoundly interesting and far-reaching change in human mating customs as feigned interest or disinterest became unviable pretenses. (As any wolf could have told us, the scent of desire can be neither faked nor masked.)

All in all an observer as impartial as Carlson imagined himself to be might have predicted that at an ultimate cost of perhaps thirty to forty percent of its population (no great loss), the world ten or twenty years After Carlson would be a much nicer place to live in.

Instead and in fact, there are four billion fewer people living in it, and in this year Two A.C. we have achieved only a bare possibility of survival at a cost of eighty to ninety percent of our number.

The first thing Carlson could not have expected claimed over a billion and a half lives within the first month of the Brave New World. His compartmentalized mind had not been monitoring current developments in the field of psychology, a discipline he found frustrating. And so he was not aware of the work of Lynch and others, conclusively demonstrating that autism was the result of sensory overload. Autistic children, Lynch had proved, were victims of a physiochemical imbalance which disabled their suppressor circuitry for sight, hearing, touch, smell, or any combination thereof, flooding their brains with an intolerable avalanche of useless data and shocking them into retreat. Lysergic acid diethylamide is said to produce a similar effect, on a smaller scale.

The Hyperosmic Virus produced a similar effect, on a larger scale. Within weeks, millions of near-catatonic adults and children perished from malnutrition, exposure, or accidental injury. Why some survived the shock and adapted while some did not remains a mystery, although there exist scattered data suggesting that those whose sense of smell was already relatively acute suffered most.

The second thing Carlson could not have expected was the War.

The War had been ordained by the plummeting fall of his flask, but he may perhaps be excused for not foreseeing it. It

28

was not such a war as has ever been seen on earth before in all recorded history, humans versus each other or subordinate life forms. There was nothing for the confused, scattered survivors of the Hyperosmic Plague to fight over, few unbusy enough to fight over it; and with lesser life forms we are now *better* equipped to compete. No, war broke out between us bewildered refugees—and the Muskies.

It is difficult for us to imagine today how it was possible for the human race to know of the existence of Muskies for so long without ever believing in them. Countless humans reported contact with Muskies—who at various times were called "ghosts," "poltergeists," "leprechauns," "fairies," "gremlins," and a host of other misleading labels—and not *one* of those thousands of witnesses was believed by humanity at large. Some of us saw our cats staring intently at nothing— and not one of us drew the obvious conclusion. In its arrogance the race assumed that the peculiar perversion of entropy called "life" was the exclusive property of solids and liquids.

Even today we know very little about the Muskies, save that they are gaseous in nature and perceptible only by smell. The interested reader may wish to examine Dr. Michael Gowan's groundbreaking attempt at a psychological analysis of these entirely alien creatures, *Riders of the Wind* (Fresh Start Press, 1985).

One thing we do know is that they are capable of an incredible and unnerving playfulness. While not true telepaths, Muskies can project and often impose mood-patterns over short distances, and for centuries they seem to have delighted in scaring the daylights out of random humans. Perhaps they laughed like innocent children as women to whom their pranks were attributed were burned at the stake in Massachusetts. Dr. Gowan suggests that this aspect of their racial psyche is truly infantile—he feels their race is still in its infancy. As, perhaps, is our own.

But in their childishness, Muskies can be dangerous both deliberately and involuntarily. Years ago, before the Exodus, people used to wonder why a race that could plan a space station couldn't design a safe airliner—the silly things used to fall out of the sky with appalling regularity. Often it was simply sheer bad engineering, but I suspect that at least as often a careless, drifting Musky, riding the trades lost in God knows what wildly *alien* thoughts, was sucked into the air intake of a hurtling jetliner and burst the engine asunder as it died. It was this guess which led me to theorize that extreme heat might disrupt and kill Muskies, and this gave us our first and so far only weapon in the bitter war that still rages between us and the wind-riders.

For, like many children, Muskies are dangerously paranoid. Almost at the instant they realized that men could somehow now perceive them directly, they attacked, with a ferocity that bespoke blind panic. They learned quickly how best to kill us: by clamping itself somehow to a man's face and forcing him to breathe it in, a Musky can lay waste to his respiratory system. The only solution under combat conditions is a weapon which fires a projectile hot enough to explode a Musky—and that is a flawed solution. If you fail to burn a Musky in time, before it reaches you, you may be faced with the unpleasant choice of wrecking your lungs or blowing off your face. All too many Faceless Ones roam the land, objects of horror and pity, supported by fellow men uncomfortably aware that it could happen to them tomorrow.

Further, we Technos here at Fresh Start, dedicated to rebuilding at least a minimum technology, must naturally wear our recently developed nose-plugs for long intervals while doing Civilized work. We therefore toil in constant fear that at any moment we may feel alien projections of terror and dread, catch even through our plugs the characteristic odor that gives Muskies their name, and gasp our lungs out in the final spasms of death.

God knows how Muskies communicate—or even if they do. Perhaps they simply have some sort of group-mind or hive mentality. What would evolution select for a race of gas clouds spinning across the earth on the howling mistral? Someday we may devise a way to take one prisoner and study it; for the present we are content to know that they can be killed. A good Musky is a dead Musky.

Some day we may climb back up the ladder of technological evolution enough to carry the battle to the Muskies' home ground; for the present we are at least becoming formidable defenders.

Some day we may have the time to seek out Wendell Morgan Carlson and present him with a bill; for the present we are satisfied that he dares not show himself outside New York City, where legend has him hiding from the consequences of his actions.

Chapter Three

From the Journal of Isham Stone

. . . but my gestalt of the eighteen years that had brought me on an intersecting course with my father's betrayer was nowhere near as pedantically phrased as the historical accounts Dad has written. In fact, I had refined it down to four words.

God damn you, Carlson!

Nearly mid-afternoon, now. The speed was wearing off; time was short. Broadway got more depressing as I went. Have you ever seen a *busfull* of skeletons—with pigeons living in it? My arm ached like hell, and a muscle in my thigh had just announced it was sprained—I acquired a slight but increasing limp. The rucksack gained an ounce with every step, and I fancied that my right plug was leaking the barest trifle around the flange. I couldn't say I felt first-rate.

I kept walking north.

I came to Columbus Circle, turned on a whim into Central Park. It was an enclave of life in this concrete land of death, and I could not pass it by—even though my intellect warned that I might encounter a Doberman who hadn't seen a Doggie Chew in twenty years.

The Exodus had been good to this place at least—it was lush with vegetation now that swarming humans no longer smothered its natural urge to be alive. Elms and oaks reached for the clouds with the same optimism of the maples and birches around Fresh Start, and the overgrown grasses

were the greenest things I had seen in New York. And yet—
in places the grass was dead, and there were dead bushes and
shrubs scattered here and there. Perhaps first impressions
were deceiving—perhaps a small parcel of land surrounded
by an enormous concrete crypt was not a viable ecology after
all. Then again, perhaps neither was Fresh Start.

I was getting depressed again.

I pocketed the grenade I still held and sat down on a park
bench, telling myself that a rest would do wonders for my
limp. After a time static bits of scenery moved—the place was
alive. There were cats, and gaunt starved dogs of various
breeds, apparently none old enough to know what a man
was. I found their confidence refreshing—like I say, I'm a
peaceful-type assassin. Gregarious as hell.

I glanced about, wondering why so many of the comparatively few human skeletons here had been carrying weapons
on the night of the Exodus—why go armed in a park? Then I
heard a cough and looked around, and for a crazy second I
thought I knew.

A leopard.

I recognized it from pictures in Dad's books, and I knew
what it was and what it could do. But my adrenaline system
was tired of putting my gun in my fist—I sat perfectly still
and concentrated on smelling friendly. My hand-weapon was
designed for high temperature, not stopping power; grenades are ineffective against a moving target; and I was lean-
ing back against my rifle—but that isn't why I sat still. I had
learned that day that lashing out is not an optimum response
to fear.

And so I took enough of a second look to realize that this
leopard was incredibly ancient, hollow-bellied and claw-
scarred, more noble than formidable. If wild game had been
permitted to roam Central Park, Dad would have told me—
he knew my planned route. Yet this cat seemed old enough
to predate the Exodus. I was certain he knew me for a man. I
suppose he had escaped from a zoo in the confusion of the
time, or perhaps he was some rich person's pet. I understand
they had such things in the Old Days. Seems to me a leopard'd be more trouble than an eagle—Dad kept one for four

33

years and I never had so much grief over livestock before or since. Dad used to say it was the symbol of something great that had died, but I thought it was ornery.

This old cat seemed friendly enough, though, now that I noticed. He looked patriarchal and wise, and he looked awful hungry, if it came to that. I made a gambler's decision for no reason that I can name. Slipping off my rucksack slowly and deliberately, I got out a few foodtabs, took four steps toward the leopard and sat on my heels, holding out the tablets in offering.

Instinct, memory, or intuition, the big cat recognized my intent and loped my way without haste. Somehow the closer he got the less scared I got, until he was nuzzling my hand with a maw that could have amputated it. I *know* the foodtabs didn't smell like anything, let alone food, but he understood in some empathic way what I was offering—or perhaps he felt the symbolic irony of two ancient antagonists, black man and leopard, meeting in New York City to share food. He ate them all, without nipping my fingers. His tongue was startlingly rough and rasping, but I didn't flinch or need to. When he was done he made a noise that was a cross between a cough and a snore and butted my leg with his head.

He was old, but powerful; I rocked backward and fell off my heels. I landed correctly, of course, but I didn't get back up again. My strength left me and I lay there gazing at the underside of the park bench.

For the first time since I entered New York, I had communicated with a living thing and been answered in kind, and somehow that knowledge took my strength from me. I sprawled on the turf and waited for the ground to stop heaving, astonished to discover how weak I was and in how many places I hurt unbearably. I said some words that Collaci had taught me, and they helped some but not enough. The speed had worn off faster than it should have, and there was no more.

It looked like it was time for a smoke. I argued with myself as I reached overhead to get the first-aid kit from the rucksack, but I saw no alternative. Carlson was not a trained fighter, had never had a teacher like Collaci: I could take him buzzed. And I might not get to my feet any other way.

34

The joint I selected was needle-slender—more than a little cannabis would do me more harm than good. I had no mind to get wasted in *this* city. I lit up with my coil lighter and took a deep lungful, held it as long as I could. Halfway through the second toke the leaves dancing overhead began to sparkle, and my weariness got harder to locate. By the third I knew of it only by hearsay, and the last hit began melting the pains of my body as warm water melts snow. Nature's own analgesic, gift of the earth.

I started thinking about the leopard, who was lying down himself now, washing his haunches. He was magnificent in decay—something about his eyes said that he intended to live forever or die trying. He was the only one of his kind in his universe, and I could certainly identify with that—I'd always felt different from the other cats myself.

And yet—I was kin to those who had trapped him, caged him, exhibited him to the curious and then abandoned him to die half a world away from his home. Why wasn't he trying to kill me? In his place I might have acted differently. . . .

With the clarity of smoke-logic I followed the thought through. At one time the leopard's ancestors had tried to kill mine, and *eat* them, and yet there was no reason for me to hate *him*. Killing him wouldn't help my ancestors. Killing me would accomplish nothing for the leopard, make his existence no easier . . . except by a day's meal, and I had given him that.

What then, I thought uneasily, *will my killing Carlson accomplish?* It could not put the Hyperosmic Virus back in the flask, nor save the life of any now living. Why come all this way to kill?

It was not, of course, a new thought. The question had arisen several times during my training in survival and combat. Collaci insisted on debating philosophy while he was working you over, and expected reply; he maintained that a man who couldn't hold up his end of the conversation while fighting for his life would never make a really effective killer. You could pause for thought, but if he decided you were just hoarding your wind, he stopped pulling his punches.

One day we had no special topic, and I voiced my self-doubts about the mission I was training for. What good would killing Carlson do, I asked Collaci. Teach' disengaged and stood back, breathing a little hard, and grinned his infrequent wolf's grin.

"Survival has strange permutations, Isham. Revenge is a uniquely human attribute—somehow we find it easier to bury our dead when we have avenged them. We have many dead." He selected a toothpick, stuck it into his grin. "And for your father's sake it has to be you who does it—only if his son provides his expiation can Dr. Stone grant himself absolution. Otherwise I'd go kill that silly bastard myself." And without warning, he had tried, unsuccessfully, to break my collarbone.

And so now I sat tired, hungry, wounded and a little stoned in the middle of an enormous island mausoleum, asking myself the question I had next asked Collaci, while trying—unsuccessfully—to cave in his rib cage: is it moral or ethical to kill a man?

Across the months his answer came back: *Perhaps not, but it is sometimes necessary.*

And with that thought my strength came to me and I got to my feet. My thoughts were as slick as wet soap, within reach but skittering out of my grasp. I grabbed one from the tangle and welded it to me savagely: *I will kill Wendell Morgan Carlson.* It was enough.

And saying good-bye to the luckier leopard, who could never be hag-ridden by ancient ghosts, I left the park and continued on up Broadway, as alert and deadly as I knew how to be.

When I reached 114th Street, I looked above the rooftops, and there it was: a thin column of smoke north and a little east, toward Amsterdam Avenue. Legend and my father's intuition had been right. Carlson was holed up where he had always felt most secure—the academic womb-bag of Columbia. I felt a grin pry my face open. It would all be over soon now, and I could go back to being me—whoever that was.

I left the rucksack under a station wagon and considered my situation. I had three hot-shots left in my Musky-killing handgun, three incendiary grenades clipped to my belt, and the scope-sighted sniper rifle with which I planned to kill

36

Carlson. The latter held a full clip of eight man-killing slugs—seven more than I needed. I checked the action and jacked a slug into the chamber.

There was a detailed map of the Morningside Campus in my pack but I didn't bother to get it out—I had its twin brother in my head. Although neither Teach' nor I had entirely shared Dad's certainty that Carlson would be at Columbia, I had spent hours studying the campus maps he gave me as thoroughly as the New York City street maps that Collaci had provided. It seemed the only direct contribution Dad could make to my mission.

It looked as though his effort had paid off.

I wondered whether Carlson was expecting me. I wasn't sure if the sound of the car I'd shot downtown could have traveled this far, nor whether an explosion in a city full of untended gas mains was unusual enough to put Carlson on his guard. Therefore I had to assume that it could have and it was. Other men had come to New York to deal with Carlson, as independents, and none had returned.

My mind was clicking efficiently now, all confusion gone. I was eager. A car-swiped lamp post leaned drunkenly against a building, and I briefly considered taking to the rooftops for maximum surprise factor. But rooftops are prime Musky territory, and besides I didn't have strength for climbing.

I entered the campus at the southwest, through the 115th Street gate. As my father had predicted, it was locked—only the main gates at 116th were left open at night in those days, and it was late at night when Carlson dropped his flask. But the lock was a simple Series 10 American that might have made Teach' laugh out loud. I didn't laugh out loud. It yielded to the second pick I tried, and I slipped through the barred iron gate without a sound—having thought to oil the hinges.

A flight of steps led to a short flagstone walkway, grey speckled hexagons in mosaic, a waist-high wall on either side. The walkway ran between Furnald and Ferris Booth halls and, I knew, opened onto the great inner quadrangle of Columbia. Leaves lay scattered all about, and trees of all kinds thrashed in the lusty afternoon breeze, their leaves a million green pinwheels.

I hugged the right wall until it abutted a taller perpendicular wall. Easing around that, I found myself before the great smashed glass and stone facade of Ferris Booth Hall, the student activities center, staring past it toward Butler Library, which I was seeing from the west side. There was a good deal of heavy construction equipment in the way—one of the many student groups that had occupied space in Booth had managed to blow up itself and a sizable portion of the building in 1983, and rebuilding had still been in progress on Exodus Day. A massive crane stood before the ruined structure, surrounded by stacks of brick and pipe, a bulldozer, storage shacks, a few trucks, a two hundred-gallon gasoline tank and a pair of construction trailers.

But my eyes looked past all the conventional hardware to a curious device beyond them, directly in front of Butler Library and nearly hidden by overgrown hedges. I couldn't have named it—it looked like an octopus making love to a stereo console—but it obviously didn't come with the landscaping. Dad's second intuition was also correct: Carlson was using Butler for his base of operations. God knew what the device was for, but a man without his adenoids in a city full of Muskies and hungry German Shepherds would not have built it further from home than could be helped. This was the place.

I drew in a great chest- and belly-full of air, and my grin hurt my cheeks. I held up my rifle and watched my hands. Rock steady.

Carlson, you murdering bastard, I thought, *this is it. The human race has found you, and its Hand is near. A few more breaths and you die violently, old man, like a harmless cat in a smokeshop window, like an eight-year-old boy on a Harlem sidewalk, like a planetwide civilization you thought you could improve on. Get you ready.*

I moved forward.

Wendell Morgan Carlson stepped out between the big shattered lamps that bracketed Butler Hall's front entrance. I saw him plainly in profile, features memorized from the Carlson Poster and my father's sketches recognizable in the afternoon light even through white beard and tangled hair. He glanced my way, flinched, and ducked back inside a split second ahead of my first shot.

Determined to nail him before he could reach a weapon and dig in, I put my head down and ran, flat out, for the greatest killer of all time.

And the first Musky struck.

Terror sleeted through my brain, driving out the rage, and something warm and intangible plastered itself across my face. I think I screamed then, but somehow I kept from inhaling as I fell and rolled, dropping the rifle and tearing uselessly at the thing on my face. The last thing I saw before invisible gases seared my vision was the huge crane beside me on the right, its long arm flung at the sky like a signpost to Heaven. Then the world shimmered and faded, and I clawed my pistol from its holster. I aimed without seeing, my finger spasmed, and the gun bucked in my hand.

The massive gasoline drum between me and the crane went up with a *whoom!* and I sobbed in relief as I heaved to my feet and dove headlong through the flames. The Musky's dying projections tore at my mind and I rolled clear, searing my lungs with a convulsive inhalation as the Musky exploded behind me. Even as I smashed into the fender of the crane, my hindbrain screamed *Muskies never travel alone!* and before I knew what I was doing, I tore loose my plugs to locate my enemy.

Foul stenches smashed my sanity; noxious odors wrenched at my reason. I was torn, blasted, overwhelmed in abominable ordure. The universe was offal, and the world I saw was remote and unreal. My eyes saw the campus, but told me nothing of the rank flavor of putrefaction that lay upon it. They saw sky, but spoke nothing of the reeking layers of indescribable decay of which it was made. Even allowing for a greenhouse effect, it was much worse than it should have been after twenty years, just as legend had said. I tasted excrement, I tasted metal, I tasted the flavor of the world's largest charnel house, population seven millions, and I writhed on the concrete. Forgotten childhood memories of the Exodus burst in my brain and reduced me to a screaming, whimpering child. I couldn't *stand* it. It was unbearable. *How had I walked, arrogant and unknowing, through this stinking hell all day?*

And with that thought I remembered why I had come

here, and knew I could not join Izzy in the peaceful, fragrant dark. I could not let go—I had to kill Carlson before I let the blackness have me. Courage flowed from God-knows-where, feeding on black hatred and the terrible fear that I would let my people down, let my father down. I stood up and inhaled sharply, through my nose.

The nightmare world sprang into focus and time came to a halt.

There were six Muskies, skittering about before Butler as they sought to bend the breezes to their will.

I had three hot-shots and three grenades.

One steadied, banked my way. I fired from the hip and he flared out of existence.

A second caught hold of a prevailing current and came in like an express train. Panic tore through my mind, and I laughed and aimed and the Musky went incandescent.

Two came in at once then, like balloons in slow motion. I extrapolated their courses, pulled two grenades and armed them with opposing thumbs, counted to four, and hurled them together as Collaci had taught me, aiming for a spot just short of my target. They kissed at that spot and rebounded, each toward an oncoming Musky. But one grenade went up before the other, killing its Musky but knocking the other one safely clear. It whistled past my ear as I threw myself sideways.

Three Muskies. One hot-shot, one grenade.

The one that had been spared sailed around the crane in a wide, graceful arc and came in low and fast, rising for my face as one of its brothers attacked from my left. Cursing, I burned the latter and flipped backward through a great trail of burning gas from the tank I'd spoiled. The Musky failed to check in time, shot suddenly skyward and burst spectacularly. I slammed against a stack of twelve-inch pipe and heard ribs crack.

One Musky. One grenade.

As I staggered erect, beating at my smoldering turtleneck, Carlson reemerged from Butler, a curious helmet over his flowing white hair. Wires trailed from it.

I no longer cared about the remaining Musky. Almost absentmindedly I tossed my last grenade in its direction to keep

40

it occupied, but I knew I would have all the time I needed. Imminent death was now a side issue. I lunged and rolled, came up with the rifle in my hands and aimed for the O in Carlson's scraggly white beard. Dimly I saw him plugging his helmet into that curious machine by the door but it didn't matter, it just didn't matter at all. My finger tightened on the trigger.

And then something smashed me on the side of the neck behind the ear, and my finger clenched, and the blackness that had been waiting patiently for oh! so long swarmed in and washed away the pain and the hate and the weariness and oh God the awful smell. . . .

Chapter Four

". . . and when I came to, Carlson was dead with a slug through the head and the last Musky was nowhere in smell. So I reset my plugs, found the campfire behind the hedges and ate his supper, and then left the next morning. I found a Healer in Jersey. That's all there is, Dad."

My father chewed the pipe he had not smoked in eighteen years and stared into the fire. Dry poplar and green birch together produced a steady blaze that warmed the spacious living room and peopled it with leaping shadows.

"Then it's over," he said at last, and heaved a great sigh.

"Yes, Dad. It's over."

He was silent, his coal-black features impassive, for a long time. Firelight danced among the valleys and crevices of his patriarch's face, and across the sharp scar on his left cheek (so like the one I now bore). His eyes glittered like rainy midnight. I wondered what he was thinking, after all these years and all that he had seen.

"Isham," he said at last, "you have done well."

"Have I, Dad?"

"Eh?"

"I just can't seem to get it straight in my mind. I guess I expected tangling with Carlson to be a kind of solution to some things that have been bugging me all my life. Somehow I expected pulling that trigger to bring me peace. Instead I'm more confused than ever. Surely you can smell my unease, Dad? Or are your plugs still in again?" Dad used the best plugs in Fresh Start, entirely internal, and he perpetually forgot to remove them after work. Even those who loved him agreed he was the picture of the absentminded professor.

"No," he said hesitantly. "I can smell that you are uneasy, but I can't smell *why*. You must tell me, Isham."

"It's not easy to explain, Dad. I can't seem to find the words. Look, I wrote out a kind of journal of events in Jersey, while the Healer was working on me, and afterward while I rested up. It's the same story I just told you, but somehow on paper I think it conveys more of what's bothering me. Will you read it?"

He nodded. "If you wish."

I gave my father all the preceding manuscript, right up to the moment I pulled the trigger and blacked out, and brought him his glasses. He read it slowly and carefully, pausing now and again to gaze distantly into the flames. While he read, I unobtrusively fed the fire and immersed myself in the familiar smells of woodsmoke and ink and chemicals and the pines outside, all the thousand indefinable scents that tried to tell me I was home.

When Dad was done reading, he closed his eyes and nodded slowly for a time. Then he turned to me and regarded me with troubled eyes. "You've left out the ending," he said.

"Because I'm not sure how I feel about it."

He steepled his fingers. "What is it that troubles you, Isham?"

"Dad," I said earnestly, "Carlson is the first man I ever killed. That's . . . not a small thing. As it happens, I didn't actually see my bullet blow off the back of his skull, and sometimes it's hard to believe in my gut that I really did it—I know it seemed unreal when I saw him afterward. But in fact I have killed a man. And as you just read, that may be necessary sometimes, but I'm not sure it's right. I *know* all that Carlson did, to us Stones and to the world, I know the guilt he bore. But I must ask you: Dad, was I *right* to kill him? Did he deserve to die?"

He came to me then and gripped my shoulder, and we stood like black iron statues before the raving fire. He locked eyes with me. "Perhaps you should ask your mother, Isham. Or your brother Israfel. Perhaps you should have asked the people whose remains you stepped over to kill Carlson. I do not know what is 'right' and 'wrong'; they are slippery terms to define. I only know what is. And revenge, as Collaci told you, *is* a uniquely human attribute.

"Superstitious Agro guerrillas used to raid us from time to time, and because we were reluctant to fire on them they got

43

away with it. Then one day they captured Collaci's wife, not knowing she was diabetic. By the time he caught up with them she was dead for lack of insulin. Within two days, every guerrilla in that raiding party had died of a broken neck. Fresh Start has not been raided in all the years since. Ask Collaci about vengeance."

"But Jordan's Agros hate us more than ever."

"But they buy our ax-heads and wheels, our neosulfa and our cloth, just like their more sensible neighbors, and they leave us alone. Carlson's death will be an eternal warning to any who would impose their values on the world at large, and an eternal comfort to those who were robbed by him of the best of their lives—of their homes and their loved ones.

"Isham, you . . . did . . . *right*. Don't ever think differently, son. You did right, and I am deeply proud of you. Your mother and Israfel are resting easier now, and millions more too. I know that I will sleep easier tonight than I have in eighteen years."

That's right, Dad, you will. I relaxed. "All right, Dad. I guess you're right. I just wanted to hear someone tell me besides myself. I wanted you to tell me." He smiled and nodded and sat down again, and I left him there, an old man lost in his thoughts.

I went to the bathroom and closed the door behind me, glad that restored plumbing had been one of Fresh Start's first priorities to be realized. I spent a few minutes assembling some items I had brought back from New York City and removing the back of the septic tank behind the toilet bowl. Then I flushed the toilet.

Reaching into the tank, I grabbed the gravity ball and flexed it horizontally so that the tank would not refill with water. Holding it in place awkwardly, I made a long arm and picked up the large bottle of chlorine bleach I had fetched from the city. As an irreplaceable relic of Civilization it was priceless—and utterly useless to modern man. I slipped my plugs into place and filled the tank with bleach, replacing the porcelain cover silently but leaving it slightly ajar. I bent again and grabbed a large canister—also a valuable but useless antique—of bathroom bowl cleaner. It was labeled "Vanish," and I hoped the label was prophetic. I poured the entire canister into the bowl.

Hang the expense, I thought, and giggled insanely.

Then I put the cover down on the seat, hid the bleach and bowl cleaner and left, whistling softly through my teeth.

I felt good, better than I had since I left New York.

I walked through inky dark to the lake, and I sat among the pines by the shore, flinging stones at the water, trying to make them skip. I couldn't seem to get it right. I was used to the balancing effect of a left arm. I rubbed my stump ruefully and lay back and just thought for awhile. I had lied to my father—it was not over. But it would be soon.

Right or wrong, I thought, removing my plugs and lighting a joint, *it sure can be necessary.*

Moonlight shattered on the branches overhead and lay in shards on the ground. I breathed deep of the cool darkness, tasted pot and woods and distant animals and the good, crisp scents of a balanced ecology, heard the faraway hum of wind generators storing power for the work yet to be done. And I thought of a man gone mad with a dream of a better, simpler world; a man who, Heaven help him, meant well.

Behind me in the far distance came the sound of a flushing toilet, followed by a hideous gargling noise, and suddenly I laughed with real amusement, choking on smoke. The sound of justice: *wooosh*-splash-*gllgh!* It was the grandest joke in the universe; I laughed until I couldn't cry any more.

Then, taking my time, I recovered the hidden pack and supplies I had cached on my way home. As I strapped up, I thought of the tape recording I had left behind on the Sony in the living room, and wondered briefly what Collaci and the Council would think of it. But I didn't really care much. For the first time in eighteen years, I was at peace. The Hand of Man had retired.

I set out for New York City.

Chapter Five

*Transcript of a Tape Recording Made by Isham
Stone (Fresh Start Judicial Archives)*

I might as well address this tape to you, Collaci—I'll bet my
Musky-gun that you're the first one to notice and play it. I
hope you'll listen to it as well, but that might be too much to
ask, the first time around. Just keep playing it.

The way I picture it, by the time this is found the Council
will have decided that I murdered Dad—both because I've
disappeared, and because the murder weapons *had* to come
from a city. You don't believe it, though, and so you've been
looking around for clues to the real identity of the killer.
That's how you ran across this tape, threaded and ready to
go. Good old efficient Collaci.

Well, I'm sorry to disappoint you, Teach', but you're
wrong. I did set the trap that killed Dad, or anyway I will after I've finished making this recording. Wha's that called?
Patricide? That sounds right, like herbicide or insecticide.

But it's gonna take a lot of talking before I've explained
why I have to kill my father, and you'll have to hear it two or
three times and think about it awhile before you'll be ready
to accept and believe. I know: it's taken me awhile. So maybe
we'd best get to it. Whip out one of your toothpicks, sit down,
and try to listen.

It goes back a couple of months, to when I was in the city.
By now you've no doubt found my journal, with its account
of my day in New York, and you've probably noticed the
missing ending. Well, here it is. . . .

I drifted in the darkness for a thousand years, helpless as a Musky in a hurricane, caroming off the inside of my skull. Memories swept by like drifting blimps, and I clutched at them as I sailed past, but the ones tangible enough to grasp burned my fingers. Vaguely, I sensed distant daylight on either side, decided those must be my ears and tried to steer for the right one, which seemed a bit closer. I singed my arm banking off an adolescent trauma, but it did the trick—I sailed out into daylight and landed on my face with a hell of a crash. I thought about getting up, but I couldn't remember whether I'd brought my legs with me, and they weren't talking. My arm hurt even more than my face, and something stank.

"Help?" I suggested faintly, and a pair of hands got me by the armpits. I rose in the air and closed my eyes against a sudden wave of vertigo. When it passed, I decided I was on my back in the bed I had just contrived to fall out of. High in my chest, a dull but insistent pain advised me to breathe shallowly.

I'll be damned, I thought weakly. *Collaci must have come along to back me up without telling me. Canny old sonofabitch, I should have thought to pick him up some toothpicks.*

"Hey, Teach'," I croaked, and opened my eyes.

Wendell Morgan Carlson leaned over me, concern in his gaze.

Curiously enough, I didn't try to reach up and crush his larynx. I closed my eyes, relaxed all over, counted to ten very slowly, shook my head to clear it and opened my eyes again. Carlson was still there.

Then I tried to reach up and crush his larynx. I failed, of course, not so much because I was too weak to *reach* his larynx as because only one arm even acknowledged the command. My brain said that my left arm was straining upwards for Carlson's throat, and complaining like hell about it too, but I didn't see the arm anywhere. I looked down and saw the neatly bandaged stump and lifted it up absently to see if my arm was underneath it and it wasn't. It dawned on me then that the stump was all the left arm I was ever going to find, and whacko: I was back inside my skull, safe in the friendly dark, ricocheting off smoldering recollections again.

47

The second time I woke up was completely different. One minute I was wrestling with a phantom, and then a switch was thrown and I was lucid. *Play for time* was my first thought, *the tactical situation sucks.* I opened my eyes.

Carlson was nowhere in sight. Or smell—but my plugs were back in place.

I looked around the room. It was a room. Four walls, ceiling, floor, the bed I was in and assorted ugly furniture. Not a weapon in sight, nor anything I could make one from. A look out the window in the opposite wall confirmed my guess that I was in Butler Hall, apparently on the ground floor, not far from the main entrance. The great curved dome of Lowe "Library" was nearly centered in the window frame, its great stone steps partly obscured by overgrown shrubbery in front of Butler. The shadows said it was morning, getting on toward noon. I closed my eyes, firmly.

Next I took stock of myself. My plugs were back in place. My head throbbed a good deal, but it was easily drowned out by the ache in my chest. Unquestionably some ribs had broken, and it felt as though the ends were mismatched. But as near as I could tell the lung was intact—it didn't hurt more when I inhaled. Not much more, anyway. My legs both moved when I asked them to, with a minimum of backtalk, and the ankles appeared sound. No need to open my eyes again, was there? . . .

I stopped the inventory for a moment. In the back of my skull a clawed lizard yammered for release, and I devoted a few minutes to reinforcing the walls of its prison. When I could no longer hear the shrieking, I switched on my eyes again and quite dispassionately considered the stump of my left arm.

It looked like a good, clean job. The placement of the cut said it was a surgical procedure rather than the vengeful hostility I'd thought of first—it seemed as though the gangrene had been beaten. *Oh, fine,* I thought, *a benevolent madman I have to kill.* Then I was ashamed. My mother had been benevolent, as I remembered her; and Israfel never got much chance to be anything. All men knew Carlson's intentions had been good. I could kill him with one hand.

I wondered where he was.

A fly buzzed mournfully around the room. Hedges rustled outside the window, and somewhere birds sang, breathless trills that hung sparkling on the morning air. It was a beautiful day, just warm enough to be comfortable, no clouds evident, just enough breeze and the best part of the day yet to come. It made me want to go down by the stream and poke frogs with a stick, or go pick strawberries for Mr. Fletcher, red-stained hands and a bellyfull of sweet and the trots next morning. It was a great day for an assassination.

I thought about it, considered the possibilities. Carlson was . . . somewhere. I was weaker than a Musky in a pressure-cooker and my most basic of armament was down by twenty-five percent. I was on unfamiliar territory, and the only objects in the room meaty enough to constitute weaponry were too heavy for me to lift. Break the windowpane and acquire a knife? How would I hold it? My sneakers were in sight across the room, under a chair holding the rest of my clothes, and I wondered if I could hide behind the door until Carlson entered, then strangle him with the laces.

I brought up short. How was I going to strangle Carlson with one hand?

Things swam then for a bit, as I got the first of an endless series of flashes of just how drastically my life was altered now by the loss of my arm. *You'll never use a chainsaw again, or a shovel, or a catcher's mitt, or . . .*

I buried the lizard again and forced myself to concentrate. Perhaps I could fashion a noose from my sneaker laces. With one hand? *Could* I? Maybe if I fastened one end of the lace to something, then looped the other end around his neck and pulled? I needn't be strong, it could be arranged so that my weight did the killing. . . .

Just in that one little instant I think I decided not to die, decided to keep on living with one arm, and the question never really arose in my mind again. I was too busy to despair, and by the time I could afford to—much later—the urge was gone.

All of my tentative plans, therapeutic as they were, hinged on one important question: could I stand up? It seemed essential to find out.

Until then I had moved only my eyes—now I tried sitting

49

up. It was no harder than juggling bulldozers, and I managed to cut the scream down to an explosive, "Uh-*huh*!" My ribs felt like glass—broken glass ripping through the muscle sheathing and pleural tissue. Sweat broke out on my forehead and I fought down dizziness and nausea, savagely commanding my body to obey me like a desperate rider digging spurs into a dying horse. I locked my right arm behind me and leaned on it, swaying but upright, and waited for the room to stop spinning. I spent the time counting to one thousand by eighths. Finally it stopped, leaving me with the feeling that a stiff breeze could start it spinning again.

All right then. *Let's get this show on the road, Stone.* I swung a leg over the side of the bed, discovered with relief that my foot reached the floor. That would make it easier to balance upright on the edge of the bed before attempting to stand. Before I could lose my nerve I swung the other leg over, pushed off with my arm, and was sitting upright. The floor was an incredible distance below—had I really fallen that far and lived? Perhaps I should just wait for Carlson to return, get him to come close and sink my teeth into his jugular.

I stood up.

A staggering crescendo in the symphony of pain, ribs still carrying the melody. I locked my knees and tottered, moaning piteously like a kitten trapped on a cornice. It was the closest I could come to stealthy silence, and all things considered it was pretty damn close. My right shoulder was discernibly heavier than the left one, and it played hob with my balance. The floor, which had been steadily receding, was now so far away I stopped worrying about it—surely there would be time for the chute to open.

Well, then, why not try a step or two?

My left leg was as light as a helium balloon—once peeled off the floor it tried to head for the ceiling, and it took an enormous effort to force it down again. The right leg fared no better. Then the room started spinning again, just as I'd feared, and it was suddenly impossible to keep either leg beneath my body, which began losing altitude rapidly. The chute didn't open. There was a jarring crash, and a ghastly *bounce*. Many pretty lights appeared, and one of the screams fenced in behind closed teeth managed to break loose. The pretty lights gave way to flaking ceiling, and the ceiling gave way to blackness. I remembered a line from an old song Doctor Mike used to sing, something about ". . . roadmaps in a well-cracked ceiling . . ." and wished I'd had time to read the map. . . .

I came out of it almost at once, I think. It *felt* as though the room was still spinning, but I was now spinning with it at the same velocity. By great good fortune I had toppled backward, across the bed. I took a tentative breath, and it still felt like my lung was intact. I was drenched with sweat, and I seemed to be lying on someone's rock collection.

Okay, I decided, *if you're too weak to kill Carlson now, pretend you're even weaker. Get back under the sheets and play dead, until your position improves.* Isham Machiavelli, that's me. You'd've been proud of me, Teach'.

The rock collection turned out to be wrinkled sheets. Getting turned around and back to where I'd started was easier than reeling a whale into a rowboat, and I had enough strength to arrange the sheets plausibly before all my muscles turned into peanut butter. Then I just lay there breathing as shallowly as I could manage, wondering why my left . . . why my stump didn't seem to hurt enough. I hated to look a gift horse in the mouth; the psychological burden was quite heavy enough, thanks. But it made me uneasy.

I began composing a square-dance tune in time to the throbbing of my ribs. The room reeled to it, slightly out of synch at first but then so rhythmically that it actually seemed to stumble when the snare-drummer out in the hall muffed a paradiddle. The music stopped, but the drummer staggered on off-rhythm, faint at first but getting louder.

It had to be Carlson.

He was making a hell of a racket. Feverishly I envisioned him dragging a bazooka into the room and lining it up on me. Crazy. A fly-swatter would have more than sufficed. But what the hell *was* he carrying then?

The answer came through the doorway: a large carton filled with things that clanked and rattled. Close behind it came Wendell Morgan Carlson himself, and it was as well that the square-dance music had stopped—the acceleration of my pulse would have made the tune undanceable. My nostrils tried to flare around the plugs, and the hair on the back of my neck might have bristled in atavistic reflex if there hadn't been a thousand pounds of head lying on it.

The Enemy!

He had no weapons visible. He looked much older than his picture on the Carlson Poster—but the craggy brow, thin pinched nose and high cheeks were unmistakable, even if the lantern jaw was obscured by an inordinate amount of white beard. He was a bit taller than I had pictured him, with more hair and narrower shoulders. I hadn't expected the potbelly. He wore baggy jeans and a plaid flannel shirt, both ineptly patched here and there, and a pair of black sandals.

His face held more intelligence than I like in an antagonist—he would not be easy to fool. Wendell *who? Never heard of him. Just got back from Pellucidar myself, and I was wondering if you could tell me where all the people went? Sorry I took a shot at you, and oh yeah, thanks for cutting off my arm; you're a brick.*

He put the carton down on an ancient brown desk, crushing a faded photograph of someone's children, turned at once to meet my gaze and said an incredible thing.

"I'm sorry I woke you."

I don't know what I'd expected. But in the few fevered moments I'd had to prepare myself for this moment, my first exchange of words with Wendell Morgan Carlson, I had never imagined such an opening gambit. I had no riposte prepared.

"You're welcome," I croaked insanely, and tried to smile. Whatever it was I actually did seemed to upset him; his face took on that look of concern I had glimpsed once before—when? Yesterday? *How long had I been here?*

"I'm glad you are awake," he went on obligingly. "You've been unconscious for nearly a week." No wonder I felt constructed of inferior materials. I decided I must be a pretty tough mothafucka. It was nice to know I wasn't copping out.

"What's in the box?" I asked, with a little less fuzz tone.

"Box?" He looked down. "Oh yes, I thought . . . you see, it's intravenous feeding equipment. I studied the literature, and I . . ." He trailed off. His voice was a reedy but pleasant alto, with rusting brass edges. He appeared unfamiliar with its use.

52

"You were going to . . ." An ice cube formed in my bowels. Needle into sleeping arm, suck my life from a tube; have a hit of old Isham. *Steady boy, steady.*

"Perhaps it might still be a good idea," he mused. "All I have to offer you at the moment is bread and milk. Not real milk, of course, but then you could have honey with the bread. I suppose that's as good as glucose."

"Fine with me, doctor," I said hastily. "I have a thing about needles." And other sharp instruments. "But where do you get your honey?"

He frowned quizzically. "How did you know I have a Ph.D.?"

Think quick. "I didn't. I assumed you were a Healer. It was you who amputated my arm?" I kept my voice even.

His frown deepened, a striking expression on that craggy face. "Young man," he said reluctantly, "I have no formal medical training of any sort. Perhaps your arm could have stayed on—but it seemed to me . . ." He was, to my astonishment, mortally embarrassed.

"Doctor, it needed extensive cutting the last time I saw it, and I'm sure it got worse while I was under. Don't . . . worry about it. I'm sure you did the best you could." If he was inclined to forget my attempt to blow his head off, who was *I* to hold a grudge? Let bygones be bygones—I didn't need a new reason to kill him.

"I read all I could find on field amputation," he went on, still apologetic, "but of course I'd never done one before." On anything smaller than a race. I assured him that it looked to me like a textbook job. It was inexpressibly weird to have this man seek my pardon for saving my life when I planned to take his at the earliest possible opportunity. It upset me, made me irritable. My wounds provided a convenient distraction, and I moved enough to justify a moan.

Carlson was instantly solicitous. From his cardboard carton he produced a paper package which, torn open, revealed a plastic syringe. Taking a stoppered jar from the carton, he drew off a small amount of clear fluid.

"What's that?" I said, trying to keep the suspicion from my voice.

"Demerol."

I shook my head. "No thanks, doc. I told you I don't like needles."

He nodded, put down the spike and took another object from the carton. "Here's oral demerol, then. I'll leave it where you can reach it." He put it on a bedside table. I picked up the jar, gave it a quick glance. It said it was demerol. I could not break the seal around the cap with one hand—Carlson had to open it for me. *Thank you, my enemy.* Weird, weird, weird! I palmed a pill, pretending to swallow it. He looked satisfied.

"Thanks, Doc."

"Please don't call me 'doc,'" he asked. "My name is Wendell Carlson."

If he was expecting a reaction, he was disappointed. "Sure thing, Wendell. I'm Tony Latimer. Pleased to meet you." It was the first name that entered my head.

There was a lull in the conversation. We studied each other with the frank curiosity of men who have not known human company for a while. At last he looked embarrassed again and tore his gaze from mine. "I'd better see about that food. You must be terribly hungry."

I thought about it. It seemed to me that I could put away a quarter-horse. Raw. With my fingers. "I could eat."

Carlson left the room, looking at his sandals.

I thought of loading the hypo with an overdose and ambushing him when he returned, but it was just a thought. That hypo was mighty far away. I returned my attention to the jar on the table. It still said it was demerol—and it *had* been sealed, with white plastic. But Carlson could have soaked off and replaced a skull-and-crossbones label—I decided to live with the pain awhile longer.

It seemed like a long time before he returned, but my time-sense was not too reliable. He fetched a half loaf of brown bread, a Mason jar of milk and some thick crystallized honey. They say that smell is essential to taste, and I couldn't unplug, but it tasted better than food ever had before.

"You never told me where you get honey, Wendell."

"I have a small hive down in Central Park. Only a few supers, but adequate for my needs. Wintering the bees is quite a trick, but I manage."

"I'll bet it is." Small talk in the slaughterhouse. I ate what he gave me and drank reconstituted milk until I was full. My body still hurt, but not as much.

We talked for about half an hour, mostly inconsequentialities, and it seemed that a tension grew up between us because of the very inconsequentiality of our words. There were things of which we did not speak, of which innocent men should have spoken. In my dazed condition I could concoct no plausible explanation for my presence in New York, nor for the shot I had fired at him. Somehow he accepted this, but in return I was not to ask him how he came to be living in New York City, I was not supposed to have any idea who Wendell Morgan Carlson was. It was an absurd bargain, a truth level impossible to maintain, but it suited both of us. I couldn't imagine what he thought of my own conversational omissions, but I was convinced that his silence was an admission of guilt, and my resolve was firmed. He left me at last, advising me to sleep if I could and promising to return the next day.

I didn't sleep. Not at first. I lay there looking at the demerol bottle for a hundred years, explaining to myself how unlikely it was that the bottle wasn't genuine. I could not help it—hatred and distrust of Carlson were ingrained in me.

But enough pain will break through the strongest conditioning. About sundown I ate the pill I'd palmed, and in a very short time I was unconscious.

The next few days passed slowly.

Chapter Six

The days passed slowly, but not so slowly as the pain. Lucidity returned slowly, but no faster than physical strength.

You've got to understand how it was, Teach'.

The demerol helped—but not by killing pain. What it did was keep me so stoned that I often forgot the pain was there. In a warm, creative glow I would devise a splendidly subtle and poetic means of Killing Carlson—then half an hour later the same plan would seem hopelessly crackbrained. An imperfection of the glass in the window across the room, warping the clean, proud curve of the Lowe Dome, held me fascinated for hours—yet I could not seem to concentrate for five minutes on practical matters.

Carlson came and went, asking few questions and answering fewer, and in my stupor I tried to fire my hate to the killing point, and, Collaci, my instructor and mentor and (I hope) friend, I failed.

You must understand me—I spent hours trying to focus on the hatred my father had passed on to me, to live up to the geas that fate had laid upon me, to do my duty. But it was damned hard work. Carlson was an absurd combination: so absentminded as to remind me of Dad—and as thoughtful, in his way, as you. He would forget his coat when he left at night—but be back on time with a hot breakfast, shivering and failing to notice. He would forget my name, but never my chamberpot. He would search, blinking, in all directions for the coffee cup that sat perched on his lap, but he never

56

failed to put mine where I could reach it without strain on my ribs. I discovered quite by accident that I slept in the only bed Carlson had ever hauled into Butler, that he himself dossed on a makeshift bed out in the hall, so as to be near if I cried out in the night.

He offered no clue to his motivations, no insight into what kept him entombed in New York City. He spoke of his life of exile as a simple fact, requiring no explanation. It seemed more and more obvious that his silence was an admission of guilt: that he could not explain his survival and continued presence in this smelly mausoleum without admitting his crime. I tried—how I tried—to hate him.

But it was damnably difficult. He supplied my needs before I could voice them, wants before I could form them. He sensed when I craved company and when to leave me be, when I needed to talk and when I needed to be talked to. He suffered my irritability and occasional rages in a way that somehow allowed me to keep my self-respect.

He was gone for long periods of time during the day and night, and never spoke of his activities. I never pressed him for information; as a recuperating assassin it behooved me to display no undue curiosity. I could not risk arousing his suspicions.

We never, for instance, chanced to speak of my weapons or their whereabouts.

And so the subconscious tension of our first conversation stayed with us, born of the things of which we did not speak. It was obvious to both of us—and yet it was a curious kind of kinship, too: both of us lived with something we could not share, and recognized the condition in the other. Even as I planned his death I felt a kind of empathy between Wendell Morgan Carlson and myself. It bothered hell out of me. If Carlson was what I *knew* he was, what his guilty silence only proved him to be, then his death was necessary and just—for my father had taught me that debts are always paid. But I could not help but like the absentminded old man.

Yet that tension was there. We spoke only of neutral things: where he got gasoline to feed the generator that powered wall sockets in the ground-floor rooms (we did not discuss where he would store the gas now that I'd ruined his

200-gallon tank). How far he had to walk these days to find scavengeable flour, beans, and grains. The trouble he had encountered in maintaining the university's hydroponics cultures by himself. What he did with sewage and compost. The probability of tomatoes growing another year in the miserable sandy soil of Central Park. What a turkey he was not to have thought of using the alcohol in the Organic Chem labs for fuel. Never did we talk of why he undertook all the complex difficulty of living in New York, nor why I had sought him here. He diverted the patient with light conversation, and the patient allowed him to do so.

I had the hate part all ready to go, but I couldn't superimpose my lifetime picture of Carlson over this fuzzy, pleasant old academic and make it fit. And so the hate boiled in my skull and made convalescence an aimless, confused time. It got much worse when Carlson, explaining that few things on earth are more addictive than oral demerol, cut me off cold turkey in my second week. Less potent analgesics, Talwin, aspirin, all had decayed quickly, and if I sent Carlson rummaging through the rucksack I'd left off campus for the remaining weed, he would in all likelihood come across the annotated map of New York given me by Collaci, and the mimeo'd Carlson Poster. Besides, my ribs hurt too much to smoke.

One night I woke in sweat-soaked agony to find the room at a crazy angle, the candle flame slanting out of the dark like a questing tongue. I had half-fallen out of bed, and my right arm kept me from falling the rest of the way, but I could not get back up without another arm. I didn't seem to have one. Ribs began to throb as I considered the dilemma, and I cried out from the pain.

From out in the hallway came a honking snore that broke off in a grunted "Whazzat? Wha?" and then a series of gasps as Carlson dutifully rolled from his bed to assist me. There came a crash, then a greater one attended by a splash, then a really tremendous crash that echoed and reechoed. Carlson lurched into view, a potbellied old man in yellow pajamas, eyes three-quarters closed and unfocused, one foot trapped in a galvanized wastebasket, gallantly coming to my rescue. He hit the door frame a glancing blow with his shoulder, overbalanced and went down on his face. I believe he came

58

fully awake a second after he hit the floor; his eyes opened wide and he saw me staring at him in dazed disbelief from a few inches away. And for one timeless moment the absurdity of our respective positions hit us, and we broke up, simultaneous whoops of laughter at ourselves that cut off at once, and a second later he was helping me back into bed with strong, gentle hands, and I was trying not to groan aloud.

Dammit, I liked him.

Then one day while he was away I rose from the bed all by myself, quite gratified to find that I could, and hobbled like an old, old, man composed of glass to the window that looked out on the entrance area of Butler and the hedge-hidden quadrangle beyond. It was a chill, slightly off-white day, but to me even the meager colors of shrub and tree seemed unaccountably vivid. From the overfamiliar closeness of the sickroom, the decaying campus had a magnificent depth. Everything was so *far away*. It was a little overwhelming. Moving closer to the window, I looked to the right.

Carlson stood before the front doors, staring up at the sky over the quadrangle with his back to me. On his head was the same curious helmet I had seen once before, days ago, framed in the crosshairs of my rifle. Its tangle of wires was plugged into the large console I recalled. I wondered again what it could be, and then I saw something that made me freeze, made me forget the pain and the dizziness and stare with full attention.

Carlson was staring down the row between two greatly overgrown hedges that ran parallel to each other and perpendicular to Butler, facing toward Lowe's mighty cascade of steps. But he stared as a man watching something *near* him, and its position followed that of the wind-tossed upper reaches of the hedges.

Intuitively I knew that he was using the strange machine to communicate with a Musky, and all the hatred and rage for which I had found no outlet boiled over, contorting my face with fury.

It seemed an enormous effort not to cry out some primal challenge; I believe I bared my teeth. *You bastard,* I thought savagely, *you set us up for them, made them our enemies, and now you're hand in glove with them.* I was stupefied by such incredible treachery, could not make any sense of it, did not care. As I watched from behind and to the left I saw his lips move silently, but I did not care what they said, what kind of deal Carlson had worked out with the murderous gas-clouds. He had one. He dealt with the creatures that had killed my mother, that he had virtually created. He would soon die.

I shuffled with infinite care back to bed, and planned.

I was ready to kill him within a week. My ribs were mostly healed now—I came to realize that my body's repair process had been waiting only for me to decide to heal, to leave the safe haven of convalescence. My strength returned to me and soon I could walk easily, and even dress myself with care, letting the left sleeve dangle. Most of the pain was gone from the stump, leaving only the many annoying tactile phenomena of severed nerves, the classic "phantom arm" and the flood of sweat which seemed to pour from my left armpit but could not be found on my side. Thanks to Carlson's tendency toward sound sleep, I was familiar with the layout of the main floor—and had recovered the weapons he was too absentminded to destroy. He had "hidden" them in a broom closet.

I wanted to take him in a time and place where his Musky pals couldn't help him; it seemed to me certain that the ones I had destroyed were bodyguards. A blustery cold night obliged by occurring almost immediately, breezes too choppy to be effectively used by a windrider.

The kind of night which, in my childhood, we chose for a picnic or a hayride.

We ate together in my room, a bean-and-lentil dish with tamari and fresh bread, and as he was finishing his last sip of tea I brought the rifle out from under the blanket and drew a bead on his face.

"End of the line, Wendell."

He sat absolutely still, cup still raised to his lips, gazing gravely over it at me, for a long moment. Then he put the cup down very slowly, and sighed. "I didn't think you'd do it so soon. You're not well enough, you know."

I grinned. "You were expecting this, huh?"

"Ever since you discovered your weapons the night before last."

My grin faded. "And you let me live? Wendell, have you a death wish?"

"I cannot kill," he said sadly, and I roared with sudden laughter.

"Maybe not any more, Wendell. Certainly not in another few minutes." *But you have killed before, killed more than anyone in history. Hell, Hitler, Attila, they're punks beside you!*

He grimaced. "So you know who I am."

"The whole world knows. What's left of it."

Pain filled his eyes, and he nodded. "The last few times I tried to leave this city, to find others to help me in my work, they shot at me. Two years ago I found a man down in the Bowery who had been attacked by a dog pack. He said he had come to kill me for the price on my head, and he died in my arms, cursing me, as I brought him here. The price he named was high, and I knew there would be others."

"And you nursed me back to health? You must know that you deserve to die." I sneered. "Musky-lover."

"You know even that, then?"

"I saw you talking with them, with that crazy machine of yours. The ones who attacked me were your bodyguards, weren't they?"

"The windriders came to me almost twenty years ago," he said softly, eyes far away. "They did not harm me. Since then I have slowly learned to speak with them, after a fashion, using the undermind. We might yet have understood one another."

The gun was becoming heavy on my single arm, difficult to aim properly, I rested the barrel on my knee and shifted my grip slightly. My hands were sweaty.

"Well?" he said gruffly. "Why haven't you killed me already?"

A good question. I swept it aside irritably. "Why did you do it?" I barked.

"Why did I create the Hyperosmic Virus?" His weathered face saddened even more, and he tugged at his beard, his voice anguished. "Because I was a damned fool, I suppose.

61

Because it was a pretty problem in biochemistry. Because no one else could have done it, and because I wasn't certain that I could. I never suspected when I began that it would be used as it was."

"Its release was a spur-of-the-moment decision, is that it?" I snarled, tightening my grip on the trigger.

"I suppose so," he said quietly. "Only Jacob could tell us for sure."

"*Who?*"

"Jacob Stone," he said, startled by my violence. "My assistant. I thought you said you . . ."

"So you knew who I was all the time," I growled.

He blinked at me, plainly astounded. Then understanding flooded his craggy features. "Of course," he murmured. "Of course. You're young Isham—I should have recognized you. I smelled your hate, of course, but I never . . ."

"You *what?*"

"Smelled the scent of hate upon you," he repeated, puzzled. "Not much of a trick—you've been reeking with it."

How could he—impossible, sweep it aside.

"And now I imagine you'll want to discharge that hate and avenge your father's death. That was his own doing, but no matter: it was I who made it possible. Go ahead, pull the trigger." He closed his eyes.

"My father is not dead," I said, drowning now in confusion.

Carlson opened his eyes at once. "No? I assumed he perished when he released the Virus."

My ears roared; the rifle was suddenly impossible to aim. I wanted to cry out, to damn Carlson for a liar, but I knew the fuzzy professor was no actor and all at once I sprang up out of the bed and burst from the room, through wrought-iron lobby doors and out of the great hall, out into blackness and howling wind and a great swirling kaleidoscope of stars that reeled drunkenly overhead. Ribs pulsing, I walked for a hundred years, clutching my idiot rifle, heedless of danger from Musky or hungry Doberman, pursued by a thousand howling demons. Dimly I heard Carlson calling out behind me for a time, but I lost him easily and continued, seeking

62

oblivion. The city, finding its natural prey for the first time in two decades, obligingly swallowed me up.

More than a day later I had my next conscious thought. I became aware that I had been staring at my socks for at least an hour, trying to decide what color they were.

My second coherent thought was that my ass hurt.

I looked around: beyond smashed observation windows, the great steel and stone corpse of New York City was laid out below me like some incredible three-dimensional jigsaw. I was at the top of the Empire State Building.

I had no memory of the long climb, nor of the flight downtown from Columbia University, and it was only after I had worked out how tired I must be that I realized how tired I was. My ribs felt sandblasted, and the winds that swept through the observation tower were very very cold.

I was higher from the earth than I had ever been before in my life, facing south toward the empty World Trade Center, toward that part of the Atlantic into which this city had once dumped five hundred cubic feet of human shit every day; but I saw neither city nor sea. Instead I saw a frustrated, ambitious black man, obsessed with a scheme for quick-and-easy world salvation, conning a fuzzy-headed genius whose eminence he could never hope to attain. I saw that man, terrified by the ghastly results of his folly, fashioning a story to shift blame from himself and repeating it until all men believed it—and perhaps he himself as well. I saw at last the true face of that story's villain: a tormented, guilt-driven old man, exiled for the high crime of gullibility, befriended only by his race's bitterest enemies, nursing his assassin back to health. And I saw as though for the first time that assassin, trained and schooled to complete a cover-up, the embittered black man's last bucket of whitewash.

My father had loaded me with all the hatred and anger he felt for himself, aimed me toward a scapegoat and fired me like a cannonball.

But I would ricochet.

I became aware of noise below me, in the interior of the building. I waited incuriously, not even troubling to lift my

63

rifle from my lap. The noise became weary footsteps on the floor below me. They shuffled slowly up the iron stairway nearest me, and paused at the top. I heard hoarse, wheezing breath, struggling to slow itself, succeeding. I did not turn.

"Hell of a view," I said, squinting at it.

"View of a hell," Carlson wheezed behind me.

"How'd you find me, Wendell?"

"I followed your spoor."

I spun, stared at him. "You . . . ?"

"Followed your spoor."

I turned around again, and giggled. The giggle became a chuckle, and then I sat on it. "Still got your adenoids, eh, doc? Sure. Twenty years in this rotten graveyard and I'll bet you've never owned a set of noseplugs. Punishment to fit the crime—and then some."

He did not reply. His breathing was easier now.

"My father, Wendell, now there's an absentminded man for you," I went on conversationally. "Always doing some sort of Civilized work, always forgetting to remove his plugs when he comes home—he surely does take a lot of kidding. Our security chief, Phil Collaci, quietly makes sure Dad has a Guard with him at all times when he goes outdoors—just can't depend on Dad's sense of smell, Teach' says. Dad always was a terrible cook, you know? He always puts too much garlic in the soup. Am I boring you, Wendell? Would you like to hear the lovely death I just dreamed? I am the last assassin on earth, and I have just created a brand-new death, a unique one. It convicts as it kills—if you die, you deserve to." My voice was quite shrill now, and a part of me clinically diagnosed hysteria. Carlson said something I did not hear as I raved of toilet bowls and brains splashing on a sidewalk and impossible thousands of chittering grey rats and my eyes went nova and a carillon shattered in my skull and when the world came back I realized that the exhausted old man had slapped my head near off my shoulders. He crouched beside me, holding his hand and wincing.

"Why have no Muskies attacked me, here in the heights?" My voice was soft now, wind-tossed.

"The windriders project and receive emotions. Those who sorrow as you and I engender respect and fear in them. You

64

are protected now, as I have been these twenty years. An expensive shield."

I blinked at him and burst into tears.

He held me then in his frail old arms, as my father had never done, and rocked me while I wept. I wept until I was exhausted, and when I had not cried for a time he said softly, "You will put away your new death, unused. You are his son, and you love him."

I shivered then, and he held me closer, and did not see me smile.

So there you have it, Teach'. Stop thinking of Jacob Stone as the Father of Fresh Start, and see him as a man—and you will not only realize that his sense of smell was a hoax, but like me will wonder how you were ever taken in by so transparent a fiction. There are a dozen blameless explanations for Dad's anosmia—none of which would have required pretense.

So look at the method of his dying. The lid of the septic tank will be found ajar—the bathroom will surely smell of chlorine. Ask yourself how a chemist could possibly walk into such a trap—*if he had any sense of smell at all?*

Better yet, examine the corpse for adenoids.

When you've put it all together, come look me up. I'll be at Columbia University, with my good friend Wendell Morgan Carlson. We have a lot of work to do, and I suspect we'll need the help of you and the Council before long. We're learning to speak Musky, you see. . . .

If you come at night, I've got a little place of my own set up in the lobby of the Waldorf Astoria. You can't miss me. But be sure to knock: I'm Musky-proof these days, but I've still got those subconscious sentries you gave me.

And I'm scared of the dark.

Chapter Seven

From the Journal of Isham Stone

Force corps ins heaven yours I go hour four fathers found dead a pond discon tune enter noon Asian. . . .

Foreskin and seven beers ago our forefingers foundered upon this condiment a ruination. . . .

Four sore and sullen years to go. . . .

The rosy glow faded, and conscious thought returned. With it came the world in all its sights and smells and sounds, replacing the glittering symmetry of hallucination, the rhythmically shifting paisley swirls and color-splashes seen palpebrally when the mind is in neutral and the eyes rolled up. I was back in my body, in lotus, on the roof of Butler Hall.

The Musky had fled.

I wondered why. My rifle seemed to be in my right hand; hair prickled on the back of neck, ancient reflex-attempt to appear an unchewable bite. With all the tentativeness of a man with third-degree burns reaching for a hot coffeepot, I flared my nostrils and cast, seeking the source of my subconscious alarm. Only the sense of self-preservation could reach me in the undermind.

Through the daily more-bearable stink of the city I isolated the spoor I sought, and grinned sourly.

What else? Collaci.

Seven others, heavily armed by the amount of cordite and magnesium I smelled, all save Collaci saturated with fear-stink. In him I detected, as usual, only the scent of hyper-alertness given off by the trained hunter, the controlled, unreadable spoor of the predator. They say that Muskies never attack Teach'—because he has no emotions for them to perceive him by.

The party were near to the southwest, coming up Riverside Drive at about 113th Street. Slowly they came, and warily, and I found their olfactory auras heartbreakingly familiar. The party was broadcasting a welter of emotions almost identical with those I had felt on my first stormy walk up Broadway nearly three months before. They'd have checked the Waldorf—they knew I was here.

A Musky drifted over St. Hilda's and St. Hugh's School onto Riverside, and the party's spoor did not change—they were all heavily plugged. The Musky started, rose abruptly skyward and caught a westerly; I sent it a fleeting hello as it shot past me over Lewisohn Hall. It inscribed a ballet figure over the Lowe Dome by way of reply and was gone. I could not tell its Name.

I put down my rifle, took the homemade stink bomb from my belt and heaved it as far as I could toward the center of the quad, feeling the irony of a Stone throwing something from this roof. It smashed on pavement, and began smoking. It would alert Wendell, wherever he was.

I took a last look at the campus that lay below me in the rich light of dawn, took my leave of ancient mighty trees and magnificent empty halls. From my high eyrie I could see a great long way, smell a longer. I had come here from my own lodging before daybreak, sensing a good morning for communication with the windriders, but now there was enough light for me to pick out the stylized letters carved in the granite face of Lowe Library:

KINGS • COLLEGE • FOUNDED • IN • THE
PROVINCE • OF • NEW • YORK
By Royal Charter In the Reign of George II

Perpetuated As COLUMBIA COLLEGE By The People of the State of New York When They Became Free & Independent—Maintained & Cherished from Generation to Generation For the Advancement Of The Public Good & The Glory of Almighty God

Such pomp for an institution that hadn't lasted much more than two hundred years.

I recovered my rifle when my nose told me that Collaci and his party had turned down 114th Street and begun an encircling maneuver around Butler. I did not need to follow that maneuver—Collaci being Collaci, he would make the most logical and effective dispersal of his forces. Two men would cover the two exits onto 114th Street. Two would watch the windows facing on Amsterdam Avenue. One would cover the entrance I had used, between Furnald and Ferris Booth halls. The last two would seal off either end of College Walk, and Collaci himself would almost certainly approach Butler alone from the north—he knew from information I'd left behind where my center of operations was. I'd expected an extra man—a utility infielder—but I didn't miss him any.

I rose to my feet and made my way downstairs, whistling through my teeth. Wendell was on his own now, as ready as I had been able to make him, and I had some talking to do.

As I descended the dusty stairways, past booby traps and deadfalls and other lethal secrets, I wondered why I felt none of the old symptoms, the old emotions at the prospect of imminent combat. No adrenaline sang through my veins, no infusion of deadly purpose, no eagerness for the kill, no drive to be about it. I rather hoped we could avoid violence altogether, though the presence of so many made it seem unlikely. Still juggling a powder keg with a hot branding iron, just like always, but not so happy about it.

Maybe losing an arm had lost me my guts.

Then again, I kept going. The emotional symbolism of the place and the presence, the mere *idea* of Wendell Morgan Carlson made for an explosive situation, and the opposition was led by the only man on earth I *knew* was a better fighter than me, but I kept going. Passing as I went the booby traps and deadfalls and other lethal secrets that might or might not cover my retreat.

I cut in the generator as I reached the ground floor, and the front door lights were blazing into life as I emerged from the lobby, rifle slung low, parallel to the ground. It had taken me some time to reach the ground from the high roof, and the absence of gunfire convinced me that Wendell had made it to cover successfully. I hoped I could shortly give the prearranged signal for him to come out of hiding. I hoped I could shortly do anything, like raise a pulse.

Out the front doors:

Waist- and chest-high grass, a mohawk strip bounded on either side by cracked concrete sidewalks flanked with overgrown hedges, the whole enclosed alley ending in steps up to perpendicular College Walk, which spans the campus east-west from Broadway to Amsterdam.

In the center of the top step, Collaci.

Lean, hollow face, apparently carved by a whittler in a hurry, all angles and planes. Deepset eyesockets, deep enough to make his brow appear broader than it was, and the incongruously rounded, thrice-broken nose from which depended a ferocious moustache. A ringer for a long-dead actor named Boone. Dressed in black as I had been, black knit cap over his crewcut. Crossed bandoliers of ammo, four grenades in sight, two concussion-type and two incendiaries. One handgun visible, a heater rather than a man-killer. But the M-60 in his arms was definitely a slug-thrower: those high-velocity shells could chisel Aristotle's name from the stone facade above my head. Or draw seven circles around Dante. Or through me.

I smiled cheerily.

"Hey, Teach'!"

"Hello, Isham." His voice was pleasant, reassuring, almost convincing. I longed for my lost arm.

"What's new?" I asked as pleasantly.

"I have one dead."

"I'm sorry." So much for the utility infielder.

He looked down at the M-60, smiled. He let it hang from its long sling and took a pipe and matches from his pocket. It was the best chance I'd ever get—both of us shooting from the hip. I thought about it.

And kept on thinking. An even chance was not enough with Collaci.

He got the pipe lit, took a deep lungful of smoke and held it. His eyes met mine. "Hell of a place to get stoned," he called, and sucked back smoke.

"It purely is."

"Somehow you want to, though." He exhaled.

"I haven't been smoking much lately. Too busy."

"First toke in four days myself."

"Enough small talk, Teach'. It's not like you. To what do I owe the etcetera?"

He took another long hit, looked quizzical.

"You were just passing through the city, huh?"

He exhaled easily. "Okay. I've been sent by the Council to bring you back with me to Fresh Start. Krish and the others want to talk with you, boy. At great length."

"What about?"

"How you clip your nails one-handed, I suppose. That sort of thing."

I nodded. "Just an errand boy, that's you—huh, Teach'? You just follow orders. So tell me about it and maybe I'll buy a piece."

"They say you talk with Muskies. This gives Krish a wish. A wish to talk with you."

"I'm the Ambassador from New York, Teach'. I want diplomatic immunity."

"Sling it over your shoulder and come along, son. I'd hate like hell to smash your only arm."

I grinned at him. "What are you offering?"

He looked tired. "Let's not, Isham. I'll get you back to Fresh Start alive, and the Council will decide the rest. It's not for me to be offering. You know that."

Gunfire came suddenly from the northeast. Collaci and I were carved of stone. Or maybe cast in iron, like twin grenades. His gaze was hooded, but then it always was. There were two shots together, then a third, a long pause and then the last two. My heart turned to ice. *So this is what it's like when a friend dies,* said a detached part of my mind, and I absently filed away an astonishing amount of grief for future perusal. I smiled at Collaci, and before that smile he winced.

"Quite a feat, Teach'. Your brave hunters offed an old man with no weapons."

"He must have tried to run," Collaci said dispassionately. "The orders read 'alive for questioning'—but that was *Carlson*. He shouldn't have spooked my men."

"Yeah," I agreed. "He should have walked over here and offered you a beer. He'd have made it."

"He would have."

"Yeah," I said again.

Another pair of shots split the stillness. My heart leaped. There was a sudden fusillade, then silence. The hedges swam like seaweed in the morning breeze, and shafts of sunlight danced on the grass between Collaci and me.

"Let's go, Isham," he said finally, flatly.

I made a rude suggestion.

"It's the only arm you've got." The automatic rifle was still slung at his hip, the pipe still in his left hand.

"There's enough food behind me for a long siege, Teach'," I called, "and this is a town full of Muskies. Come in after me and see what you've taught me. Or put up that cannon and leave your weapons at your feet and come on inside for negotiation."

He shook his head once.

"Standoff, then."

Footsteps came faintly to the left of him, and a man's head appeared above the chest-high wall of College Walk, jogging toward Collaci. I could have put a slug through his right ear, but it wasn't my business to teach Collaci's newest pupils theirs.

"Boss," said the newcomer, "he got away. Subway."

I remembered the IRT station on Broadway and felt a half ton lighter—thank God! Wendell was safe: men who smelled as scared as this joker would not relish following the devil himself into a subway—their plugs might as well be earrings for all the good they'd do down there.

Collaci frowned, poised on the brink of issuing an order that would not be obeyed. But he was too smart for that, too smart for me.

"Cover him," he rapped, and was suddenly flat on his stomach. I sensed rather than saw the oncoming grenade and spun on my heels, diving for the safety of Butler. But I had strayed too far from first base, and Collaci had picked me off.

The grenade went *past* me, over my head, and went up in

my face as I hurtled toward the doorway. A giant slapped two boulders together, and I flipflopped in the air, landing on my back about where I had started.

Incredibly, I was still conscious, but I could not get through to my body. I saw hedges sway above me, felt flames lap my ankles, and wished I could whistle. "Born to Lose" was on my mind.

The sun went out gradually, as if someone were slowly turning down its rheostat.

Regaining consciousness in Butler Hall can get to be boring, if you do it often enough. But this was easier than the first time. As my eyes opened I checked my equipment immediately, and discovered to my considerable relief that I had everything I had started with. I was stiff as a February breeze, but my strength was with me and my head was clear.

Collaci sat beside the bed, perennial toothpick in his mouth, a .45 held lazily in his bony-knuckled hand. As my eyes opened he lined up the pistol with them, and being reminded thereby of a subway tunnel I rejoiced, remembering Wendell's escape.

But grinning hurt my face, so I stopped. Collaci saw this and lowered the gun. "Anything feel broken inside?"

"Just my heart, Teach'." I felt light-headed and vaguely aware that that was suspect.

Collaci thought so, too. "How many fingers?" he asked, and held up his free hand. I read the number of fingers and gave him the same in reply, putting my arm into it. He barked a laugh and brought up the gun again. "You'll do," he said, grinning fiercely. *Sonofabitch is pleased*, I thought dizzily. So was I, come to think.

I suddenly realized where we were—my old room—and how far into the building. Those booby traps had been pretty good. "How many did you lose?" I croaked.

His grin disappeared. "Two. Counting the one you scragged before you jumped."

I had?

"Pretty good, Isham. I guess I should be proud of you."

I guessed so, too. Reflexes that operate without even notifying you are impressive indeed. I told him so.

72

"You don't look happy," he observed.

"Funny thing happened to me on my way to New York," I said. "I stopped getting off on killing people."

He nodded slowly. "Bound to happen to me someday. Soon after that someone'll explode a grenade in my face. You were actually hoping I'd just go away, weren't you?"

"Well . . . I had hopes."

He regarded me for a moment with eyes like chips of obsidian. "You've changed." A sneer. "Gone pacifist, boy?"

"Not exactly. Put that forty-five caliber advantage back in its holster and I'll break both your arms for you with one of mine. On the other hand, I'd like you to know that if you close the door behind you on the way out, a shape charge in the door frame will snap your spine."

A normal man would have started or jumped. Collaci looked intrigued. "The difference?"

"I still understand revenge and self-defense. But I'll stop short of killing if I possibly can. It's too final. You never have all the facts and you can't undo it afterward."

"You regret killing Jacob?" he asked distantly.

"No."

He seemed somehow happy about that, but I couldn't read the why on his chiseled face. He stood, spat out a mangled toothpick and twitched the .45 a millimeter toward the door. "Let's go, Isham."

"Eh?"

" 'We're blowin' this burg.' Come on, come on. I mean to be out of town by nightfall."

I started to rise, then bit off a scream and fell back, holding my middle. "My gut!"

Collaci's eyes narrowed. " 'Up' I said."

"Can't . . . can't make it, Teach'."

Thunder filled the room. Three slugs ripped into the bed, each a foot closer to my crotch. I flopped weakly and yelped. The forth failed to smack into my belly.

"I guess maybe you *are* hurt," Collaci mused.

A short man ducked into the room and tossed a grenade onto the bed. Collaci looked startled.

I swept it toward the window and sprang, heard glass shatter as I landed, rolled into a ball, behind a file cabinet.

There was no explosion.

Instead I heard Collaci chuckle. "Thanks, Joe. Well, Isham? Coming? Or do I start breaking fingers?"

I rose cursing to my feet and preceded Collaci down the hall to the crisp afternoon outdoors vastly chagrined. Good old subconscious sentries—smart as turnips.

Collaci left the door open behind him.

The day was sunny, and the breeze was from the east, a breeze ridden only by birds. Five guards sat around a campfire on the broad concrete sward in a rough circle, eating field rations and managing to look sullen, scared and salty all at the same time. Three I knew slightly, and two appeared to be hill-folk from the mountains north of Fresh Start. These latter, set apart by their tied-back swaths of long hair, would be the most superstitious, the most spooked. But the three who came from my own home, the last bastion of scientific thought, gave off the smell of fear just as strongly. This devil city had taken three of their comrades.

And I was, in their minds, its most recent avatar.

They rose raggedly as we approached, and I heard growls, saw hands go to weapons. Of the three Fresh Starters, the one I knew best was ignoring his sidearm entirely and fondling his knife with dismaying fervor. Joe, the hill-man who had hurled the phony grenade, looked from me to Collaci and murmured, "Anybody say we got to bring *all* of him home, boss?" They didn't seem like friends for the making.

And Collaci barked once and the five came to something very like attention. He stood before them with fists on his hips and spoke, his voice like cold steel. "This man is under my care. The Council of Fresh Start wishes to have speech with him. And that makes his life worth more than yours—at the moment. You'll guard him like hawks, and you'll die for him if you must. Anybody got a beef?"

Nobody had a beef.

We sat out for Fresh Start.

After we cleared Passaic, New Jersey wasn't too hard to take. It was good to see countryside again, hills and patches of earth, and even the highway we sort of followed had poplars growing right up out of it at fairly regular intervals. Some of them housed birds, who sang. Long-abandoned automobiles lent a note of color, mostly rust-red, and were arranged singly and in bunches with the randomness of true natural beauty. But it was the trees beside the road that held my eyes—while I had toiled in the city, autumn had been spraying latex around the land. It seemed that no two leaves were the same color.

We marched in silence. I limped for all I was worth, but I didn't seem to impress anyone very much. No, take that back—I impressed the hell out of *me*. As I hobbled through growing darkness I thought often of Alia, wondered for the thousandth time what name you could give to the thing that had happened to us on our last night—the night before I set out to track and kill Carlson, months ago. I wondered what she thought of me, when she did, if she did. I wondered what I thought of her, and knew I could not postpone finding out much longer. She had come to my home when I first returned from the city, but I had had Dad send her away. She never returned, and I left her as my only loose end when I left home again shortly thereafter. Seems like you just shouldn't ever leave a world behind with loose ends in it— you might not be back.

Here I was doing it again.

Long after sundown Collaci called a halt beneath a half-crumbled overpass and announced we were camping for the night. Bedrolls were opened and canteens passed round. Nobody offered me a drink. I collapsed where I stood, a hair too melodramatically if my tailbone had anything to say about it, and made my eyes unfocus as I stared at Collaci. He laughed and threw something at me—I had ducked and caught it with my outflung arm before I realized I'd been suckered again.

It was a four-day-old edition of *Got News*, the weekly my father and two other men had begun nearly two decades ago, when they began consolidating Fresh Start and feeling the need for a public-relations arm. Lately it was a photo-offset eight-pager, nearly half that classified ads.

But page one was still the traditional spot for news. The 36-point bold head said: "JACOB STONE DEAD." Beneath

75

it a subhead added: "Founding Father of Fresh Start Found Apparently Slain."

I scanned the copy. Jacob Stone, respected leader and thinker, had been found dead in his home. Foul play was suspected, but there was no clue to the identity of his assailant, if any. Further details would be forthcoming; Security Chief Collaci had promised to issue a statement soon etcetera.

For a story that said nothing, it sure said a lot.

No mention of my tape or manuscript, no mention of my name anywhere. Not even so much as a description of the cause of death. That tight a lid on a story of this magnitude was almost incredible—hell, I guess Dad was one of the most respected men in the world. A lot of people must be finding this story baffling. The cover-up could not last: soon the Council would have to (a) publish the truth, or (b) offer up a fall guy. It seemed from the events of the past twelve hours or so that my name was patsy. By why, dammit, wouldn't the truth serve?

Sure it would shock a lot of people. But truth is truth. Or so I believed.

I decided to ask Collaci. I looked up to see him lying about ten yards from me, cocooned in his sleeping bag, facing the other way. A foodtab dinner had taken him no longer than reading the paper had taken me. The odds were even that the old hunter was sound asleep—he had that predator's ability to sleep where and when it was safe, instantly—with the corollary ability to come awake just as instantly. But I was burning to hear some kind of explanation for the things I had read—I decided to risk approaching the sleeping wolf from behind.

I didn't actually tap-dance to him, but no one could have said I was tiptoeing. Or pussyfooting. A pussy in platform shoes would have made less noise approaching Collaci than I did. None of the guards he had inevitably posted nor the other eating, resting members of the hunting party even felt it necessary to raise their weapons, growl, or even glance my way. We were in the country, plugless all, and they knew I knew they could track me perfectly by scent.

As of course could Collaci, even sound asleep. And my self-esteem rose some trifling fraction when he troubled to

76

roll over and face me, gun preternaturally occurring in his fist, before I had covered half the distance between us.

"Sorry to wake you, Teach'," I said, pitching my voice for his ears only.

"What do you want?"

I sat down beside him. "Been reading the paper."

He grunted.

"Mighty interesting lead story. All that's missing is the story."

He grunted again.

"What kind of shit is that, anyway?"

He looked at me for a long moment, weighing something, and then his lip curled. "You're young, boy," he said sourly, "and I've been missing my two flankers and tailgunner all day, so I'm not inclined to grow you up politically tonight. Figure it out." And with that he rolled over savagely and shoved the gun back under his pillow, leaving me with venom dripping out of my ears, mightily confused. He must have had some reason for showing me the paper in the first place. I couldn't decide if he loved me or hated me.

It occurred to me that I never *had* known.

A large man with a face like an underdone turnip tossed me a bedroll, and as I bent to lay it out and unzip it, added a tin of K-rations with considerable vim. The tin caught me on the tail, which smarted enough already, and I spun angrily. He was covering me with a reconditioned Winchester, grinning. Have you ever seen a turnip grin? I thought longingly of turnip stew, then gave it up and sat down to eat.

It was a wonderful meal, with the consistency of old stove cement and a flavor between shoeleather and toasted mucus. I washed it down with spit and thought hard. By rights, by all logic, Collaci should have had a million questions to ask, about my claim that Wendell and I could communicate with Muskies, if nothing else. But he displayed no curiosity, no inclination to swap stories—or even civilities. I could imagine him deciding that the story I'd left behind for him was a fiction. I could picture him deciding to put the arm on me for murdering Dad. But I couldn't picture him behaving the way he was now—it didn't fit, it didn't jibe. If Collaci had a theory that featured me as a liar, he'd be testing it, asking

77

probing questions, interrogating me. As far as I knew he was the last living, Pre-Exodus cop in the world—and he was acting more a dog fetching a stick.

An hour's thinking produced no results. I swore softly for a while in Swahili and slept.

And woke, unknown time later, into an uproar of gunfire and shouting men.

Hot-shots split the darkness, and brilliant yellow-green flame blossomed in the trail of one of them, leaving a momentary ghastly view of men struggling from sleeping bags, firing as they came. Then blackness fell again and only the hot-shots and muzzle-flashes were visible.

You don't need to see to fight. My nostrils flared even as I wriggled one-handed from my sleeping bag, and I counted at least eight Muskies, at such close quarters it was impossible to pin down the number with accuracy. Jerked from sleep, surrounded by shouting, shooting men, I could not easily enter the undermind state, but I tried. If my complexion had allowed it, I would have paled. The fragmentary interface I achieved indicated nearly a full Name of windriders within a three-mile radius!

We were outgunned.

Outgunned? I didn't have a *match*. But then, I didn't want—or need—one. If I could reach Collaci at once, and make him believe me.

I threw back my head and bellowed. "Heeeeyyyy RUBE!" I don't know what the hell it means, but it fetched him like it always does. He reared up out of the gloom, a smoking Musky-gun in his hand, and pulled one from his belt for me.

I didn't have time to be flattered or grateful. "Teach', hear me good," I rapped. "Have your men hold their fire."

He gave a full second to staring at me, then snarled and began to turn away. I grabbed his shoulder. "Teach', I know what I'm doing! There's a couple dozen of 'em—*let me parley or we're dead.*"

He started to pull away, and my heart sank. Then he checked, turned back. "What do I do?"

"Thank God! Get your men to hold fire, shut up and stand still."

78

He opened his mouth, then shut it and turned to the chaotic battle raging in the night. "Freeze!" he roared.

Discipline pays off—all firing ceased, and the shouts were supplanted by the sound of men falling where they stood, then by silence. "Start an Om," I hissed, seating myself in hasty half-lotus.

"What the—"

"Do it," I whispered savagely.

Collaci sat beside me in classic za-zen posture, filled his gut with air, and began:

"AAAAAAAAAAAAOOOOOOOOOOOOOMMMMM . . ."

For long startled moments he was alone, his men wondering if the Boss had cracked. Then two voices joined him, one on the same note and one on the tonic. As the rest came in, I turned inward and entered the undermind.

Four score and seven years ago our forefathers founded upon this continent a new nation, conceived in liberty and dedicated to the proposition that all men are created equal . . .

Forze corinze heaven years I go arf ore fathers found it a ponthisk on tin enter noon hay shun . . .

For scorin' savin' years Agro are forefingers . . .

(astonishment)[28]

(*greeting*)

(interrogative)[28]
(*identity*)
(confusion)[28]
(*identity*)
(suspicion)[28]
(*IDENTITY*)
(identity)[28]

pause.

(interrogative)[28]
(*incomprehension*)
(interrogative)[28]
(*incomprehension*) (*receptivity*)

(interrogative)[28] (hate)[28]
(*comprehension*) (*love*)
(astonishment)[28]

another pause, and an added depth of communication.

(Name?)[28]
(*Wendell Morgan Carlson*)
(sudden comprehension)[28] (sympathy)[28]

Thank God!

(requests?)[28]
(*go in peace*)
(it is done)[28]
(*wait*) (*Name?*)
(it is proper)[28] (Sirocco)[28]
(*identity*) (*farewell*)
(identity)[28] (farewell)[28]

   . . . *con sieve din libber tea end dead a cay to tooth a proper zish in that Allman are creative sequels* . . .
   Fore scorn's heaven years aglow . . .
   The group Om-chant pillowed me gently back to reality like a psychic parachute, and I was back in my conscious, the consciousness-occupying word games gone, no longer needed. The night sky no longer smelled musky.
   The Sirocco Clan had gone.
   As his own nostrils confirmed this, Collaci stopped Om-ing beside me. I wondered if I should tell him that he had just joined the Carlson Clan.
   "Anyone hurt?" he called softly. The Om ceased; stillness returned to the night.
   "All here, all whole, major," came a hoarse voice.
   "Shift guards and sack out," he ordered and was obeyed. There was no conversation, and not because the Boss wouldn't have liked it.
   He turned to me then, and looked at me in silence through the dark for a long time. He passed me his pipe and lit it for me. I nearly choked: it was hash. And as a I sucked deep on

the token of friendship he began to talk softly, speaking at first of apparently unrelated things. It was his way of saying thanks—I guess he hated losing men under his command. I kept my lip buttoned and both ears open, and by dawn I understood why the Council had decided that I must die.

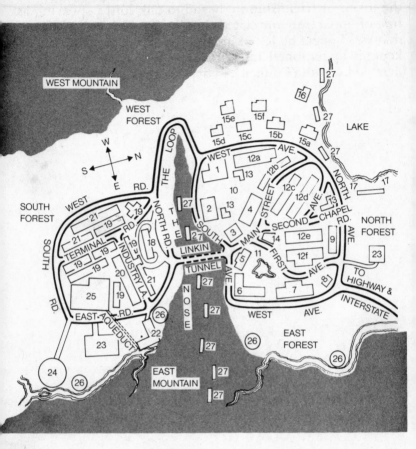

1 The Tool Shed
2 The Pantry
3 Hospital
4 The General Store
5 Security HQ
6 The Ad Building
7 School (P.S. 1)
8 The Gate
9 Theater (planned)
10 Sports Field
11 Town Square & Pond

12 Dormitories:
  a) Hilton b) Sheraton
  c) Statler d) HoJo Inn
  e) Ritz f) Holiday Inn
13 Public Showers
14 Church
15 Private Homes:
  a) Store b) Krishnamurti
  c) Phinney d) Dalhouse
  e) Collaci f) Gowan
16 Stone Study

17 Public Beach
18 Motor Pool
19 Factories
20 Munitions
21 Research Labs
22 Distillery
23 Sewage-Methane Converter
24 Fuel Dump
25 Power Plant
26 Water Towers
27 Windmills

Chapter Eight

Excerpts from The Building of Fresh Start, *by Jacob Stone, Ph.D., authorized version: Fresh Start Press, 2001*

Although Fresh Start grew slowly and apparently randomly as personnel and materials became available, its development followed the basic outline of a master plan conceived within a year of the Exodus. Of course, I had not the training or experience to visualize specifics of my dream at that early stage—but the basic layout was inherent in the shape of the landscape and in the nature of the new world Carlson had made for us all.

Five years prior to the Exodus, a man named Gallipolis had acquired title, by devious means, to a logged-out area some distance northwest of New York City. It was an isolated two hundred-acre parcel of an extremely odd shape. Seen from the air it must have resembled an enormous pair of green sunglasses: two valleys choking with new growth, separated physically by a great perpendicular extrusion of the eastern mountain range, almost to the western slopes, leaving the north and south valleys joined only by a narrow channel. The perpendicular "nose" between the valley "lenses" was a tall, rocky ridge, sharply sloped on both sides, forming a perfect natural division. The land dropped gently away from the foot of this ridge in either direction, and dirt roads left by the loggers cut great loops through both valleys. The land was utterly unsuited for farming, and too many miles from nowhere for suburban development—it was what real estate brokers called "an investment in the future."

Gallipolis was a mad Greek. Mad Greeks in literature are invariably swarthy, undereducated, poor, and drunk. Gallipolis was florid, superbly educated, moderately well off and a teetotaler. He looked upon his valleys and he smiled a mad smile and decided to hell with the future. He had a serviceable road cut through the north forest past the lake, to a lonely stretch of state highway which fed into the nearby Interstate. He brought bulldozers down this road and had six widely spaced acres cleared west of the logging road loop in the north valley, and a seventh acre on the lakeshore for himself. On these sites he built large and extremely comfortable homes, masterpieces of design which combined an appearance of "roughing it" with every imaginable modern convenience. He piped in water from spring-fed streams high on the slopes of the Nose (as he had come to call the central ridge). He built beach houses along the lake shore. It was his plan to lease the homes to wealthy men as weekend or summer homes at an exorbitant fee, and use the proceeds to develop three similar sites in both valleys. He envisioned an ultimate two or three dozen homes and an early retirement, but the only two things he ultimately achieved were to go broke before a single home had been leased and to drop dead.

A nephew inherited the land—and the staggering tax bill. He chanced to be a student of mine, and was aware that I was in the market for a weekend haven from the rigors of the city; he approached me. Although the place was an absurdly long drive from New York, I went up with him one Saturday, looked over the house nearest the lake, made him a firm offer of a quarter of his asking price, and closed the deal on the spot. It was a beautiful place. My wife and I became quite fond of it and never missed an opportunity to steal a weekend there. Before long we had neighbors, but we seldom saw them, save occasionally at the lake. We had all come there for a bit of solitude, and it was quite a big lake—none of us were socially inclined.

It was for this wooded retreat that my family and I made in

84

the horrible hours of the Exodus, and only by the grace of God did we make it. Certainly none of the other tenants did, then or ever, and it must be assumed that they perished. Sarwar Krishnamurti, a chemist at Columbia who had been an occasional weekend guest at Stone Manor, remembered the place in his time of need and showed up almost at once, with his family. He was followed a few days later by George Dalhousie, a friend of mine from the Engineering Department to whom I had once given directions to the place.

We made them as welcome as we could under the circumstances—my wife was in a virtual state of shock from the loss of our eldest son, and none of us were in much better shape. I know we three men found enormous comfort in each other's presence, in having other men of science with whom to share our horror, our astonishment, our guesses and our grim extrapolations. It kept us sane, kept our minds on practical matters, on survival; for had we been alone, we might have succumbed, as did so many, to a numb, traumatized disinterest in living.

Instead, we survived the winter that came, the one that killed so many, and by spring we had laid our plans.

We made occasional abortive forays into the outside world, gathering information from wandering survivors. All media save rumor had perished; even my international-band radio was silent. On these expeditions we were always careful to conceal the existence and location of our home base, pretending to be as disorganized and homeless as the aimless drifters we continually encountered. We came to know every surviving farmer in the surrounding area, and established friendly relations with them by working for them in exchange for food. Like all men, we avoided areas of previous urbanization, for nose plugs were inferior in those days, and Muskies were omnipresent and terrifying. In fact, rumor claimed, they tended to cluster in cities and towns.

But that first spring, we conquered our fear and revulsion with great difficulty and began raiding small towns and industrial parks with a borrowed wagon. We found that rumor had been correct: urban areas were crawling with Muskies. But we needed tools and equipment of all kinds and descriptions, badly enough to risk our lives repeatedly for them. It went slowly, but Dalhousie had his priorities right, and soon we were ready.

We opened our first factory that spring, on a hand-cleared site in the south valley (which we christened "Southtown"). Our first product had been given careful thought, and we chose well—if for the wrong reasons. We anticipated difficulty in convincing people to buy goods from us with barter, when they could just as easily have scavenged from the abandoned urban areas. In fact, one of our central reasons for founding Fresh Start had been the conviction that the lice on a corpse are not a going concern: we did not want our brother survivors to remain dependent on a finite supply of tools, equipment and processed food. If we could risk Musky attack, so could others.

Consequently we selected as our first product an item unobtainable anywhere else, and utterly necessary in the changed world: effective nose plugs. I suggested them; Krishnamurti designed them and the primitive assembly line on which they were first turned out, and Dalhousie directed us all in their construction. All of us, men and women, worked on the line. It took us several months to achieve success, and by that time we were our own best customers—our factory smelled most abominable. Which we had expected, and planned for: the whole concept of Fresh Start rested on the single crucial fact that prevailing winds were virtually always from the north. On the rare occasions when the wind backed, the Nose formed a satisfactory natural barrier.

Once we were ready to offer our plugs for sale, we began advertising and recruiting on a large scale. Word of our plans was circulated by word of mouth, mimeographed flyer and short-wave broadcast. The only person who responded by the onset of winter was Helen Phinney, but her arrival was providential, freeing us almost overnight from dependence on stinking gasoline-powered generators for power. She was then and is now Fresh-Start's only resident world-class genius, a recognized expert on what were then called "alternative" power sources—the only ones Carlson had left us. She quite naturally became a part of the planning process, as well as a warm friend of us all. Within a short time the malodorous generators had been replaced by water power from the streams that cascade like copious tears from the "bridge" of the Nose, and ultimately by methane gas and wind power from a series of eggbeater-type windmills strung along the Nose itself. In recent years the generators have been put back on the line, largely for industrial use—but they no longer burn gasoline, nor does the single truck we have restored to service. Thanks to Phinney, they burn pure grain alcohol which we distill ourselves from field corn and rye, which works *more* efficiently than gasoline and produces only water and carbon dioxide as exhaust. (Pre-Exodus man could have used the same fuel in most of his internal combustion engines—but once Henry Ford made his choice, the industry he incidentally created tended of course to perpetuate itself.)

This then was the Council of Fresh Start, assembled by fate: myself, a dreamer, racked with guilt and seeking a truly worthwhile penance, trying to salvage some of the world I'd helped ruin. Krishnamurti, utterly practical wizard at both requirements analysis and design engineering, translator of ideas into plans. Dalhousie, the ultimate foreman, gifted at reducing any project to its component parts and accomplishing them with minimum time and effort. Phinney, the energy provider, devoted to drawing free power from the natural processes of the universe. Our personalities blended as well as our skills, and by that second spring we were a unit: the Council. I would suggest a thing, Krishnamurti would design the black box, Dalhousie would build it and Phinney would throw power to it. We fit. Together we felt *useful* again, more than scavenging survivors.

No other recruits arrived during the winter, which like the one before was unusually harsh for that part of the world (perhaps owing to the sudden drastic decline in the worldwide production of waste heat), but by spring volunteers began arriving in droves. We got all kinds: scientists, technicians, students, mechanics, handymen, construction workers, factory hands, a random assortment of men seeking Civilized work. A colony of canvas tents grew in Northtown, in cleared areas we hoped would one day hold great dormitories. Our initial efforts that summer were aimed at providing water, power and sewage systems for our growing community, and enlarging our nose-plug factory. A combination smithy-repair shop-motor pool grew of its own accord next to the factory in Southtown, and we began bartering repair work for food with local farmers to the east and northwest.

By common consent, all food, tools, and other resources were shared equally by all members of the community, with the single exception of mad Gallipolis's summer homes. We—the Council members—retained these homes, and have never been begrudged them by our followers (two of the homes were incomplete at the time of the Exodus, and remained so for another few years). That aside, all the inhabitants of Fresh Start stand or fall, eat or starve together. The Council's authority as governing committee has never in all the ensuing years been either confirmed or seriously challenged. The nearly two hundred technicians who have by now assembled to our call continue to follow our advice because it works: because it gives their lives direction and meaning, because it makes their hard-won skills useful again, because it pays them well to do what they do best, and thought they might never do again.

During that second summer we were frequently attacked by Muskies, invariably from the north, and suffered significant losses. For instance, Samuel Pegorski, the young hydraulic engineering major who with Phinney designed and perfected our plumbing and sewage systems, was cut down by the windriders before he lived to hear the first toilet flush in Northtown.

But with the timely arrival of Philip Collaci, an ex-Marine and former police chief from Pennsylvania, our security problems disappeared. A preternaturally effective fighting man, Collaci undertook to recruit, organize and train the Guard, comprising enough armed men to keep the northern perimeter of Fresh Start patrolled at all times. At first, these Guards did no more than sound an alarm if they smelled Muskies coming across the lake, whereupon all hands made for the nearest shelter and tried to blank their minds to the semitelepathic creatures.

But Collaci was not satisfied. He wanted an offensive weapon—or, failing that, a defense better than flight. He told me as much several times, and finally I put aside administrative

88

worries and went to work on the problem from a biochemical standpoint.

It seemed to me that extreme heat should work, but the problem was to devise a delivery system. Early experiments with a salvaged flamethrower were unsatisfactory—the cone of fire tended to brush Muskies out of its path instead of consuming them. Collaci suggested a line of alcohol-burning jets along the north perimeter, ready to guard Fresh Start with a wall of flame, an idea which has since been implemented—but at the time we could not spare the corn or rye to make the alcohol to power the jets. Finally, weeks of research led to the successful development of "hot-shot"—ammunition which could be fired from any existing heavy-caliber weapon after its barrel had been replaced, that would ignite as it cleared the modified barrel and generate enormous heat as it flew, punching through any Musky it encountered and destroying it instantly. An early mixture of magnesium and perchlorate of potash has since given way to an even slower-burning mix of aluminum powder and potassium permanganate which will probably remain standard until the last Musky has been slain. (Long-range plans for long-range artillery shot will have to wait until we can find a good cheap source of cerium, zirconium or thorium—unlikely in the near future.) Hot-shot's effective range approximates that of a man's nose on a still day—good enough for personal combat. This turned out to be the single most important advance since the Exodus, not only for mankind, but for the fledgling community of Fresh Start.

Because our only major misjudgment had been the climate of social opinion in which we expected to find ourselves. I said earlier that we feared people would scavenge from cities rather than buy from us, even in the face of terrible danger from the Muskies who prowled the urban skies. This turned out not to be the case.

Mostly, people preferred to do without.

Secure in our retreat, we had misjudged the *zeitgeist*, the mind of the common man. It was Collaci, fresh from over a year of wandering up and down the desolate eastern seaboard, who showed us our error. He made us realize that Lot was probably more eager to return to Gomorrah than the av-

89

erage human was to return to his cities and suburbs. Cities had been the scenes of the greatest racial trauma since the Flood, the places were friends and loved ones had died horribly and the skies had filled with Muskies. The Exodus and the subsequent weeks of horror were universally seen as the Hammer of God falling on the *idea of city* itself, and hardcore urbanites who might have debated the point were mostly too dead to do so. The back-to-nature movement, already in full swing at the moment when Carlson dropped the flask, took on the stature and fervor of a Dionysiac religion.

Fortunately, Collaci made us see in time that we would inevitably share in the superstition and hatred accorded to cities, become associated in the common mind with the evilsmelling steel-and-glass behemoth from which men had been so conclusively vomited. He made us realize something of the extent of the suspicion and intolerance we would incur—not ignored for our redundance, but loathed for our repugnance.

At Collaci's suggestion Krishnamurti enlisted the aid of some of the more substantial farmers in neighboring regions to the east, northeast, and northwest. He negotiated agreements by which farmers who supported us with food received preferential access to Musky-killing ammunition, equipment maintenance and, one day (he promised), commercial power. I could never have sold the idea myself— while I have always understood public relations well from the theoretical standpoint, I have never been very successful in interpersonal diplomacy—at least, with nontechnicals. The dour Krishnamurti might have seemed an even more unlikely choice—but his utter practicality convinced many a skeptical farmer where charm might have failed.

Krishnamurti's negotiations not only assured us a dependable supply of food (and incidentally, milled lumber), it had the invaluable secondary effect of gaining us psychological allies, non-Technos who were economically and emotionally committed to us.

Work progressed rapidly once our recruiting efforts began to pay off, and by our fifth year the Fresh Start of today was visible, at least in skeleton form. We had cut interior roads to supplement the northern and southern loops left by gyppo loggers two decades before; three dormitories were up and a fourth a-building; our "General Store" was a growing commercial concern; a line of windmills was taking shape along the central ridge of the Nose; our sewage plant/methane converter was nearly completed; plans were underway to establish a hospital and to blast a tunnel through the Nose to link North- and Southtowns; the "Tool Shed," the depot which housed irreplaceable equipment and tools, was nearly full; and Southtown was more malodorous than ever, with a large fuel distillery, a chemistry lab, and glass-blowing, match-making and weaving operations adjoining the hotshot and nose-plug factories.

Despite these outward signs of prosperity, we led a precarious existence—there was strong public sentiment in favor of burning us to the ground, at least among the surviving humans who remained landless nomads. To combat this we were running and distributing a small mimeographed newspaper, *Got News,* and maintaining radio station WFS (then and now the only one in the world). In addition, Krishnamurti and I made endless public relations trips for miles in every direction to explain our existence and purpose to groups and individuals.

But there were many who had no land, no homes, no families, nothing but a vast heritage of bitterness. These were the precursors of today's so-called Agro Party. Surviving where and as they could, socialized for an environment that no longer existed, they hated us for reminding them of the technological womb which had unforgivably thrust them out. They raided us, singly and in loosely organized groups, often with unreasonable, suicidal fury. From humanitarian concerns as much as from public relations considerations, I sharply restrained Guard Chief Collaci, whose own inclination was to shoot any saboteur he apprehended—wherever possible, they were captured and turned loose outside city limits. Collaci argued strongly for deterrent violence, but I was determined to show our neighbors that Fresh Start bore ill will to no man, and overruled him.

In that fifth year, however, I was myself overruled.

Collaci and his wife Karen (a tough, quiet, redheaded

woman) had been given one of Gallipolis's uncompleted cabins, the one farthest and most isolated from Northtown's residential area. A volunteer house-raising had finished it off handsomely the previous spring. It was either bad judgment or ignorance that brought the seven-man raiding party past the Collaci home on their way to blow up the Tool Shed. But it was unquestionably bad judgment that made them kidnap Karen Collaci when they blundered across her in the forest. She was diabetic, and they had no insulin.

Collaci left his duties without authorization and pursued them, found her body within a few days. He tracked the seven guerrillas over a period of a week. Although they had split up and fled in different directions, those seven days sufficed him. He exacted from them penalties which cannot be repeated here, left each nailed to a tree, and upon his return to Fresh Start slept for three consecutive days.

Collaci's understandably impulsive action seems in the light of history to have been more correct than my own policy of tolerance. At any rate, we have never been raided since.

With the advent of Dr. Michael Gowan, a former professor of psychology from Stony Brook who undertook to create and administrate an educational system, all the necessary seeds had, to my mind, been planted. Barring catastrophe, technological man now could and would survive. Someday, perhaps, he might rebuild what had been destroyed.

And then, one day in 1999, I interviewed and "hired" a new arrival named Jordan Washington. . . .

Chapter Nine

Breakfast had been ominously superb. After four days of foodtabs, it could hardly have helped it. One of the nice things about eating real food indoors is that the aromas remain, lingering on the palate long after the last bite has been consumed. The other comfort of home I really appreciated was having been allowed to bathe. Our group had spread out considerably in the last twenty miles or so, and not from fear of attack. *Gee, it's great to be back.*

The room was one I knew well, although I hadn't seen it for years. It was large and comfortably furnished. Three walls were stacked floor to ceiling with a mighty collection of books that spilled over into a series of standup library shelves on the opposite end of the room. Escher and Frazetta prints lined what free wall-space there was, and there was not an uncomfortable chair in the room. From the huge curtained picture window on my right, dawn splashed the long oak table at which I sat, with the remains of my breakfast scattered before me.

I had spent a good many hours of my life sitting at that table, often alone with a book, as often with the owner of books, table and room: Dr. Michael Gowan, Fresh Start's Director of Education. The room held his spoor, and I wondered where he was, now that his home had been picked for V.I.P. prison.

Collaci watched in impassive silence while I ate, ate in silence while I watched. Since that one burst of loquaciousness after the Musky attack three days before, I hadn't been able to get a rise out of him. He didn't seem to regret having explained the facts of life to me—but his interest in further conversation was negligible. I wondered if he had opened up that night from a sense of obligation, payment of a debt of honor—Teach' hates to lose men under his command. The notion left me feeling cheapened, as if he'd left fifty dollars on the bed on his way out.

The two armed Guards also watched me in silence, as they had since we arrived in the middle of the night, and there was never the faintest chance of suckering anyone into the line of fire. I had dozed off in the uncanny stillness before dawn, but I'm certain no one else gave sleep a thought. Four days and three nights of good behavior hadn't earned me so much as an inch of slack, and if I wanted to get a high-velocity slug through my head, all I had to do was look clever when I buttered my toast. Collaci might have been sneakingly grateful for my pacifist powwow with the Sirocco Brothers, but his hired guns appeared to lack the imagination. If anything, their fear-hate had smelled stronger than ever lately. They had seen me commune somehow with things that mankind had sensed, feared, and loathed for centuries, and the happy outcome was irrelevant. *If he's on our side* went one grumble I had overheard on the trek home *whyn't he line them Muskies up where we c'd pick 'em off?*

Of course, they were by no means an accurate reflection of the kinds of minds I'd have to deal with when the Council convened, but they were a depressing preview of the sort of grass-roots reaction I could expect. It soured the maple syrup right on the pancakes.

All that silence got oppressive, so I got up and heated up Dr. Mike's radio (which he still calls a "tuner," even though the useless tuning knob has long since been removed for salvage). But it didn't help much. Dan O'Connor, who replaced me at the board when I split for New York, had become just as rotten a DJ as I'd known he would. His voice was a thin monotone over the AR-4s, and he had apparently decided on a morning program of Latin music. Worst, he forgot to change the selector when he shifted from disc to tape, and let a good twenty seconds of dead air go out before he noticed the absence of signal.

I switched off in disgust, sat down again, and watched Col

laci gulp the remains of his coffee, which unlike my own was still hot. Mine had been given to me with too much milk, too cool to seriously discommode anyone if I happened to spill it in their eyes. It's those little ego-boosts that keep you going.

"Hey Teach'," I asked him cheerily, "can I call you for a witness?" I wanted to needle him, to break through that impenetrable cool and wrest from him a genuine emotion, any emotion at all. Fat chance.

"Son," he said, looking me in the eye, "you can call Wendell *Carlson* for a witness. You can call Marie Antoinette, or the Spirit of Christmas Past. No one'll stop you."

I nodded. "It is expedient that one man should etcetera."

He nodded right back at me. There was just enough expression on his face to half-fill a gnat's pocket. If Teach' had any feelings at all, they were so well shielded a telepath might have missed them. I felt a surge of anger, and sat on it fast. *Who's needling who?* I asked myself. *Keep your cool, my man.*

Myself replied that it made no slightest bit of difference whether I was calm in the next few hours or not—it would have made precious little difference if I'd been unconscious, or absent. The script's conclusion was written; this was only the performance, and to a closed house at that.

So sometimes the ad-libs make the show. Nobody listens to an angry man, and Wendell is counting on you.

Footsteps sounded outside the window, heard through the open doorway. A group of people crunching up the gravel path. One of the Guards left the library on cat feet, and the one covering me went that one last increment toward becoming one with his weapon. Teach' himself sat motionless, a granite promontory carved by the pounding sea into a remarkable likeness of a man.

"It begins," I said, and was annoyed at the hoarseness of the first syllable.

"Yes," he said, and his voice was just as hoarse.

The guard returned almost at once, with the three people I had been expecting: Dalhousie, Phinney, and Krishnamurti. The Council of Fresh Start. There ensued a long pause, during which all three busied themselves with not meeting my eyes or each other's, which was ludicrous enough to restore my good humor.

George Dalhousie clumped in first, the doorway fitting

him as snugly as ever. George is no bigger than a Kodiak bear, and I've seen oxen I believe were stronger. He wore his usual faded denims, and an ancient cracked leather jacket against the morning chill. Big mud-stained engineer's boots encased his feet. His square tanned face was deeply lined, the eyes bagged. His shapeless cap of pepper-and-salt hair was still damp from the shower, and he had shaved hastily. His expression and spoor were not hard to read: George was horribly embarrassed.

Next came Helen Phinney, as immaculate as ever. Her grey hair was yanked back into its customary tight bun, and her lipstick had been drawn with the same precision as one of her circuit diagrams. She smelled mad. As I had expected, she wore black, and her carriage was rigid, as though she were maintaining her organic integrity by an effort of will. I read her hollow eyes and the set of her mouth, and knew that she had loved Dad very much. (He and I spoke of it once. I asked him why he hadn't ever married Helen. "She's white," he had said shortly and changed the subject). I wondered if she had heard my tape—or even listened to it. She glanced at my stump, then away, and I'd have sworn I saw her smile.

Last to enter was Sarwar Krishnamurti, a man cross-filed under several headings in my mind. Systems Planning Chief. Friend of Jacob Stone. Founding Uncle of the Techno Philosophy. Present unofficial mayor of Fresh Start: the man minding the store, anyhow.

And father of Alia.

He looked as crusty as ever (dammit, all three of them were "as ever." It seemed to me they ought to be changed somehow, marked by the decision to take my life. Did I look the same to them as before I'd killed Dad?) He was nearly as tall as Dalhousie, massed perhaps half as much, yet there was nothing gangly about him. His Fu Manchu moustache emphasized the lean planed length of his face and the elongated neck. He wore a tweed suit with vest and a wide necktie, which contrasted ludicrously with his leather sandals. From a mouth like a slit in a piece of paper jutted an empty meerschaum identical with the one my father had been smoking the last time I saw him. He had been more than Dad's second in command—had in some ways been almost a spouse. The

96

two thought alike, dressed alike, worked together, shared so many mannerisms that it was impossible to tell who had originated which. Seeing him I felt just a bit like Hamlet in the first act. Which made his customary expression—purest scorn—more sardonic than ever. He took in my stump, with all the rest of me, in a single sweeping look.

He glanced at his two companions as if realizing for the first time their utter incompetence for the task ahead, which is how he looks at everybody, all the time, and motioned curtly to Collaci. The lean security chief left at once without a backward look, followed by the two Guards. I started to speak, and then subsided, concentrated on measuring my breaths.

The three seated themselves at the opposite end of the table. Dalhousie placed a battery-operated cassette-corder on the table between us and made a few quick level tests, then sat back and left it purring.

Well, pal, here you go. Tell 'em what they have to know. "Howdy, folks."

"Isham Stone," Krishnamurti began formally, "we the Council of F . . ."

"Cool it, Krish. Nobody here but us chickens. You aren't gonna make Nixon's Mistake and put that tape in the archives, so why bother pretending this is a legitimate session of the Council? You're Uncle Krish, Uncle George and Aunt Helen, and my name is Mud—let's get on with the killing."

Dalhousie clouded up, but Krish restrained him with only a shadow of a gesture. "What makes you think this is not a legitimate Council session, Isham?"

I didn't want to get Teach' in trouble (although I couldn't quite remember why not), so I skipped the main reason. "The time. The location, and its owner's mysterious absence. The absence of audience, secretary, Guards and counsel. The ridiculous look on George's face . . . shall I go on?"

"That will not be necessary," Krish said drily. "You are correct. This is a closed session."

"Star chamber—isn't that the phrase?"

"Now listen here," Dalhousie began indignantly.

"Shut up, George," Phinney told him.

"But Helen, he's implying . . ."

"Save it. He's right. Let's get on with it." Dalhousie still looked indignant, but he shut up.

"We shall require from you," Krish went on as if there had been no interruption, "all the data you have acquired regarding the Musky race."

I showed him my teeth. "And if you get it—?"

Dalhousie boiled over. "You want a *reward* for aiding your own race against those living farts?" he roared. "You're going to withhold vital strategic information and *bargain* with us?"

"Well, I confess I had some small hope of coming out of this alive, yes." That jolted him, bringing the guilt back to his face. "*If* it looks like that can be arranged, and *if* you manage to convince me that you're capable of using the data wisely, I might be persuaded to tell you what I know. But frankly I find both propositions dubious."

"What makes you think that we intend your death, Isham?" Krish asked, utterly poker-faced.

"I'm a big boy now, Krish. Look me in the eye and tell me I'm wrong."

He steepled his fingers and frowned. "You do seem less naïve than the boy who made that tape recording," he acknowledged. "It is a shame that you came to wisdom *after* murdering Jacob."

"Executing," I corrected. Helen went white, but Krish cut her off.

"If I allow the correction, it makes you no less a fool. Who appointed you judge, jury, and executioner?"

"My father," I said simply.

Three mouths opened and shut.

"Dad was the fool," I went on, "and his stupidity, coupled with pesky bad luck, destroyed most of the world and ultimately himself. It may yet destroy *me,* and the rest of the human race. But not if I can get you three to *listen* to what I have to say."

"Then you will talk?" Dalhousie asked.

"If you can convince me there's any percentage in it."

"What will it take to convince you, Isham?" Krish asked smoothly. "A guarantee of your life?"

98

"No, that'd convince me that you were lying. I'd like you to answer some questions."

"This is ridiculous," Phinney burst out. "We don't need his cooperation. Send for scopalamine and peel him like a grape." Her eyes were bright.

"*Shut up, Helen,*" Krishnamurti snapped. "What are your questions, Isham?"

"What will you do with the information if I give it to you?"

They left it up to Krish. He took his time answering, which pleased me—I didn't want a knee-jerk response. But of course it made little difference.

"You have apparently learned how to communicate with the Muskies," he said with an expression of distaste. "We feel that in so doing you may have gained information which will help turn the tide in the present combat before our race is annihilated. We need an edge, Isham. Perhaps you can give it to us. If so, it is your duty as a human to do so. And if it is a spectacular enough edge, from a public relations point of view, we may—I say 'may'—be able to grant you your life."

Boy, I was tempted. "And your ultimate intentions toward the Musky race?"

His answer was immediate. "Its destruction."

Here it came. The big question. Everything depended on their answers—and whether or not I believed them.

"What if I could bring you—not victory, but peace?"

That rocked all three. They all began talking at once, and it was a while before Krish was able to silence the others. When he had, he paused himself for a long moment, a new expression on his swarthy face. It was the one I had hoped against hope to see, the expression of a man reexamining his axioms.

"The possibility had never occurred to me," he admitted to me at last. "I'm not certain I believe you. Do you seriously contend that a human-Musky treaty could be negotiated?"

"I think there's a chance. Do you want to hear about it?"

"Yes."

Dalhousie started to speak, then thought better of it. He obviously had reservations, but just as obviously he intended to keep them to himself if it would get me to talk. Helen

99

Phinney's expression was unreadable. Dammit, I could be playing into their hands—but if there was ever to be a chance, it was now. I had to gamble. "All right. Here's the story."

Krish's face was absolutely expressionless, an irregularity on the front of his skull.

"First I must tell you why the War started. Muskies have been around for longer than we have. A lot longer. Their race was born in the days when Earth was still a volcanic hell with an unbreathable atmosphere, and in those days they flourished. Their First Golden Age ended at roughly the same time that life as we know it began to evolve on the planet's surface, and their numbers gradually fell to a fraction of a percent of what they had once been. But they did not vanish. Their race survived, with the merest shadow of its former glory. Christ only knows how they reproduce, but evolution somehow thoughtfully cross-wired the process to the available food supply—something that might have saved our own race endless centuries of war and bloodshed. On a geologic time scale, they adjusted to the new conditions quite easily. For thousands of years, their 'food' supply remained small but relatively stable. So, therefore, did their numbers.

"Then came the change.

"It was shockingly sudden, by their standards, because their individual life-spans are so many times longer than our own. I don't think they ever fully understood it. In a mere couple of hundred years—practically overnight—the available 'food' supply increased hundreds, then thousands of times. Sheer reflex triggered off a breeding explosion, and in the last fifty years their population began to climb drastically, in inexorable geometric progression. Slowly the Muskies came to understand that this demographic upset had been brought about by creatures living on the Earth's surface—the ones whose emotional broadcasts had been entertaining them for so long. For some reason humans had—from the Musky point of view—chosen to interfere drastically with their destiny."

"Wait a goddamned minute," Dalhousie blurted. "I don't get it. How did *we* make their food supply increase? What the hell *do* they eat?"

I grinned at him. "Helen's figured it out. Haven't you, Helen? Tell Uncle George what Muskies eat."

"Air pollution," she said, whitefaced.

Dalhousie's face went utterly slack; simultaneously his shoulders knotted and swelled under the leather. The effect was so fascinating I almost missed the way Krishnamurti's eyes narrowed to slits. I wondered if he'd made the intuitive leap to the solution I meant to propose. I went on.

"See the implications, George? Those funny ground-huggers took to gathering together in bunches and mass-producing food. And then, when they'd artificially boosted the Musky population to an ecologically dangerous level, utterly disrupting an ancient and stable culture, *they cut off the food supply literally overnight.* The sulfur dioxide, the lead oxides, all the tasty hydrocarbons, all vanished instantly and for keeps. And at the same time all those Indian givers began going berserk, filling the emotional 'ether' with broadcasts of terror, agony and despair. They began to slay each other, themselves, and—astonishingly—Muskies. For the first time in history, humans revealed an ability to perceive Muskies, and used it to kill.

"So what did the Muskies do? What would you do, George?"

"My god," he said hoarsely, and swallowed. "No wonder. No wonder."

Helen Phinney was tougher; her face was almost unnaturally composed. "It explains much," she said softly.

"It damned well does," Dalhousie exclaimed. "That Agro charge . . ."

"Shut up, George!" Krishnamurti rapped.

"Yeah, George," I agreed. "You almost slipped and told me that we've always known Jordan's right when he claims that Musky raids tend to center around Fresh Start."

"Who told—? Oh!" Krishnamurti looked disgusted.

"Right, Krish—Dad again. Ever since Jordan made that charge two years ago, our P.R. department—pardon me, our Good Neighbors Bureau—has been blandly falsifying statistics to prove it's all a lie. I *know*—I work in the radio station, remember? Only it ain't a lie. *The Muskies hang around downwind of Fresh Start because it's a soup kitchen.* And they hang

101

around cities for the same reason. When I first breathed New York air unplugged, it seemed worse than it could naturally be after twenty years—and so it was. The Muskies figured some way of hermetically enclosing the city, sealing in the last of the 'food,' and they've been rationing it out ever since.

"But we're probably the only place on earth producing new food. In small quantities, yes—but producing."

"Then you're with Jordan," Dalhousie barked. "You're saying we should shut down Fresh Start, let technological civilization die forever and go back to the Stone Age." His face was reddening.

"Nuts," I replied. "I'm saying we should export smog."

Dalhousie and Phinney went into the jaw-dropping routine again. Krishnamurti's eyes still looked like paper cuts. *Hit 'em while they're groggy, my man.* I plowed on urgently.

"Think about it, George—Helen—Krish. Think of the kind of work you could accomplish if you didn't have to have three men guard every one working, if you didn't have to waste time and materials and power Musky-proofing every work-zone, if you didn't have to devote so much energy to mass-producing hot-shot and compatible weaponry, if you didn't keep losing good men to Musky raiders. How much more could you accomplish if the farmers and Agros who live around this burg weren't half-crazy with fear? How would you like free safe access to the tools and equipment of the cities? How would you like to be able to walk safely outdoors with a head cold? *How would you like to stop all the killing?*" I was startled by my own vehemence, and discovered that I was bathed in sweat.

"What sort of . . . treaty are you proposing?" Krishnamurti asked quietly.

"A simple symbiosis. If the Muskies promise to leave us alone to rebuild a technology, we promise to do it. We work *with* them, work out ways to expand at a stable, even rate beneficial to both sides. Dammit, if we use our fucking brains we can have industry and clean air both—the Muskies'll eat our pollution for us. But it'll call for understanding and good communications."

"Which you can provide?" Krishnamurti asked just a hair too smoothly.

"Hell, no," I said. "I've been working on talking to Muskies for weeks now and I haven't gotten past the 'Me Tarzan—you Jane' stage. And that ain't even the big problem."

"Explain."

"Look: Muskies come in groups, called Names. Each Name contains anywhere from three to forty Muskies, and each individual *is* the Name—talk to one and you're talking to them all. It's a group-mind, with certain qualifications that are so subtle I don't understand them myself." *Sure giving away a lot of free information, old son. Fuck it, I've got to convince them.* "But there are thousands of Names still living, the survivors of starvation and human firepower—and communication *between* them can only be accomplished through the High Muskies."

"What the hell are High Muskies?" Dalhousie snapped.

"The aristocracy, George. The elders, the older and wiser heads. The Musky Council, if you will. Their diminished mass keeps them mostly in the upper stratosphere, though I'm not certain whether that's a matter of preference or necessity. I can't tell you why they can communicate with any Musky while the Names can't communicate with each other. I can't explain the relationships between High Muskies and Names. I can't even tell you for sure how much of this is fact and how much is guesswork—the distinction gets vague when you're talking with a Musky. But I can tell you with intuitive emotional certainty that the High Muskies are the key to ending the War. We've *got* to get to talk with one, people, and soon."

"What do you propose?" Krishnamurti asked again.

"Drop everything and begin constructing some sort of flying machine," I replied at once. I'd had the walk from New York to perfect this. "From what I know of Fresh Start's technical capabilities I would suggest a balloon, capable of lifting two or three people and about fifty pounds of electronic equipment. While that's being done—in fact, before it's begun—send an expedition to New York to work with Wendell Carlson." Phinney sucked air through her teeth. "I know we haven't got any semanticists or philologists, but *some*body better qualified than me has to learn to talk with the windriders. I'd recommend Dr. Mike, and anybody else

103

we've got who's good with languages. No sense sending 'em an embassy if the ambassadors can't speak the lingo."

"And when the . . . ambassadors have learned the 'lingo,' and the balloon is ready?" Krish prompted, Eastern features impassive.

"Send 'em up and have 'em start learning High Musky. If they can accomplish that, they can try to work out some sort of peaceful coexistence agreement."

"And their chances of surviving?"

"I believe excellent. No Musky with whom I've 'spoken' has displayed the slightest aggression. *I* don't know what goes on in whatever they use for heads, but apparently the ability to communicate is enough to raise you from the class of 'them damn crazy vermin' to 'potential people.' I can't say I've ever really *communicated* with them—half the time both sides get confused as hell—but we always part amicably. Our ambassadors may be a long time getting understood, but they'll be safe enough while they're trying. They might even be able to get an interim cease-fire in Fresh Start and surrounding areas."

I paused, took a deep breath and looked carefully at all three. "So there you go, people. There's the story, there's the chance of peace and the hope of the race. What do you say to a way to end the War and give the survivors—for the first time in history—clean technology, not to mention a new and rich culture to exchange with and learn from? The Muskies are an ancient and wise people who never knew war until men taught it to them—let's make peace with them and get on with the business of rebuilding the world. What do you say?"

And so it was all said, and I shut up to give them time to think it over. In the sudden silence, I saw Dalhousie's features go slack again, a sure sign that he was thinking at full speed. Phinney was frowning furiously, chewing hell out of a good lipstick job and drumming silver fingernails on the tabletop. Krishnamurti stared with a fixed intensity at that same tabletop, as if fascinated by the interplay of grain on its surface.

It was the noisiest silence I ever heard.

And while I was supposed to be studying my inquisitors, I

104

found myself distracted by my own thoughts and emotions. The sincerity in my last words astonished me. To be sure, my life literally depended on the Council's decision—but I was startled to discover the priority that had in my feelings. With something like shock I discovered that ending the War was more important to me than my personal survival, that I would willingly die to bring about peace. The suspense I felt in regarding my inquisitors was not for myself alone but for my people, for the idea of humankind. For someone like me it was a hell of a realization. I wouldn't have been willing to die to kill Wendell Carlson, back when that seemed the prime motivation of my life—I undertook the task because I believed I could do it. *Hara-kiri's* not my style—or at least, it hadn't been. *Altruism at your age, old son? You've been hanging around Wendell too long.*

Or maybe just long enough?

I yanked my attention back to the tactical situation, confused and off-balance. Krishnamurti was looking directly into my eyes, and I started.

"A very good try, Isham," he said slowly, and my heart sank. "It very nearly worked. Your story has a kind of internal consistency which belies its basic absurdity. But it won't wash."

Dalhousie had been ready to agree; he back-pedaled mentally. "What are you saying, Sarwar?"

Krishnamurti smiled for the first time that morning. "Come now, George. You haven't been taken in by this ridiculous story? Use Occam's Razor, for heaven's sake. Isham here is sent to New York to execute Carlson. He returns, admitting that he failed and was held prisoner for an indefinite time by Carlson and his Musky friends, admitting that they drugged him, and the first thing he does is to murder his father. He flees back to his alien companions and the exiled renegade, and is brought back here only by force, over Musky opposition from what Collaci told me last night. In defense of all this he claims that Jacob was a madman, Carlson is a saint, and the Muskies are misunderstood creatures with whom we picked a fight. He advises that we drop our defenses and make a peace which will in one stroke solve all the problems of mankind. Isn't it obvious he's been brainwashed in some way by Wendell Carlson? Isn't it obvious that he is a tool in that psychopath's plan to destroy his own kind, a plan that *began eighteen years ago and is not yet complete?*"

"But . . ." George began.

"Think, man," Krishnamurti pushed on, with just a bit too much determination for a man interested in examining a question fairly. "Think. Did you really believe the tape that Isham left behind after he murdered Jacob? Do you believe that Jacob Stone, who built Fresh Start with his own two hands, was the madman, and a bearded hermit in New York the savior of mankind? Do you—?"

"It's true," I said flatly, hopelessly. "Guilt built Fresh Start. Dad's guilt. And Wendell's may yet save it."

"A good try indeed, Isham. I wish we could take the time to reverse your brainwashing and return you to sanity. I really do; I've always rather liked you. But it is a matter of urgent political necessity that we execute you at once." His lips curled up in the ghost of a sad smile. "Perhaps it is as well. If I had murdered the most loved and needed man in the world, I would rather die convinced my action was correct."

"I would rather," Phinney said icily, "that he die in full knowledge of his crime."

"Now, Helen," Krishnamurti soothed, "vengeance is pointless; if Jacob had realized that, he might be alive today. Reparation will do quite nicely. Let's patch up the mess his death caused and get on with the job."

"Get Collaci in here," I said suddenly.

"Why?"

"I want him for a witness."

Krishnamurti frowned. "I see no useful purpose . . ."

"You're going to take my life and I don't get to call a single witness?"

This time it was Dalhousie who spoke. "Dammit, we're dragging this out. We've heard what he has to say, Sarwar, and we know what we have to do. Let's finish up."

Krishnamurti nodded. "Isham Stone," he began formally, "You have been tried for the murder of Jacob Stone and found . . ."

"Excuse me," I said. No point in yelling "Hey rube," with the door closed the room was soundproof. I rose, turned my back on them and grasped my chair with my only hand. I came around fast, whipping the chair like a flail and letting it go at once. It cleared Krishnamurti's head by three inches, so quickly he never had time to duck, and shattered the picture window. As glass exploded out into the garden I continued my pivot, springing headlong toward the library door. It opened as I was in mid-air, the two Guards spilling into the room with rifles at the ready. But I was already between the jutting barrels, clamping one head under my stump and slapping the other into it savagely. The impact carried all three of us out into the hall, where we landed in a heap. The Guards stayed down. I was up at once, my hand prominently empty.

Collaci came through the shattered window in a ball, rolling as he hit the floor. He finished on his feet half-shielded by a bookshelf, and if I'd even looked like having a weapon the machine pistol in his hand would already have cut me in half. I grinned at him.

"Hiya, Teach'. I wanted you here, and they wouldn't call you."

He nodded. "So you did. You always did have a weakness for histrionics, son." He turned to Krishnamurti, who still sat frozen in the same position he'd held when the chair whistled past his ear. "Not trying to shut me out, are you, Krish?"

Krishnamurti began furious denials, and my grin widened. My primary purpose in summoning Teach' was already fulfilled—he'd listen to the "trial"-transcript tape now if he had to steal it, and perhaps he'd have brains enough to see that my proposal was logical and necessary. "What do you want, Isham?" he asked, cutting off Krishnamurti's excuses, and I went on to my secondary purpose—the faint hope that I might still reach the Council.

"I want to ask you a question, Teach', a question neither Dad nor these three would ever have asked, even of themselves. In your professional opinion as Chief of the Guard, as a Musky-fighter of twenty years' experience, *how much longer will the human race survive if the War continues?*"

He was startled, but he didn't need to make any calculations. His eyes got hard and cold, and his voice came out like computer-construct. "Without a major breakthrough in

107

long-range detection and destruction, a maximum of ten to twelve years."

Dalhousie and Phinney paled, but I could see Krishnamurti deciding to disbelieve. No good—for now, at any rate. "I advise negotiation, folks," I said, and gave up. I'd done my best. I could only hope they'd think over what I'd said.

"Take this man away and guard him well," Krishnamurti snapped at Collaci. "He stands condemned. Execution will be tomorrow at dawn in front of the Gate. Don't allow him to speak with anyone—at all."

Teach' looked at him for a long time, no readable expression on his face. "You're the boss," he said at last, and waved the machine pistol at me. "Let's go, son."

"Sure thing," I agreed, and we started for the door. As we reached it, a thought struck me and I turned, slowly enough to avoid startling Collaci's trigger finger.

"Helen," I said softly, and she looked up in surprise. "I'm sorry, Aunt Helen." I wasn't entirely sure what I meant—but I meant it.

She bit her lip. "Go away, Isham."

I nodded and left the Council behind, heading for the light of day. I hoped Teach' had a joint on him. I needed one.

Chapter Ten

There was a terrible hollow-gut feeling in me as I left Gowan's house. Very little of it had to do with the awareness of mortal danger. The largest element was ego-bruise. People who knew me had ordered my death. Hell, they were practically my aunts and uncles—they'd watched me grow up. They say an impersonal killer is a terrible thing—Collaci makes a lot of folks uneasy. But as we walked through the cool quiet of the West Forest I reflected that personal involvement doesn't make killing much prettier. A vagrant flutter of thought began: *Who are you to talk?* but something smothered it before it really came to my attention. My limp increased.

Collaci took his instructions literally. Krishnamurti had said "Let him see no one," and Teach' did his level best. We collected two entirely trigger-happy Guards outside the house and, rather than going straight to West Avenue and through the heart of Northtown, Teach' led us through the forest, around behind his own house, turned east past Dalhousie's place and brought us out of the forest at the big intersection of the Loop with South and West avenues. At that hour it was deserted—the herd going to work had passed nearly an hour ago. I heard the truck in the distance, but it was heading away from us.

Where we stood the huge granite foot of The Nose took a big bite out of the southern sky (if you'll pardon a triply-mixed metaphor); beyond it, downwind of course, lay the factory-lab complex of Southtown. In that complex the bulk of Fresh Start's population were now hard at work rebuilding the world—or trying to. I felt sudden kinship with them, and fear for them.

To our left, the two-story bulk of the Tool Shed cut us off from the view of any slugabeds in the dorms of Northtown. The Shed is an immense brick warehouse in which virtually all precious and irreplaceable scientific equipment and tools are stored when not in use—everything from titration flasks and microscopes to metric wrenches and thermocouples. Given the universal antipathy toward cities and other Pre-Exodus centers of civilization, those tools are just too precious to risk. The Shed has a small stockade on its flat, high roof, from which a Guard with some excellent firepower was regarding us with a bored eye. Another sign of unrest in the kingdom. The building had survived countless Agro raids in the old days, but it had not been deemed necessary to man the battlements for years now. It gave me a hell of an idea.

The trigger-happy Guards actually made it easier. As I was trying to work out a plausible approach, I stepped quite accidentally in a pothole. With a small cry of genuine fear, I went down heavily. Knowing the Guards were on edge, I rolled sideways as I hit, which would have been fine except that Collaci also knew his men were edgy and struck both their gun barrels aside as I went down. One flailing barrel tracked me as I tumbled, and a slug smacked into the earth by my head. I lay still, oh very still, and blinked at Teach'.

"You didn't think I'd let these clowns shoot me?" I asked plaintively.

"You didn't think *I'd* let them?" he returned sourly, and glared at his men. "Come on, son. On your feet."

I got up, limped tenderly off the road and sat down in the shade, next to a bracing strut of the right-hand loading dock.

Collaci looked disgusted. "Isham . . . "

"Teach'," I broke in wearily, "you can pick me up and carry me the last couple of hundred yards, or you can wait two minutes while I get my breath back. Besides, I think my heel is coming off."

He sighed, and turned to the ape who'd nearly shot me. "Go to the Hospital and have a paramedic sent to Gowan's home—Cole and Jalecki'll be needing skull transplants. Then go on home and get some sleep." The man turned to go at once, mortally embarrassed. "Andrews." He turned back. "Your reaction time is commendable. But next time just kick his teeth in—it's not such a final mistake."

"Yes, sir."

"Get." Teach' came and sat near me, sitting with instinctive caution on my armless side. My idea was taking shape. A flat stone under my right thigh decided me. I shifted slightly so that the stone was between my legs, then pulled my left foot up on my lap with a great show of weariness.

"Feet hurt," I wheezed, and examined the shoe mournfully. The heel was indeed coming off—I decided I was a hot-damn commando but a terrible cobbler. "Now I've gotta walk around like a duck." I worked the heel the rest of the way off.

"Not much further."

"You know, Teach', a few months ago I'd have been good and pissed of at old Andrews there. But I did a very similar thing myself in New York when I first arrived." I inspected the heel and its protruding nails disgustedly, and dropped it in my lap. It slid to the ground between my thighs. "It's not good to think with your adrenals—but sometimes you can't help yourself." I gazed at the mountain, and shielded my eyes against the sun. "Got a joint?"

"Smoking a lot lately," he said, lighting and passing a rather large doobie.

"Only when I get uptight." I took a deep hit, carbureting with air, and passed it back.

"Ride your nervous system," Collaci advised. "Don't let it ride you."

I exploded. It was easy—I actually was a bit uptight. "God DAMMIT," I bellowed, "I have lost an arm, killed my father, found out that my best friends on earth are Wendell Carlson and the Muskies, been busted and dragged a couple hundred miles, been condemned to death by my aunts and uncles, and my fucking *heel* has come off!" I reached between my legs, grabbed the flat rock and hurled it at the mountain. "I don't need a laconic flatfoot telling me to stay on top of things!"

It was a critical moment. I had no idea how closely the stone resembled a broken-off heel—for all I knew it was bright blue—nor could I sneak a glance as I flung it. I used

111

my eyes to hold Collaci's—but what about the remaining Guard?

At any rate, my aim was good. Instead of landing on rock, where it would have made the wrong sound, the stone landed in a patch of scrub grass where it made no appreciable sound at all. " . . . See?" I finished, hoping he didn't.

He looked at me evenly, not speaking, and I flushed convincingly. He passed me the joint. I took another toke and stared at the ground.

"I think you've got your breath back, son," he said finally, and rose, unholstering his pistol. I made a song and dance out of getting to my feet, managing to palm the heel and slap it against the underside of the loading dock without being seen—difficult without another hand to misdirect with. To my intense relief the nails sank relatively silently into the big platform, nothing shuffling my feet couldn't cover. The heel remained when I took my hand away, visible only to a man lying full-length under the loading dock.

Since all this involved leaving the joint hanging from my mouth, I took another huge hit. Then, under the prodding of Teach's gun, I started walking east again, straining to still look harassed when I felt triumphant. Trying to walk with one leg stiff and the other missing a heel supplied the necessary irritation—a double limp that wasted energy and slowed me up enough to keep Collaci chivvying me to hurry. We passed the empty athletic field, the Pantry (an enormous food warehouse bursting with fruits, grains and vegetables), and finally the Hospital, just short of the mouth of the Linkin' Tunnel. It was there that Teach's luck ran out.

Three people stood just inside the Hospital door, two visiting farmers and a Techno woman. Since the Hospital must always be well ventilated, the door was naturally open, and they saw us at once.

I guess there just aren't too many one-armed black men around—they recognized me, and their conversational buzz died as though the needle had been lifted off the record. There went the secrecy—for efficient information dispersal, you just can't beat idle chatter.

I felt a brief impulse to shout out the results of my trial, and I believe if I had been acquainted with any of the loiter-

112

ing three I would have. Even less than I liked the idea of my execution did I like the idea of a lid on it. *Let the people know the truth.*

But I reflected, and the impulse passed. An informed populace would be no help to me in the next twenty-four hours, and a pissed-off Collaci would actively hamper me. *The hell with the people. Hi there. Just out for a walk with my good friend Teach', and this gorilla here kindly consented to carry my bazooka for me. Say, have you seen my keen new stump?* I gave the three what I hoped was an enigmatic smile and passed on. Collaci said nothing, but the idlers scattered when they saw his face.

On the opposite corner of Main, beyond the tunnel, stood Security Headquarters, a rather small sturdy ferrocement building colloquially known as "the cop on the corner." Directly across South Avenue, to our right, a wooden stairway led up the steep slope of the Nose to a heaped-rock emplacement on the north face. From this bunker embrasures ran in either direction, disappearing almost at once among the rocks—Line Two, Fresh Start's second line of defense. Any Musky raiding party that gets past the armed men at Line One (between Northtown and the Lake) runs into more sharpshooters and a wall of alcohol-jet flame when it reaches the Nose—only rare individual Muskies ever threaten the dozens working, plugged, in Southtown.

I took one last deep toke, gazed wistfully at the Nose while I held it, then pinched and pocketed the roach. Sighing, I preceded Collaci and the Guard into Security HQ. *Do not collect two hundred dollars.*

It was darker indoors—my eyes were a moment adjusting. "Hi, Shorty," I called out, smelling an old friend. "What's new?"

"Howdy, Isham. Noth—"

"Shut up, Shorty," the Guard behind me snapped. "This son of a bitch talks to nobody. Krish's orders."

Shorty Pfeil looked him over, got up from behind his desk and smiled. They call him Shorty because he stands six-five. If you shipped a barrel inside Shorty, it'd rattle a lot. "Cal," he said gently, "that running of the mouth'll land you in the Hospital yet." Cal shut up. "As I was saying, Isham: 'Nothing much, what's new with you?'"

"They shoot me tomorrow morning."

He nodded. "Yeah, if it ain't one damn thing it's another. We're on the downhill slope; got to run faster all the time just to stay on our feet. He get the executive suite, chief?"

Collaci nodded.

"TV's busted, Isham, and I'm afraid room service ain't what it used to be—but for you, it's on the house."

"I'll take it, Shorty," I said. "Thanks." I really was grateful—Shorty's chatter was the first friendly words I'd heard all week. I thought of a leopard in Central Park, and smiled. I was glad I'd left my heel at the Tool Shed. It didn't belong here.

He produced a ring of keys and opened up the larger of the two cells that make up the rear of the building. It was a stone cube with a barred window on the far end. Mattress on the left, toilet on the right, three feet of clearance in the middle. My nose told me that the last tenant had been Marv Cassidy—drunk again. The door was a really impressive steel-bar affair that must have weighed a quarter ton. If Fresh Start were suddenly overrun by rampaging brontosaurs, I'd be perfectly safe—but by and by I'd get hungry. I stood in the entrance for a moment, feeling decidedly at bay. On the other hand, that mattress looked mighty good. I entered the cell. But there was one last bit of business to be played out first.

Teach' followed me in, and stood waiting. "I don't tip bellboys," I said. "No luggage."

"That's what interests me," he admitted. "Let's have that belt, son."

"Eh?" Shrewd bastard.

"Open it. Slowly."

I complied. There wasn't any way to hide the knife blade built into the buckle. I looked disgusted and passed over the belt. My scalp itched.

"Christ, Isham," Collaci said, shaking his head. "I *taught* you that gag." I nodded ruefully. "And I also taught you that one concealed weapon isn't enough."

That shrewd. Damn him.

"Let's see. A smart young fella like you would probably

114

pick a place you expect people's gaze to avoid. Let's unpin that empty sleeve."

What do you know? There was a sap strapped to my stump. I tried to look unconcerned, but Teach' was cannier than I'd expected. My scalp itched something awful.

He stepped outside and closed the door, which snapped shut with a meaty *thunk*. I sank down wearily on the mattress, feet under me in lotus. "Don't forget that transcript, Teach'."

He paused on his way out. "I don't expect any surprises."

"Uncle Phil . . . do you like to fight? Or do you just like to win when you must fight?"

The question took him by surprise; I hadn't called him that in ten years. He got a thoughtful look. At last he said, almost to himself, "I think you have to get to where you like it, if you intend to keep on winning, every time." He frowned, and his voice softened. "Sometimes I get to thinking I'd like to kick the habit and lay up awhile. But it seems like they just keep a-coming. Fights, I mean, one kind or another. If I ever get me a sustained break, maybe I'll—" He frowned and grinned at the same time, squinting his wolf's eyes. "Yeah, I like it. Why?"

"You looking forward to the next twelve years of it?"

He pursed his lips. "Isham, every morning I get up and I put my pants on one leg at a time."

"And then strap on an arsenal and you're ready to shave. You sleep with one eye open and you never use plugs, even when the wind's from the south. I grew up with this crazy world, but don't *you* ever get tired? You told the Council and you told 'em true. It gets worse from here."

"So?"

"Play the transcript."

"I will. But I'm dismally afraid you've figured out How to Save the World."

"And that in your considered opinion can't be done? May we quote you, Chief Collaci?"

"So long, Isham." He left, Cal following like a well-trained gorilla. I'd done the best I could, sown all the seeds I'd brought with me.

As soon as Shorty Pfeil took his traditional siesta, I shook

115

the lockpicks out of my afro and tried them, pausing to scratch my scalp thoroughly. The third pick worked, the same one that had let me into Columbia University a hundred years ago. I pulled the door closed again, replaced the picks in my hair, and then *I* went to sleep. I had a long night ahead.

The first visitor didn't blow my mind at all. In fact, I'd been expecting him.

Dr. Michael Gowan arrived late in the afternoon, just as I was waking up. As usual, he managed to make stained overalls into a Techno Tuxedo. I've seen him look dapper in the shower, and dammit, he's too *old* to be dapper. Not many real blonds can carry off a Van Dyke, but he manages. A rather short man, elegant and awesomely learned. With a variable staff, he's kept school running at Fresh Start—a school open to anyone, Techno, farmer or Agro alike—for over fifteen years, constructing curricula, organizing softball teams, teaching endless tireless hours, riding hard on a gang of yahoos with fairness and dignity and turning them into educated adults. He always has a spare half an hour for you, and as far as I know he sleeps on every third Thursday. He was my teacher all my life, my personal tutor through early adolescence, and the first adult I ever relaxed with. If Dad was the father of my body, "Docta Mike" was the father of my mind.

On my sixteenth birthday, he and I got drunk together on his home-brewed beer, went for a walk in the woods with three jugs of home-foam, and woke up two days later in an abandoned warehouse miles from home. The warehouse turned out to be the Hudson Valley Textbook Supply repository—that is to say, about half of what you'll find in the School Library today. We stayed for a week, and both caught hell from Dad when we returned.

I had drifted away from Gowan in the last few years. Dad subtly disapproved of the things he taught me, and saw to it that I spent an equal amount of time with Collaci. Both tutors challenged my intellect, but Collaci was clearly the more glamorous role model—and cynicism a more attractive posture to a young man. And so I stopped coming by the

116

book-filled library with the picture window, tapered off the evenings of conversation and discussion, ducked the pesky questions I could not answer about the thing I *had* to do. Collaci's kind of teaching was easier to reconcile with the indoctrination I was getting at home.

When I blinked away the thick fog of sleep and saw Gowan standing at the cell door, I discovered with a detached amusement that I had missed him very much.

"Hello, doc. Sorry I bust your window."

"The pain was transient."

"No puns, please. A mouse has died in my mouth. We missed you at homeroom."

"You think I enjoyed being evicted at two in the morning? Had the misfortune to be the only window lit when they needed a place to park you. Shorty, old fellow, a glass of water for Isham here. I spent the night on Krishnamurti's couch and the day asking questions that didn't get answered. Fortunately I had the sense to bug my own study before I left."

"Doc," I said with genuine relief, "you've just saved me *pages* of dialogue." I was a little tired of recapitulating the events of recent months.

"You should have saved them this morning. Really, Isham, were you that naïve? Or was it simple ignorance?"

"The old college try. The truth shall make you free."

"If you can say things like that, I can make puns. Isham, the Council, individually and as a group, *had* to ignore your words."

"I know—Collaci has explained the political situation. Jordan's Agro gang is bigger than ever; they've been raiding some of the smaller farmers that trade with us and threatening the bigger suppliers. One of those suppliers was killed by Muskies last week, and public sentiment is turning against us. To announce that our founding father was the man who dealt this mess in the first place, and that his son has been collaborating with Muskies, would be asking to have this place burned to the ground."

"Spurious argument, Isham."

"Say what?"

"Specious and spurious. And probably exactly what those

117

three have been telling each other all day. 'Expediency—that's why we closed our minds.' Claptrap! A good politician can sell anything—even the truth."

"What do you figure, then? Please don't tell me they have a vested interest in anti-Musky munitions."

"Any of them would infinitely rather be producing solar-power units—which we can't spare the time or manpower for now. No, Isham. Politics is made of people."

"Explain."

"Each of the three members of the Council has their own reason for reaching this morning's decision. Their motivations are subtly different but amount to the same thing: they will let no political, social or moral considerations prevent them from punishing you for Jacob's death."

"Look, Dr. Mike, at this point anger would be a comfort. But I can't see them as that hypocritical. Maybe it'd be simpler and easier to look on them as villains—but I don't."

"Good lord, boy, neither do I. They're *people*. People always do what they must—you of all people should know that. Don't interrupt. You hit each of those three in a vital spot, the kind of hurt they can't consciously admit because that would involve recognizing and acknowledging the vital spot. You opened scars they do not wish to remember they have. And so they find other, urgently necessary reasons to crush your head between two boulders. That's not hypocrisy—just rationalization. Which may be just as frustrating to deal with, but not as culpable—the subconscious can plead self-defense."

"They loved Dad that much?" I was not convinced. Helen aside, there had been no great warmth between Dad and his lieutenants. Respect, sure; friendship, certainly. The four were together a long time, went through a lot together while I was still learning to use the potty. But not warmth. Hell, *I'd* never gotten any real warmth from Dad—bare approval was an achievement.

"Perhaps Helen's prime motivation is close to love—in the fifteen years since your mother died she's never stopped believing that one day Jacob would warm to her and return her love. And then you went and cut him down before he could. If you're ever captured, don't let them give you to the women. Not alive.

"But equally important, Helen *cannot* accept the new version of Jacob. She's a proud woman, boy—you'd have to know how women used to be treated to understand how proud. If what you claim of Jacob is true, then she displayed execrable judgment in falling in love with him, in failing to see through him all these years. She can't accept that. So you *must* be a liar."

"All right. That figures. But what about George and Krish?"

"George is the one you couldn't have known about . . . though you might have guessed. Not many celibates around these days."

"I don't get you. So George is a loner. . . . "

"George is exclusively homosexual. Was, I should say, as he hasn't functioned sexually at all in all the years I've known him."

"So what?" I was mildly surprised, but I knew what homosexuality was; I'd seen and smelled it in animals. Only the "exclusive" part puzzled me. Seemed silly.

"Isham, the kind of persecution such people used to incur is another of those things you'd have to have lived through to understand. We don't seem to have homosexuals anymore—it must be a Civilized luxury—but when we did we hated them. They were called sick, evil, degenerate, deranged—and indeed many were driven off the rails by inner or outer pressure. It was infinitely harder for such a man or woman to find a satisfactory partner, to build a lasting relationship.

"George was apparently one of the very lucky few. In his late teens, he met and ultimately moved in with an engineer named Tom Wocjik, and they lived together for nearly ten years. Wocjik was driven into autism by the Hyperosmic Plague. George kept him alive somehow for six weeks until a Musky got him while George was out foraging. He returned in time to kill the Musky with a cutting torch."

"So George isn't disposed to make peace with Muskies. But you say he wants to punish me for killing Dad. Do you mean he has the same motivation as Helen?" The notion seemed weird—unsettling, somehow.

"No, Isham. But when your father first began organizing Fresh Start, George's sexual orientation caused some controversy. Sarwar learned of it somehow and argued that

George should be driven out as an 'undesirable.' You know George—he'd die without projects to boss. Your father spoke up for him, with considerable fervor, and told Sarwar that if he ever mentioned George's sexual proclivities again, *he* would be asked to leave."

"Oh." Light dawned.

"Yes. With the passing of years, George and Sarwar seem to have buried the hatchet—but I suspect that a bit of the handle is still visible. George was extremely grateful to Jacob; thanks to you he's now under the direct authority of a man who, he believes, considers him less than a man."

I felt a flash of pity for George, but it didn't last long. *Poor old fellow has to kill me; how sad for him.* I laughed.

"Pretty ironic, doc. One of the most crucial people in human history blows the big one on account of a taboo that's been dead for twenty years. Civilization persists in completing its suicide." He didn't seem to appreciate the humor. "How about Krish?"

"Sarwar's case is an altogether subtler one." Gowan studied his fingernails. "His biochemical knowledge aside, Isham, your father was a dreamer of magnificent scope—but a shockingly undereducated man. His first big dream resulted in the world we live in today." Well, at least one person believed me. "Fresh Start was a better dream, but he was no more equipped to execute it than he was the first time around. Again, he needed a stooge. He was the dreamer— but Sarwar was the planner, the systems specialist, the design engineer. Tell him you want living quarters for a hundred fifty technicians, and he'll devise buildings and water and sewage systems to your parameters. Tell him you want a newspaper, and he'll locate presses, form a staff, arrange distribution. He's a realizer of dreams.

"But he's not a dreamer. Faced with hostile neighbors, it took him to get *Got News* and WFS working—but it took Jacob to think of them. Sarwar lacks originality, and his vision is of a unique kind, as limited in its way as Jacob's. He tends to see the inside, the workings, whereas Jacob saw the outside, the goal. Without Jacob, Sarwar is a man with his head cut off. He has no dreams to forge."

"And I cut off his head, and rubbed his nose in the fact

120

that even with that head, all he ever was was the second Wendell Carlson. Oh, Jesus!" It all fit now, and the completed jigsaw picture was sickening. What a tangled concatenation of bullshit for the fate of the race to be decided by! I began to get angry, a deep anger I didn't entirely understand. "I felt better thinking they were just stupid and ruthlessly practical. That's a dumb bunch of reasons to die you just gave me, Dr. Mike. Why, they're worse than hypocrites, they're—they're—"

"Human. Just like Jacob was human, lad. Just like you."

"Me?" I leaped to my feet, enraged.

Gowan stood his ground. "What other reason did you have for killing Jacob than personal outrage? Don't tell me you really believe that 'Hand of Man' guff he used to give you? Have you really 'slept easier' lately?"

My voice was low and dangerous. "That's none of your goddamn business."

"Suffering Jesus, boy, how can you condemn the Council for their rationalizations when you won't look at your own? All right then, tell me: why *did* you kill Jacob?"

"Hey, listen—he loaded, cocked, and aimed me. All I did was go off."

"Oh, crap! You're a man, not an artifact; you made a free-will choice. The cleverness of the method used shows that you applied your reason to the matter—do you seriously claim you're a tool of your conditioning? Is that why you associate with our enemies and try to sell a peace nobody wants?"

"Shut up." I blazed, startling myself considerably. I don't think I'd ever said that phrase before in my life. "I don't need this shit! What I need is someone to help me get through to the Council, not somebody to tell me they're just as right to kill me as I was to do what they're killing for."

"What you need, Isham, is to learn to forgive them—and your father. If you don't, you can't justly forgive yourself—and if you can't do that, you might as well not wait until tomorrow morning to die."

I didn't plan on dying any time in the near future, but I couldn't say that with Shorty listening—he's my friend, but he has a strong sense of duty. Besides, it was irrelevant. I stood clutching the bars of my cell with my one hand, and for an awful moment I was back on top of the Empire State Building, reeling at a great height. *It may be necessary, but is it right? As you sow, so shall you reap. One good burn deserves the other cheek for an eye have been used goddammit used by that sanctimonious* . . . I burst into angry tears and sat down hard on the stone floor.

"Isham, one of the hardest things for a young man to realize and accept is how many of his father's worst traits he has acquired unconsciously." Gowan's voice was soft, compassionate. "Perhaps there are valid grounds for execution—perhaps they even obtain in your case. But you killed Jacob for personal reasons."

"As he would have had me kill Wendell," I muttered into my lap.

"Precisely."

The knot in my gut *refused* to loosen. In all the weeks since I had booby-trapped the bathroom I had, by an effort that only now seemed remarkable, entirely avoided thinking about the matter at all. Poor Wendell had accepted the news with no comment at all—I don't suppose he felt qualified to make moral judgments anymore. And so there were no rationalizations to surrender, no defenses to come tumbling down around my ears. There was only the pain, the horror and the pain that formed a molten lump in my belly. It was plenty.

The words clawed themselves up my throat with ragged talons, pried open my teeth and escaped. "I loved him! I l-loved him. The bastard, the *motherfucker*, I loved him. Cold-hearted self-serving madman I loved him killed him HATE HIM!" I was screaming, beating my thigh with my hand, stump flailing.

Gowan reached through the bars and captured my hand in his. I'd never thought of him as a strong man, but his grip was unbreakable. The painful pressure of his fingers was an input from the world outside my skull, and I could not break the connection; it anchored me to reality. All the tension that made my body shiver and spasm seemed to drain off down my arm and into those clenching fingers. For an endless time I seemed to be dangling from them over some bottomless abyss, and just as the pain reached the breaking point it began to ease, until finally I was only sitting on a hard floor with a wet face and a sore arm.

"'Can any man,'" Gowan quoted softly, "'be asked to be more than a man?' You did what you had to do, Isham. You were who you were, and are now someone different in consequence." His voice was somewhat hoarse. I smelled sweat, glanced up and saw his face beaded with it, his hand white in my grip. I released it hastily.

He held my eyes, and suddenly he laughed and stood up. "First my window, then my hand. You've got a blacksmith's grip, friend."

I seemed to be looking up at him out of a well. "I had the idea *you* were holding *me*." I wiped my nose.

"I guess I was, at first."

"I . . . I'm glad you came."

"How do you feel?"

I thought about it. "At peace," I said at last, surprised. "First time in—a long while."

"Then I'm glad I came too. I was going to bring you some books, but I forgot. I'll come back with them tonight. Have you read *The Count of Monte Cristo?*" He winked gently on the side away from Shorty.

It was beautifully done. The sudden chatter sounded natural after the extreme intensity of the moment past—and Shorty is completely illiterate.

"As a matter of fact I already have, yes," I told him, smiling. "I liked old Valjean—he did things for himself." *No, I don't need any help in escaping.*

"I should say so. Well, do you need anything, then?"

"No, thanks. You've given me the only help I needed."

His lean face lost twenty years' worth of tension. "I'm glad, Isham. I'm glad. You always were one of my brighter pupils. If only you weren't so utterly undisciplined . . . "

I waved my arm in silent pantomime, mouthed *"Avoid the Tool Shed"* with exaggerated clarity.

" . . . you might have amounted to something," he continued without missing a beat, nodding when I finished.

"Not me. I'm going to be a teacher when I grow up," I replied aloud.

He grimaced. "Enough of my pupils are Stoned already, thank you."

I awarded the pun a wince. "As opposed to cap-and-Gowaned?" I asked, then peered at him closely. "Your pupils don't look stoned to me." He winced right back, and we almost smiled.

"Enough of this chitchat, Isham. I've got Sarwar's ear to bend, and George's, and especially Helen's. In fact, I believe I'll see her first. Tomorrow is a long way off. Be of hope."

"I am, Dr. Mike. Thanks for stopping by."

"Be seeing you, lad." He left with his usual jaunty stride, and the memory of his smile, framed in wispy blond beard, stayed with me longer than his spoor.

I went to the cell window. It faced on Town Square and the Pond, a macabre touch. I spent about ten minutes watching children sail small wooden boats in the shade of the weeping willows, wishing for a good case of amnesia.

I found myself thinking of Wendell. I was desperately anxious to know if he still lived. He was an old man; his heart wasn't up to running around the city, jumping in and out of subway tunnels. But the transmitter which had been causing me to limp for so many miles had barely enough range to set off the bomb at the Tool Shed, and no receiving capacity. There's a limit to how much you can build into a hollow heel, even if you know what you're doing and have all the resources of New York City to draw from. There was no way for Wendell to tell me if he lived.

I gave it up and put in an hour's hard thinking on Gowan's words.

Chapter Eleven

It was the second visitor that surprised me.

I'd just finished a tolerably good Last Meal, and from a strong sense of tradition as much as from prudence I ate heartily. Being upwind of the building's front door, I didn't even get spoor warning. I simply looked up and Alia was there.

A giant punched me under the heart with considerable vim, and the overseer part of my brain that wanted to slam the cerebrum into high gear was informed that the cerebrum was not accepting calls at this time. I rummaged desperately in my bag of wisecracks and grabbed the first one I found.

"If Shorty's had his dessert, would you ask him to come in?" I rolled to my feet.

"Isham, I . . . "

"Aren't you the heroine who brings the prisoner a Pfeil with a cake in it? You *can't* be the prison chaplain, and Collaci doesn't wear his grenades under his shirt like that. I know you're not my lawyer, or they wouldn't let you see me. What *are* you here for?"

"I came to hear a babbling idiot do vaudeville routines," she said drily.

"Den you in de right place. Fus' dey gimme ten years in Leavenworth. Den dey gimme 'leven years in Twelveworth. Now I gets five and ten in Woolworth, and do you *know* how much wool worth these days? Say, why haven't you asked me to shut up by now? It sure is a hell of a note when you can't even piss people off any . . . "

"Isham, please shut up."

I shut up, and we looked each other over for a hundred years or so. My first conscious thought was that she looked

125

different somehow, the first person I had seen who didn't look precisely as they had before I'd left home to go shorten Wendell. I couldn't nail down the difference, and, finally controlling my funk, looked closer.

The hair was the same, soft brown wings falling from a center part, worn just a bit longer than was practical. The line of her jaw was as regally strong as I remembered it. Same almond eyes, with that improbable tiny red splotch next to the left pupil and no eyebrows worth mentioning. Same slender neck, skin the color of coffee extra light disappearing beneath the familiar blue turtleneck. Powerful shoulders, hands callused but surprisingly graceful for a blacksmith's, with long spatulate fingers. Same generous, low-slung breasts, the right still markedly larger than the left. Same wide hips, soft belly and pouting mound under the very same patched jeans I had last seen pooled at her feet, four months ago. . . .

I ceased my catalog hastily; a breeze was blowing and I was upwind. And as my eyes traveled prudently upward, I saw the little things I had missed, the subtle differences. At the place where waist became hips, two pads of flesh that I didn't recall distorted the twin curves. The belly and breasts appeared fuller, more padded. The mouth, for which I had never found any adjective but "chewable," now had firm things happening in the corners—as if it'd done some chewing of its own. That, combined with the fact that the almond eyes were bloodshot, made her overall face subtly older, stronger somehow but in a melancholy way. There was something about those eyes. . . .

"You've changed, Isham."

I snorted. "Yeah. I used to be bilaterally symmetrical."

"Stop it. I don't mean your arm, and I don't mean the changes losing an arm makes in your face and in the way you carry yourself. I was expecting them."

"What do you mean, then?" Dammit, I was trying, consciously, to make my voice soft, but the edge just would not come off it.

She lowered her eyes. "I don't know. Forget it."

"Okay. You've changed too." *For Christ's sake, say something nice.* "You're getting fat."

She shook her head. "Getting thin. I've lost five pounds in the last two weeks. I got fat while you were away."

"I must say I'm astonished to see you."

"You are?" Her face fell. "Didn't you know I'd—"

"Hell, I was surprised they let Dr. Mike in, and your father can reasonably rely on him to keep his mouth shut. But you?"

Her face got up again. "What do you mean? Keep my mouth shut about what?"

"Whoa. Back up. What *do* you know about why I'm here?"

A muscle tightened in her jaw. "Papa says you admitted murdering Dr. Stone. And some foofooraw about collaborating with Muskies."

"He say anything about Carlson?"

She paled a little, but her voice was steady. "He says Carlson has brainwashed or subverted you in some way, that he made you kill your father."

"Mmm-hmm. And you know my sentence?"

"Yes."

"I don't understand it. Krish must be nuts to let you speak with me. He must know in his heart that I can convince you of the truth in about ten minutes, and that no power on earth will shut you up. He *can't* let the true story get out—folks might not . . . "

"Isham?"

" . . . unless—yes?"

"What makes you think Papa knows I'm here?"

I blinked. "But Shorty would never let you back here unless—"

"—unless I told him that Papa authorized it. So I did."

"Oh." *Prison life is making you stupid, old son.* "Suppose he'd checked?"

"I leaned on him just a little. I told him Papa'd written out the authorization, and showed him a memo about a crew chiefs' meeting with Papa's signature on the bottom."

"And Shorty *bought* it?"

"He can say he did—if anyone ever asks. Who's going to mention it—you?"

"Shorty's a nice fella. I'm gonna be extra careful not to get him hurt."

127

Her eyes widened, and I was somehow subtly pleased at the operating speed of her uptake. Interesting datum, that pleasure.

"Need any help?"

I hesitated, and she sensed my distress. "Shorty's stepped out for a breath of air."

"Shorty is a gentleman and no I don't think I need any help." Her face once again landed on its face. *Dammit, she wants to help. Make nice—need something, for Chrissake.* "No, wait—if you can occupy Teach' somehow between, say, midnight and one tonight, without sticking your neck out—"

"It's done."

"And for the love of Carlson, stay away from the Tool Shed!"

"Damn." She grinned. "Dr. Gowan hinted about that. I should have added two and two." I liked the grin.

"Oh, the doc he is a subtle man." In the same funny way as before, I was pleased at the questions she wasn't asking. *Never rains but it pours, does it?* I was sort of out of things to say; we sat in silence for a measureless space, whirling thoughts surely hidden behind both sets of eyes. We were taking each other's measure.

I began to speak, telling her the story she had not yet heard, recapitulating all the events that had led me to where I was. And as I spoke, my thoughts kept returning to where I'd been, to the even earlier events which had led me to the start of the road whose journey I was recounting.

Specifically the ones having to do with Alia. We have known each other forever, and shared some intensely traumatic times, good and bad. She was, for instance, there when Mom was cut down by a Musky on the Lake shore before our eyes, and we cried together all that day. I was, for instance, there with her on the day when her mother died by her own hand, and we both took guilty comfort in having another before whom we did not have to cry and look sad. We were together much, feeling somehow closer to each other than to the other children of Fresh Start, whose fathers were not movers and shapers. And somehow it was not until we both were fourteen that we first made love.

I understand by Pre-Exodus standards that's shockingly

young, and I guess I believe it. But things are different nowa-
days—in fact, Alia and I were a trifle backward. By virtue of
our parentage, we probably got a better sexual education
that most do these days—but only from the academic standpoint. We were playmates for years before we caught on that
those particular scents meant *that*.

From there, of course, it is a short step to combining the
scents to see what results. As it happened, it was Dr. Mike
who found us, in the woods east of the Lake, lost in the wonders of scientific inquiry, covered with mosquito bites and
hickeys. He apologized for disturbing us, we told him that
was all right, and he went back to his walk, looking thoughtful. We too returned to our exercise, and thought no more
about the encounter. But that night we each walked into the
windmill back at our respective homes.

Characteristically, Dad had never given my sexual identity
a thought—it was after all right under his nose. Alia's dissim-
ilar plumbing had, on the other hand, literally rubbed
Krish's nose in the matter some years earlier—but he had
been too embarrassed to do more than give her a coldly fac-
tual lecture on procreation and genetics that went in one ear
and out the other.

That night, though, both our fathers suddenly discovered
a great deal they had meant to say, all of it intensely personal
and personally intense. I remember Dad's oration very well.
He could be pretty Old Testament when he put his mind to
it, and I got both barrels that night.

The basic theme was that a warrior can't afford to go and
get himself entangled with no women—at least not until he's
discharged his duty. "With Civilization gone, there just isn't
any kind of contraception left, Isham—*except self-control!* I
know you're reaching the age when girls will seem like the
only thing in the world—but there's another thing in the
world, and its name is Wendell Carlson, and it *must be destroyed.* If I hadn't had you and your mother to care for, I'd
have gone after Wendell myself long since. I, I nearly did
when Barbara died . . . well. I'm an old man now, son, and
our revenge won't wait much longer. If you think for one
minute that you can . . . "

You get the idea. I certainly did—by the time Dad had

finished pulling all the stops on the emotional organ, I was sobbing with remorse, and shaking with fear that Alia and I had already made a baby. I avoided her, and all women my age, like plague vectors for months thereafter, practicing my karate and becoming preternaturally adept at masturbation.

I never did learn what Alia's father told her, but I gathered it was more racial in theme. At any rate, she and Tommy Ostermyer had an abortion together the next spring (which I was *not* supposed to know about and never let on I did), and she was thereafter seen in the company of other young men, all of them white. If this bothered me, I didn't tell myself about it.

It was, oh, *years* later that we were next within twenty yards of each other.

I had actually left Fresh Start on my way to New York City for my destined meeting with Wendell Carlson, loaded down with good wishes and bad advice and grim courage and growing terror, and made my first camp about twenty miles to the south with the onset of evening. I intended to take my time and arrive fresh and full of beans, and so I went to sleep soon after supper.

Sometime in the small hours I found myself awake with Musky gun in one hand and knife in the other. The moon was full, the night crisp and still. I saw her at once, *much* closer than she should have been able to get without waking me. She stood quite still, a few yards from my feet, and her eyes gleamed unnaturally bright. She was naked, her clothes pooled at her feet. I had the idea she'd been standing there for some time.

As I stared, unable to shake off the unreality of the moment enough to speak, she began walking toward me, slowly and with grace. I smelled the scent of her, pungently female. I felt myself harden in response. I saw the muscles of her thighs ripple under skin the moonlight had turned to new meerschaum. I heard the whisper of her feet on soft earth. I tasted desire, harsh behind my tongue.

The glistening at her eyes spilled over and ran down her cheeks as she knelt at my feet, but she made no sound. She grabbed the end of my sleeping bag and pulled, slowly and firmly. As it slid downward I said something like "Hey." I

130

dropped my weapons, but did not grab the sleeping bag. She tossed it carelessly into the darkness, breasts jiggling, and sat on her heels staring up the length of my body. Her lower lip hung slack and her head seemed too heavy for her neck to support; my head swam with the scent of her. The ground was cold beneath me.

I spoke her name, a dry croak around a leather tongue. She almost smiled.

"They can't say I kept you from going, now," she whispered huskily. "And you might not be back."

And all at once she swarmed up my body and sealed my mouth with her tongue, and she was warm and wet and urgent. She rode me like a succubus, demanding and insistent, the way men take women in all the books, her own climaxes coming in clusters as she rocked on my groin. White heat boiled my brain and ecstasy nailed me to the ground. I spasmed, screamed, spasmed, arching back lifting us both from the earth, clutching fingers prying at her shoulder blades. And fell, boneless like a Jell-O man, through an endless sea of black molasses, gasping for air.

The second time was slower, longer, much more tender, and infinitely sweeter, the first truly profound thing I had ever known. The crashing chord of its resolution blended indistinguishably into total sleep without ever permitting even momentary return of conscious thought.

And in the morning she was gone, and the road was before me.

I told her of that road now, and where it had led me. I sat within a stone cube in my own home town, and through the bars I told her of Dad and Wendell and Muskies and of the strange place that was New York, of the hate and guilt and madness that went back twenty years, that had made the world we lived in. I found to my surprise that I was telling her a different story than the one I had given the Council. Instead of talking of interspecies conflict and the precious hope of peace that lay within our grasp, I spoke of the gentle, calm, yet inexplicably *different* nature of the Muskies I had met, of the soft inquisitive touch of them in my mind. Instead of dwelling on the rage and hate that had led me to

131

booby-trap the bathroom, I spoke of Wendell, of his contradictions and paradoxes and his strange, funny blend of incompetence and wisdom. Instead of bitterly attacking her father and the Council and Dad and Collaci, I found myself speaking of a dead Persian tom and a decrepit leopard. There was something I was trying to tell her, a message I recognized only subliminally. It would not even jell in my mind as "what I would say to her if I had the guts" or anything like that—I just kept on talking and talking and hoping that somewhere between the lines I was saying what I wanted to. I stared at the floor as I spoke, and wondered what my spoor was telling her. I wished I could read hers.

She absorbed the story in silence, which should have surprised me and didn't. The story of Dad's treachery must have turned her world-view as violently upside-down as it had mine—like finding out that fresh air causes cancer. But she made no sign. For my part I was staggered to discover the new perspective problems can take on simply because a woman listens to them. I experienced a steadying effect like six quick hits of reefer, a calming and centering of my energies I had not experienced since my last talk with the Sirocco Brothers. The confusion and unacknowledged pain of the last few days stopped being the whirlpool I was drowning in, became only the situation I had to work with.

Somewhere in there a thing was decided, an agreement was made between us, unnamed in any of the words I spoke. We both knew it.

At last I was talked out. We sat in silence together, sharing the stillness, until loud ahem-ing and Shorty's returning footsteps brought us back to an awareness of our situation.

"'Bout ten minutes more, Miz Alia. Your father's due at ten-thirty, and it's almost ten now."

"Thanks, Shorty. You are a good friend." He smiled sadly, shook his head and left, whistling "Salt Peanuts."

"He sure is," I agreed. "Knew he was downwind, and so he took the trouble to make noise coming back. Instinctive courtesy."

She nodded. "Your father had that, Isham."

"And Judas was kind to midgets" is what I started to say,

132

but before the words reached my mouth my anger melted, and what I said was, "Yes, he did."

After a pause, she caught my eyes and said, "My father is partly right, too, Isham. The Agro situation really is becoming unstable. Public opinion has been running high against us since your father's death—he was the figurehead for the whole community. People were willing to accept us eggheads as long as we were governed by a man they liked. They respect Papa, as a negotiator, but they don't like him. He . . . doesn't inspire love."

"Do those hayseeds think that all Dad's ideas and ideals died with him? Don't they still want hot-shot, and safe child-birth, and—"

"People have short memories, Isham."

I was unsettled to find myself hotly championing Dad's ideals, but there it was. "Collaci gave me the broad outlines. What are the specifics?"

"Well, the usual, of course: spot raids, handwritten broadsides, whispering campaigns. But they've opened up some new fronts. They're getting more confident now.

"First they held a huge meeting, a week after Dr. Stone died. Jordan spoke, at length. The vicious Technos had done away with your father because he had finally discovered their conspiracy to enslave everyone else. He claimed Papa was in radio contact with Wendell Morgan Carlson, and had been for some time. He repeated the charge that Muskies raid most near us, while we never get hit. He said that proved we could control Muskies. He called on every able-bodied man within a hundred miles to leave his farm and join the 'Agro Army,' a group he proposes to train and lead. In return he promised them food, quarters, protection for their wives and families—and a slice of the pie, though not in so many words."

"What pie? Those idiots believe they could *conquer* Fresh Start, and *run it themselves?*"

"That's just what they believe, some of them. Jordan'd be happy just to keep the hot-shot plant in operation, and maybe the ice-cream maker. He has no use for the research or agricultural labs, or for the power plant or the distillery, or even my smithy. Back to nature: muscle power and a thirty-year life span."

"Look, I know Jordan's a musclehead and his followers suffer from rectocranial inversion. But did any of our neighbors *swallow* that bilge?"

"The musclehead was smart. He gave an oration that appealed to people's fear, threw in half-truths and hinted at the other halves—and *didn't* call for a show of hands. He thanked everyone for listening and sent them home.

"A few days later, some of his bravos started going door to door. 'Why aren't you joining, Mr. Jones? Your neighbor Sam Smith is.' Then, when you've signed him up, trot over to Sam Smith's and use Jones's name to sign him up. Some of the smaller holdouts got roughed up just a little."

"Christ!"

"Lately, even big suppliers have been having mysterious bad luck. Amos Lewis's barn happened to catch fire. The Crows Hollow gang couldn't get their tractor to start one morning and there turned out to be sugar in the tank. A rockslide on a sunny day almost got Mr. Rosenberg and his son."

"Yeah, Teach' told me about that one. Jordan's getting bold. Maybe too bold. Is his location known?"

"He's still at Salt Mountain, in the old mine. But they say he has nearly a hundred and fifty with him."

"Whoo-ee. All fighting men?"

"Most of them. Isham, it really hurt us when the Muskies got Mr. Hardy. One of our biggest suppliers, on his way here with a load of rye, and he's killed a quarter-mile from the Gate. Mrs. Hardy went strange, sent her four sons off to join Jordan, and burned the homestead flat. Old Man Barton from across the river came to the Gate the other day, screamed incoherently for ten minutes, and stumped off home again. People are in an ugly mood."

"And the true story about what went down in New York wouldn't help much. I know."

"And Carlson can't—and Wendell can't get the Muskies to stop their attacks and help us?"

"Not without help from Fresh Start. Your father isn't inclined to give it."

"I'll talk to him."

"Talk to Dr. Mike first—he may help you keep your foot out of your mouth. He extracted mine pretty smoothly."

"I will. Is there anything else I can do?"

"Just what I said. Keep Teach' occupied for an hour or so. Then when you hear a very loud noise, act surprised. I . . . I'll get back to you as soon as I can. Maybe not in person for awhile, but . . . "

"Isham?"

"Yes?"

"Thanks for trusting me."

All of a sudden that uncomfortableness was back between us again, stronger than ever. I didn't know why. "Why shouldn't I? You once gave me the best going-away present I ever got."

"You too."

"Eh?"

"Never mind. You've got things to do, and so do I. Time I got to them."

I found I was reluctant to let her go. "How're things at the smithy?"

"Busy. The bellows busted and I got backed up, and then my damnfool apprentice ran off and married a chemist. But I've got a new helper now, the Taylor boy. I think he'll work out; he can pound sand. I . . . I'd like to meet Wendell some day. He sounds like a very nice man."

"He is. I hope you get the chance real soon, Alia. I hope he's still al—"

And I stopped speaking, just shut up like a broken tape. The wind had suddenly backed, uncharacteristically for that time of day, and I found myself dumbstruck. Alia sensed it at the same instant I did, tried briefly and without success to keep her features straight. She swore bitterly and burst into tears.

"Damn, damn, damn, shit. I didn't mean for you to know."

I was cunningly constructed of corn flakes and stale glue. The steering was out and the brakes wouldn't work. The only slug left was jammed in the firing chamber. The last step wasn't there. I had swallowed a giant ice cube and my stomach was shrinking around it. "When are you due? Asshole question number one; March, isn't it? I *thought* you were getting fat."

Dr. Mike's pedagogical voice sounded distantly in my ears. *"The distinctive, identifiably feminine scent of woman arises in large part from glandular changes based on the ovulation cycle. . . . "*

She was actually wringing her hands, a gesture I'd read of but never really seen. "I thought if I came after supper, the wind would stay hard north."

"This time of year it was a good bet. There you go."

There seemed only so long I could avoid making some kind of statement, some declaration of where I was at. Where the hell was I? *Teach' is right. Sometimes it seems they just keep a-comin' at you.*

I didn't know the half of it.

"Isham, I don't . . . you can't . . . I won't have you . . . " She couldn't get it out, and I wanted to interrupt her so she wouldn't have to, and I didn't know what to say, and prayed for a distraction of any kind at all, and instantly there was a sound like the trump of doom heard from arm's length. *Thank you.* The floor danced and Alia screamed.

Chapter Twelve

My second thought was that the charge I'd planted at the Tool Shed had gone off prematurely, but as I hit the floor I realized the three discrepancies. The blast was entirely too loud, by a factor of five; it was too far away; and it came from the north. *North? What the fuck is north?*

But my *first* thought, before I went down, was to poke my leg through the bars and kick Alia's feet out from under her. I didn't know enough about her reflexes to depend on a shout. We landed roughly simultaneously, and she did it damned well.

Shorty came in the door at a remarkable speed for a man of his mass, grabbing a Garand and diving behind the desk. The spoor of the blast said mortarfire. *Mortars?*

"Aw, *shit*, Isham!" Shorty yelled reproachfully.

"Not my doing, Shorty. Watch your ass."

"Worse and worse. Want me to fetch you a gun?"

"Wait a minute, I'll come get it." I retrieved the pick from my afro and reached up to the lock, keeping as much of me as possible on the floor. Gunfire had been coming from the north since the moment of the explosion, and by now the stink of cordite had reached us. People-killing iron. Alia kept her mouth shut.

Shorty was waiting with a pistol for me. "Match weapon," I said appreciatively. "Thanks, pal." It was considerate of him to pick something I could fire one-handed.

"You take west and north windows; I'll cover east and the door?"

"Solid."

"Some fine turnkey I turn out to be."

Alia had crawled near; she started to rise as I did. "Give me a gun—I can shoot."

"Stay the fuck down, woman!" I bellowed. "You're pregnant."

"Yes, Isham." She dropped back on her precious belly and crawled behind a file cabinet. Oddly pleased, somehow feeling more dangerous, I looked around the room.

An alcohol lamp glowed low; the room was alternating butter and chocolate. Defensive props were at a premium: Alia was behind one and Shorty was just crawling out from behind the other. The Ashley furnace near the twin cells was too small to provide effective cover from any direction. There were six rifles of varying potency racked against the south wall beside the doorless door, but they had no slings—I couldn't use them. Likewise the big-bore Musky-guns on the other side of the doorway, even if they'd had the range I wanted.

Shorty was busy underneath the Musky gun-rack. He kept a fair-sized mirror around so weekend drunks like Marv could repair their appearance before going home to their wives or husbands, and he was hastily improvising a stand for it: a good way to cover two directions from one position. He got it the way he wanted it and began pushing it into the doorway with the barrel of his Garand. He saw me watching, paused a moment to grin, and said a very strange thing. He said, "That's a good woman you got there, pal." Then he went back to his task.

The mirror started to fall, and he risked a quick lunge. His balding head exploded like an egg and yanked him a full yard into the room, slamming him against the floor. I suppose there was a noise. Things splattered. I screamed, an inarticulate wail of fury, and Alia gasped. The room suddenly smelled of excrement.

Shorty's dying spasm had swept the mirror in my direction—I lifted it to the east window and scanned the rocky slope of The Nose. From the angle of impact, the shot could have come from nowhere else. I saw him. A short man with some kind of rifle, crouching behind a boulder. From the doorway he'd be covered, but I was just that hair to the side: his silhouette was a textbook target against the moonlit sky.

I had a handgun I'd never used before. Everybody knows you can't hit anything with a handgun. I was firing uphill,

138

with a corner of my eye. Everybody knows you can't hit anything firing uphill. It was dark out. I stuck my right hand through the bars of the window, bent it awkwardly backward to aim to the right, and shot him dead. I knew he was dead even before I saw the limp, heavy, bag-of-clothes way he rolled down the scree slope, landing in a clatter of gravel in the ditch along South Avenue. I'd known it before I stuck the gun out the window.

I saluted Shorty with the pistol. "I didn't think I believed in vengeance anymore, Shorty," I told him, "but I'm glad you won't go to hell alone."

Behind her file cabinet, Alia said nothing.

I used the desk to build me an alcove from which I could cover the door, and settled down to wait. As an afterthought, I retrieved Shorty's Garand and laid it across the desktop so that its field of fire encompassed the window of the cell I had vacated.

More gunfire had been going on during all this, still mostly to the north, but it got right quiet now. I wondered where Teach' was, and what he thought of the fireworks in this corner of the world.

"Isham Stone!"

Holy smoke, Jordan himself? "Yah."

"Come on out with you hands empty. We get you out of here, get you to the mountains." It sure sounded like tapes I'd heard of Jordan.

I said something along the lines of "be fruitful and multiply," without actually implying a partner.

"The Man gon' kill you, boy, where you at? We on your side."

"Then get off of it."

"Crazy muthafucka, you want to die?"

"Looking forward to it, ugly man."

There was a silence; when he spoke again his voice was dark with anger. *Jordan, all right.* "We c'n roll grenades through that door all day, *father-killer.* I want your ass, an' I want it now."

Why the hell? "Roll away." I thought I was being canny—it seemed obvious that whatever he wanted my ass for, it wasn't hamburger. He wasn't about to get gay with greandes.

139

So my heart nearly stopped when a pineapple-sized object sailed through the door frame. I leaped on it to smother the blast, instinctively, and that was my undoing. For instead of grenade, Jordan had hurled a much more ancient and child-ish weapon.

A stink bomb.

It burst beneath me. The smell tore my nose like a dozen immense fishhooks of varying sharpnesses. It brought the shock-paralysis of any sensory overload, the same piteous mewing and spastic clutching you see in a man who's stared at magnesium combustion or stuck his head in the fire-horn. I didn't even wish for my plugs—it was far too late. I wished for oblivion, and was heard. *Thanks again.*

I came back to something like consciousness to find the world upside-down. Slowly I realized I was slung over a broad, anonymous shoulder, being carried at a dogtrot. I was breathing in great spasmodic gulps, and I hadn't the strength to do anything else. I decided my respiratory system had gone on strike under intense pressure from the olfactory center, and was now working overtime to fill the backlog of orders. The worst of the stink was past.

I was vaguely aware that Alia was near, looking right-side-up and therefore being carried like me. She was uncon-scious. Light-headed and foolish, I tried to tell her captor to watch out for our baby, but I couldn't get air allocated for the purpose. *Who's in charge here?* I wondered, and what a ques-tion that was.

A flat, sharp voice came from the right—Collaci's, of course. "You die first, Jordan."

The man carrying me froze, as did all I could see. To give them credit, none tried to dive for cover. It would probably have been fatal.

"The Stone boy die second, pig." Jordan's voice held no fear, but there was anger. I noted vaguely that he smelled a lot like Collaci.

Teach' chuckled. "I class him as pretty expendable." *Hmmph.* Through my fog I was vaguely annoyed.

"Maybe the new boss-man's daughter take his place, then."

"Fine. Then I won't have to aim this Browning so careful."

140

Jordan was plainly discomfited—this script wasn't following the expected pattern. And a Browning is a hell of a lot of gun. He growled deep in his chest.

"That's the trouble with hostages," Collaci remarked conversationally. "They're like flashbulbs—use 'em once and they're gone. I'd rather have her on my conscience than hanging over my head. Next time the stakes might be higher."

"Then why ain't you shootin'?"

"Let her go and you can walk. With him, if you want him. You know my word is good."

"White man's word," Jordan spat, but he sounded tempted. He should have been—it was a good deal. But as he was deciding . . .

"No, Collaci!" came a breathless shout that could only have been Krishnamurti. "Let them go!"

Jordan's voice swelled with triumph. "That smell like the new boss-man, pig. I guess we walk after all."

There was a long pause, and then Collaci sighed disgustedly. "I guess you do."

Throughout all this I had been listening with imperfect attention and no sense of personal involvement. It had been a day so full of changes that my mind was numb. Since breakfast I had (a) been interrogated, (b) been condemned to death, (c) lost weeks of peachy rationalizations about Dad's murder, (d) discovered I loved Alia, (e) discovered Alia loved me, (f) discovered Alia was pregnant, (g) seen a good friend's brains splattered on the floor, and (h) taken a stink bomb at close range. An overloaded brain seized on the last of these as a perfect excuse to retreat from reality, into a warm, dark, safe place altogether to be preferred. Being head-down probably didn't help either.

At a command from Jordan, the man carrying me began jogging again. This made things hurt, and I decided to retreat that last little bit. I turned out the lights behind me and left the world.

It all got sorted out somehow while I slept. I woke clear-headed and alert, cataloging bruises and contusions before I opened my eyes. When I did, they were little help—it ap-

141

peared to be midnight in the coal cellar. Alia was near. Save for her, my nose said it was an empty coal cellar, in which used sweatsocks, diapers and sanitary napkins had been stored for the last forty years. My ears, when I moved, said it was a cave. Except for the shoes, the clothes I wore were not my own.

I was ravenously hungry.

I don't know if you've ever been in a cave. Your eyes just don't adjust—it stays *dark*. I used thrown pebbles to define the size and shape of the place—walking around seemed entirely too much trouble. It was about the size of Gowan's study, shaped (and scented) like a wedge of limburger, with a roughly ten-foot ceiling. There appeared to be an exit tunnel at one corner, and I didn't smell a guard. But with the background stench, that wasn't too surprising—I assumed there was one out there somewhere.

Alia began making waking-up noises a few feet to my left and I surprised myself a bit by dropping my survey of the tactical situation and rolling over at once to throw an arm over her. I didn't want her to wake alone in a strange place.

It didn't seem to help much—as soon as she came fully awake, she began to sob quietly. I found myself completely a a loss, so I tightened my grip and held on. "Cry it out, baby," I heard myself whisper, "Cry for me, too." I guess she did; i lasted awhile. It came to me during that time that spinning helplessly in a maelstrom is not as bad if someone else is spinning with you. It was a new and profoundly interesting thought, to me, and I took time to taste its fullness. *You're no just you anymore. Perhaps you never should have been.*

With the end of tears came the beginning of desire, and we made love with the quiet, purposeful intensity of people in bomb shelters, sinking ships and cul-de-sacs before us. I was, as has been noted, a way of telling Death to get fucked, a desperate and defiant affirmation of living. It made an enormous difference somehow that there was already a bab planted and growing in that womb—we felt its presence, and welcomed it.

"One of the startlingly many nice things about being dextrous as opposed to ambidextrous"—I said a long time lat

142

er—"is that you can lie on your side holding your lady without your left arm going to sleep."

She snorted and made a face (which I knew in the dark only because our faces were touching). "But you won't be much help changing the baby."

"Gee whiz, that's a shame."

"That's all right," she decided. "I'll rig a clamp over the toilet for the dirty diapers, and let you scrape them off into the bowl. I don't want you to feel left out."

"Gosh, hon, you're a brick. Still, if I'm going to be in a partnership, I don't guess I want to be any more than an equal partner, at that. If it's all right, though, I'll leave nursing to you."

Alia nodded, and we both rose into sitting position by unspoken agreement (another one, that is). "How do you feel?" I asked.

"Oh." Her hands left my shoulders. "I wish you hadn't asked me that." Her voice was odd.

"Eh?" She was gone. From a far corner came the sound of retching. "Oh, my god! Morning sickness." I wanted to laugh, but nothing much struck me funny. "Can I help?" She managed to convey a negative, which left me feeling even more helpless.

Then I began thinking about the few times I had ever been nauseous and alone, with no one to hold my head while I vomited, and scuttled across the rock floor to her side. She protested weakly, but gave in so quickly I knew I had chosen rightly.

So then I started thinking about just how few times I *had* ever been nauseous and alone. It came to me of a sudden that although Dad had never given me a lot of emotional support (my memory banks claimed "none"), still one way or another throughout my childhood he had always been right there when I really *needed* him—even in emotional matters. For the second time in a couple of months I flashed on the day I'd watched a chicken being slaughtered and, remembering Izzy's death struggles, freaked out. Although Dad had never in his life cared for touching or being touched, when I woke from my coma it was to find myself in his arms. And he

143

had made a point of bringing me back to the same farm to witness another hen's death, so that I could learn the difference between that and my memory-trauma. *Change the records. The accused has been found innocent of one count of the charges against him. Posthumously.*

That did strike me as funny, but laughter didn't seem appropriate. To cover my confusion I went back to my assessment of strategic considerations—mildly startled at how long it had been since I'd given them a thought—while a part of my mind kept stroking Alia's forehead and brushing the hair back from her face.

I took a quick inventory of my assets. I had (a) a pregnant woman, (b) a radio transmitter in my right heel which ought to set off any radio-detonated explosives that happened to be on the right frequency for two miles in any direction—with no warranty, (c) a collection of peachy lock-picks, in case I ran across a lock, (d) teeth, (e) toenails, (f) one fist, and (g) the strength of ten because my heart was pure. My nose plugs were gone, and my coil lighter was probably with the rest of my clothes—wherever they were.

As an afterthought, I struck (g) from the list.

I went over it again, looking for components with which I could build a death ray and a flashlight, and found slim pickin's. I had neither the tools nor the equipment to either boost the transmitter's range or alter its frequency (so that increased range might accomplish anything more useful than blowing the loading dock off the Tool Shed back home). For that matter, I wasn't sure the thing was still in working order. *Something* had been rattling faintly as I walked on it for the last twenty-odd miles, making me limp so theatrically. Nor had I been anxious to make the only test possible.

Alia's spasms had subsided while I pondered, the sour reek hanging almost motionless in the air and expanding slowly to fill the available space. We both returned to the spot where we had made love and reclaimed our borrowed clothes, dressing in silence.

"Say, Alia?"

"Yes, Isham?"

"Will you marry me?" *Some agreements ought to be spoken.*

"Yes, Isham."

144

Well, at least that's one thing settled. You're just a romantic at heart. There was silence again for awhile.

"What are you thinking about Isham?"

"Wondering."

"About what?"

I sighed, and came all the way back from my thoughts. "Oh, about where I'm going to get you pickles and ice cream. Where Wendell is, and what progress he's made getting through to the High Muskies. Where Dad is these days, and how soon I'll be joining him. Where I am."

"I can answer the last one. We're in Agro Headquarters— the old abandoned mine-cave network at Salt Mountain. About twelve miles from home."

"I know—that isn't what I meant."

"Oh."

"But you raise an interesting point. I believe we're the first Technos Jordan has ever invited home. I hope we're invited for dinner. I'd clean up afterward and do the dishes. I'd even put on a tux and wash my hand. Say, did you ever try to wash one hand? Easier to clap."

"Isham . . . you don't have to wisecrack to keep my morale up."

"I know that. It's *my* morale I was thinking of."

"Oh again. Well, I've got a better morale builder than silly cracks."

In spite of the distraction her feathery fingers began to produce in my trousers, I was about to make a terrible pun in reply—when my nostrils flared. I rose to a crouch, back hairs bristling. There was a ghost in the coal cellar.

The ghost-glow brightened gradually, solidified, became the lantern-lit far wall of the tunnel that curved away to the right from the exit. Footsteps and spoor arrived roughly simultaneously: Jordan and two others. *Plug-uglies seem to come in pairs. Must be a union regulation for spear-carriers.* These two gave off the attack-pheromones of angry, frightened bumblebees, a faint acrid smell. But Jordan literally exuded confidence. His spoor again reminded me of Collaci, and, not being dazed this time, I was disturbed. He was a dangerous opponent. At the same time I was eager to see him in the flesh, to see for myself if all the stories were true. "Let me do the

145

talking, hon," I whispered, and she nodded. (I spared a second to enjoy having light to see her by again.)

I didn't bother with stand-beside-the-doorway-and-clobber-them-as-they-step-through routines. For one thing, such gambits don't work so well against three people. For another, if Alia and I weren't both in plain sight when they arrived, Jordan could simply throw rotten eggs through the entrance until I capitulated.

Sure enough, he had one in his hand when he appeared. He pocketed it when he saw me and stepped into my parlor. The two goons that followed him carried enough ordnance to make my corpse weigh twice what it did at the moment, but I had the notion that he'd only brought them along out of respect for tradition, or that union reg.

Jordan Washington was purely the most impressive man I have ever seen in my life.

He was gigantic, just impossibly tall and broad, like something out of one of Dr. Mike's lovingly preserved comic books. You could have hung a saddle over each massive shoulder without impeding his arms. Those arms looked like legs, and his legs looked like fifty-year oak. He moved all this with a whiplike speed and precision that made me wonder if he ate coal and drank kerosene. He made Shorty look like a dwarf. In the harsh lantern light he looked coal-black; his skin was at least three shades darker than mine. His head was shaved bald. He wore handmade black leather boots, extremely baggy pants, and a handmade white tunic. He looked like a sultan, and the long knife at his hip (his left hip, my tactical computer noted) supported the image.

But the single most striking feature, aside from his sheer bulk, was the wide white mask that fell from the bridge of his nose, obscuring his entire lower face.

I'd heard it described, of course—but it had an impact that words won't carry. There was a deep horizontal indentation in the nose for the upper edge of it, for one thing—gruesome hint of the horrors beneath. It was pure, dazzling white for another, in stark contrast with the skin of his forehead and throat. Another part of the impact had to do with the fact that I customarily watch people's mouths more than their eyes. I find a mouth much more expressive of inner emotion than eyes are said to be in books—to be confronted with an antagonist whose mouth I couldn't see was somehow uniquely disturbing.

But these things were trimmings. The real impact of the mask was that it said the twisted ruin underneath was so horrible that it could not even be made worse by covering it up.

Jordan was a Faceless One.

His eyes were wry and wise, vastly amused by something. I tried to look as though I shared the joke, but I don't think I pulled it off. Although you usually don't notice your own spoor, I was aware that I smelled battle-ready—and afraid. When you're keyed up enough to betray it in your spoor, you're in trouble. When you betray it enough to notice it yourself, you're in bad trouble. I ordered my medulla to calm down and start regularizing my breathing, and both the fear and its effluvium began to subside.

"Hello, Isham," he said, in a deep baritone that no other chest could have produced.

I showed him my wisdom teeth. "Howdy don't."

"My, my." He shook his great head. "My, my. Lots of confusion in my mind, son. Got me puzzlin' for sure. They say you off your daddy, an' I say whee, we got us a brother in the smelly place. Then they say you get busted, get dragged back from the graveyard to get shot, an' I say woo-*ee*, gotta go spring my man from the smelly place. Then I come to the smelly place, an' you burn my friend Sylvester while he tryin' to set you free. Make me use a stink bomb on you, when I was lookin' to be your friend. You know all of us had to burn our clothes? Yours too. Where's that at?"

"I thought you were someone I owe money to."

"Why you kill your daddy?"

"He snored."

"Pretty heavy way to kill a man. Hear tell he looked like me when they buried him—only all over. Closed coffin."

"*What?*"

"That chlorine gas, it's a mean mother. Eat skin like boilin' water on a snowman."

I'd know that chlorine gas was deadly poison, and how to produce it, but I hadn't known that. *Dad always said your education was incomplete.* I felt sick to my stomach. "He snored loud."

Jordan shook his massive head and chuckled indulgently.

"Well, you had your reasons, I expect. Like to've offed that man myself—he was the whitest nigger I ever saw. What I wonder, what is it you *really* don't want to tell me?"

"Say what?" He *couldn't* suspect—could he?

"I ask you a little thing, and you got nothin' to say. I think you got a big somethin' you don't want to talk about, an' you jus' gettin' in training. Somethin' about your eyes say so. You evade all my questions, I don't notice which particular questions you evade."

What a canny son of a bitch. As a wolf senses a trap, he had sensed that I was holding out on him—which told him the terribly damaging fact that I had something to hold out on him. The Council hadn't been that bright; they'd thought I'd told them the whole truth. My fear-sweat came back—which was all the proof he needed. *Shit!*

"Yeah, you a boy with a secret, all right. Somethin' big. Damn big. Got something to do with the sky devils; hear you talk with them fuckers."

"Where'd you hear that?" Was there . . . ahem . . . a nigger in our woodpile? How had he learned that chlorine gas killed Dad?

He ignored the question. "So let's play poker, boy. I got all the aces—but I'm a reasonable man." His eyes smiled. "Tell me somethin' heavy."

So I tried a couple of lies, and they didn't work worth shit, and after a while I tried half-truths and they worked worth half a shit, and when Jordan inevitably got around to pointing out that the white lady smelled to be pregnant and pregnant ladies often have accidents, and my bluff of disinterest about that didn't work, I finally got around to telling him the truth. Not the whole truth, and not nothing but the truth—but he got as much as I'd given the Council, which was a lot. A damn lot. I felt like a rabbit conversing with a snake, off-balance and scared, and sorely hampered by the presence of my mate.

But it took him so long to get that much (even after he had given his word to let Alia go in exchange), and my reluctance was so obviously genuine, that he decided he had the whole package—at which I was very careful to feel no relief; that tricky bastard would have smelled it.

It was not hard to project dismay. The story of Dad's

treachery was just the P.R. angle Jordan needed to drive a final wedge between Fresh Start and the surrounding community, if not the world at large. Oh, I could refuse to corroborate the story publicly, and it's hard to force a man to be a good material witness against his will—but all he had to do was demand a public exhumation to see whether Dad had died with adenoids in his head. I wished I hadn't been such a clever murderer.

But I had to give Jordan *something*, something I could plausibly be very reluctant to tell him. The only other secret I had on me was too dangerous to tell *anyone*, just at this point in history.

And so I gave him Dad.

He was gleefully triumphant. "I knew it! I knew that nigger was a liar! Whoo Lord, but I never figured him for that much of a liar. Set the whole thing up to make himself a big frog in a small puddle, an' his karma come back on him. Lord, lordy-lord, I—am—*avenged*!" He rocked with gargantuan laughter that beat at the walls of the small cave, and his plug-uglies grinned with him.

I was salty; I'd been psychically outgunned before my woman, maneuvered into disclosing more than I'd wanted to, and it rankled. "Look, Jordan, you came to us looking for work. We put you to work at an honest wage. You volunteered for plugged work, for the high pay, and your number came up. My father didn't blow off your face—you did."

I didn't see the fist coming. It felt like a home-run clout from an oar, and it lifted me clean off my feet. Being shy one wing loused up my aerodynamic stability and I landed badly, cracking the back of my head. The ceiling peeled off the cave and the stars fell in on us. Alia screamed, and there was the sound of a scuffle that didn't last long. *Steady, boy. She's all right.*

"Don't you ever talk about my features again, *boy*." There was a curious emphasis on the last word that I didn't understand. "What happened to me was my karma, for associatin' myself with them nature-killin' Technos! I'm straight with Pan now, and I don't take no shit from no Fresh Start Stone boy. I reaped what I sowed—an' now I'm gonna plow the mothafucka *under*!"

I blinked up at three of him, decided to deal with the one

in the middle. "You really believe all that Pan stuff, don't you?"

His voice and manner changed dramatically. He squatted down and sat before me in lotus. "Isham, what do you know about Pan?"

Something in his eyes made me answer honestly. "Not a lot. Life Force, isn't he?"

"Pan be the force behind all that lives, yes," Jordan said quietly. "Pan be the burstin' of the earth with life, the thing that make a tree come bustin' up through a sidewalk and the thing that make a kitten struggle. He the changin' of the seasons, an' the risin' of the tides an' the sap in the trees. He be nature, Isham, the god our fathers forgot, an' he live in the soil an' in the sea. He live in the five-acre garden I work with my own two hands."

I felt the same weirdness I had felt making small talk with Wendell while planning his assassination, the same lingering aura of unreality. I was sitting in a hole in the ground with the faceless giant who was my kidnapper/jailer, discussing theology, while my wife squirmed in the clutches of a lesser gorilla.

"It ain't right for us to turn away from that force, Isham. Plastic an' concrete an' metal an' glass, they the straitjacket we built for Pan, the thing we pave him over with. Man try to be god, he do a damn poor job. Them things you people make in the smelly place, they ain't natural."

"It ain't natural to take aspirin, but I wish I had some right now."

"Hell it ain't. Ever hear of sassafras? Grow right up out of the ground, an' the tea you make from it cure any headache in the world. That tek-knowledge-y shit make it so any weak ignorant idiot can survive, life-stuff Pan woulda scrapped an' started over. Ever since they turned their back on Pan, people been gettin' weaker an' weaker, leanin' on their false god, their tek-knowledge-y."

"So we go back to stone axes and handsaws?"

"Damn right. Indians was hip to Pan before the white man come, livin' in balance with the world. Then come Mister Charlie with pop'lation explosion an' atom bombs an' seas of concrete. Gotta get back in planetary rhythm, gotta put our

150

faith in in Pan. Tek-knowledge-y mean cities, an' *everbody* know where they was at."

I couldn't answer that. I couldn't answer anything he said; my thoughts had that soap-slippery elusiveness that talking theology always gives them. Then I saw a hole in his logic.

"Are Muskies part of Pan, too, Jordan?"

"I wondered about that considerable, for many many years," he said slowly. "Seemed like they was an' it seemed like they wasn't. But you give me the answer tonight. Sky-devils feed off of what you do in the smelly place, so they anti-Pan. Sky-devils be the force of anti-nature itself, grown so evil it poisonin' itself. What you people call entropy. They the proof that science be no friend to us—they Satan chewin' his own leg in frustration. They'll go when the smelly place go."

"So where's the consistency? You don't want anything to do with Fresh Start—but you buy our Musky-killing ammo through middlemen, and use it in weapons that are a far cry from stone axes."

"Self-preservation, boy. When you fightin' evil itself, you use its own weapons if you can. Day comin', won't need nothin' from you. Then we can lay down our guns an' go back to tillin' the soil."

"By hand."

"Boy, I lived in New York City when there was such a place, an' I'd rather break my back in the fields than see that evil come again."

"It's not just your own back that you're proposing to break."

He flared up. "I'm sick of talkin' to you. You talk like a white boy, like your daddy." He stood up angrily. "I thought maybe you could see his evil—but you shot through with it yourself. I think you need a little meditation, a little time to open up so Pan can come into your soul and give you guidance. In fact, just to help you, I gonna arrange a little fast for you." I gasped in dismay; I was starving. "Say a week." He turned to the guard who was not holding Alia. "See that they get water—nothin' else." The guard grinned. Jordan turned to go, and the two gorillas watched me for a false move, the second one releasing Alia to free his hands.

151

I didn't feel much like moving at all, especially if the raging hunger in me was not to be sated for a week. But I had some unfinished business to transact. "Jordan." I stood up.

He turned back. "What?"

"What about Alia? You gave your word to let her go if I spilled my guts."

He paused a moment in thought, nodded briefly. "I'll think about it."

"*Think* about it?" I snapped. "I thought you were a man of honor." It was a risky thing to say with witnesses present, but it didn't faze him at all.

"Boy," he said, eyes twinkling above his ghastly mask, "What I am, I'm a *practical* man. End justify the means."

"Feed her, Jordan. Or there'll be death between you and me." He saw my eyes then, and his stopped twinkling.

"I'll do what I'll do," he said curtly, and left.

Chapter Thirteen

I didn't know whether Jordan sincerely believed that we could be converted to Pan worship, or whether he had some planned P.R. purpose for hanging on to us, or whether he was just keeping us on ice. To tell the truth I didn't especially care. I was about at the end of my psychological rope: just too many traumatic things had happened to me in too short a time. I told myself that Jordan had had me over a barrel by possessing Alia as a hostage, but I was nonetheless filled with bitter shame and chagrin at the way he had opened me up like a clam. I could have reminded myself that Jordan was a much older, more experienced man whose particular genius lay in the ability to manipulate people into serving his ends. But instead I allowed myself to be demoralized. I was feeling my calendar age, the confidence of pseudomaturity gone, feeling adolescent for the first time since I'd been fifteen.

My only consolation was that I hadn't spilled that last secret which would have made utterly certain Jordan's victory in the battle for the hearts and minds of surviving mankind. But almost, I wished I had told that secret to the Council. I had decided—correctly, I still believed—that they would use the knowledge for the wrong ends just as surely as Jordan would. But possessing it might have evened the odds in the coming crisis in their ideological struggle with Jordan.

Crying over spilt milk, yeah: I did a lot of that during my first day of fasting. About the only thing I did that didn't fall under that heading was futile—I tried to escape. There was no guard immediately outside the exit from our prison-cave, and the tunnel beyond it was mighty dark. I figured I would see a guard silhouetted by light behind him better than he could see me, and tried tip-toeing out into the tunnel. The

153

darkness covered sight, and extreme care covered sound, but there was nothing I could do about smell. Before I'd gotten ten yards up the passageway a bullet came spanging around the gentle curve of the tunnel from the darkness ahead, whined past my ear like an angry bee and went through a really amazing number of ricochets inside the cave where Alia waited before spending itself.

I followed it, in a similar hurry. Alia was shaken but unhurt.

That was my only quote constructive act unquote. After water had been fetched for us by a grinning Agro, Alia and I spent the rest of that first day sitting together in silence and thinking about soyburgers and hamburgers and ham with brown sugar and pineapple gravy and mashed potatoes with butter and carrots and rice and turnips and parsnips and buckwheat and lentils and cabbage and steak and onions—oh god, onions—and apple pie and chili and milk and beer and garlic and honey and ice cream and beets and corn and pancakes and eggs fried in bacon grease and drip coffee and squash and peppers and cheese and trout in lemon sauce and bananas and chocolate and peanut butter and strawberries and peas and stringbeans and cauliflower and lettuce and molasses and broccoli and celery and radishes and tomatoes and spinach and tofu and popcorn and bread and chapatis and cornbread and beans and raisins and peanuts and cashews and walnuts and almonds and peaches and pears and plums and grapes and cherries and wild raspberries and blueberries and a big heaping steaming bowl of oatmeal with maple syrup. We made love repeatedly that night, but sating one hunger only stoked the other.

On the morning of the second day (according to our biological clocks) even thinking about food was intolerable, so we talked. I told her more about Wendell, and a lot about what had happened to me during those years she and I had been keeping out of touch. She told me of her own experiences during those years (including the straight of what had happened with Tommy Ostermyer), and we spoke, as lovers will, of what fools we had been to wait so long.

"Isham," she said suddenly, "there's something on your

mind that you aren't talking about—something you didn't tell Jordan."

I said a filthy word with considerable volume. "Good old Isham Stone! If he's not around to tell a secret to, you can always make it into a musical and take it on the road. Thirty-six point Times Roman lettering across my forehead. *Fuck!*"

She moved closer and put a hand to my cheek. "You're wrong, Isham. There's nothing written on your poker face—anyway, with your complexion, it'd have to be written in chalk. What Jordan read was the handwriting on the wall, there for all to see. What I read is the writing on your heart—which only I can see. You needn't tell me your secret."

"I don't see why not. Pan never created hidden microphones, as far as I know, and nobody's in smell." I was considerably mollified, and I needed to share my burden. "It's a secret I didn't dare tell your father or the Council, the most potentially destructive piece of information I know, and I can say it in three words:

"Muskies are plasmoids."

She made a puzzled noise. "I don't understand."

"Hmmm. Look, do you know about the four states of matter?"

"Four? I thought there were three."

"And here I thought Dr. Mike was giving you kids an education. Okay. For centuries it was thought that there were only three states of matter: solid, liquid and gas.

"Then about twenty or thirty years ago, someone remembered the silly superstition of the ancients, who spoke of earth, air, water *and fire*. Fire doesn't fit under the heading of solid, liquid or gas—it's a fourth thing: a plasma. So is ball lightning. Plasmas are ionized gases . . . you savvy 'ionized'? Good. It was the understanding of the existence of plasmas that made those last exploratory efforts with fusion power possible, just before physics went to hell with the rest of the world. Because plasmas have certain qualities that gases don't have. One of them is that they can be affected by electromagnetic fields. For fusion reaction you need such uniformly hellish temperatures that you can't let the target matter contact the walls of a container—heat loss at the fringes

155

kills the reaction. So you use a plasma, and suspend it within an electromagnetic field—to oversimplify it enormously.

"Well, Muskies are plasmoids—masses of ionized gas held together by a self-generated magnetic bottle."

"Then Muskies can be affected by electromagnetic fields?" Alia interrupted. "That's why you couldn't tell Papa and the Council—because you were afraid they'd used EM as a weapon against the Muskies?"

"Close, but no cigar. Right now, using hot-shot, you can kill a Musky that's at the limit of your olfactory detection range—EM alone wouldn't make that much difference. But the reason I couldn't tell the Council about Wendell's attempts to contact High Muskies with EM, the reason I concocted that ridiculous scheme about building a balloon, was that I didn't dare let them suspect that Muskies are plasmas rather than gases, didn't dare let the concept come into their minds. Men have thought of Muskies as living gas-clouds for years, and it had to stay that way.

"Because *plasmoids show up on radar.*"

She gasped as the implications struck her.

"Plasmoids," I went on, "were one of the phenomena that the Air Force dug up to explain flying saucers, years and years ago. That theory differed from weather balloons and thermal inversions and such only in that it was correct. It simply never occurred to the Air Force that the plasmoids were sentient."

"Oh, lord," she whispered. "That increases detection range from a couple of hundred yards of smell to . . ."

"Miles, baby. Lots of miles. If the Council learned that, in its present state of mind, there'd be such a Musky pogrom as would likely make peace forever impossible. Conceivably the Musky race could be exterminated—Wendell thinks EM of the right type and frequency will disrupt a Musky quicker'n hot-shot. Radar-aimed, that'd be pretty unbeatable."

"But . . . but . . . Isham, my mind is spinning, but . . . why mustn't you let Jordan find out? He's fanatically opposed to any kind of technology. He knows nothing about how to reactivate radar, or run it if he did."

"He's a 'practical man,'" I quoted. "He'd learn. That knife at his hip was Sheffield steel, and that carbine that blew off

Shorty's scalp was government issue. He's willing to compromise to an extent—he thinks it's only for the time being."

"But how could he learn something so complex?"

"There are quite a few military installations and airports within walking distance, and *lots* of libraries, public and private. If necessary he could kidnap all the Technos he needs. He's got two already," I added bitterly.

"Then . . ."

"So he becomes the world's most efficient Musky-killer. *Then* who are the Saviors of the World: Technos or Agros? Our popularity declines by an enormous percentage, and the bottom falls out of the hot-shot market. Bye bye Fresh Start."

"But Fresh Start has *much* more to offer the world than just ammunition. Medicine, commercial power . . ."

"Baby, the man who rids the world of Muskies can name his own price. All we have to offer folks is brotherly love and convenience. Hate wins hands down."

"Oh God, Isham, this is terrible. You *mustn't* tell Jordan. You . . . you shouldn't have told me."

I took her by the ear, smiled fondly (and invisibly) and said softly, "Don't be a jerk. I'd watch you flayed alive with our baby inside you before I'd spill *this* secret—and you'd do me the same favor."

I felt her nod. "Yes, I would. Thanks—for the second time—for trusting me."

I shook my head. "Don't thank me. It's not as if I could help it."

And after a remarkably short transition we were making love again. The sharing of the secret had brought us even closer than plighting our troth, and making love was only the symbol. But there was nothing else about it that was "on-ly"—I took most of the remaining skin off my knees, and didn't notice till hours later.

The next few days were very disjointed; our emotions went through vast manic-depressive cycles, that only occasionally coincided. After a time the manic part stopped happening so much.

The overriding keynote at first, of course, was hunger—a hunger such as neither of us had ever experienced or ima-

157

gined before. Then we woke from our third or fourth sleep with the sharp, clear awareness that we weren't much hungry for anything at all—except intellectually. Our bellies had given up caring whether or not they ever got filled again, and turned to meditations of their own.

It didn't make me feel much better. I don't know about Alia, but I passed the silent times I had previously spent daydreaming of food in mourning. Just mourning, for anything and everything. I mourned my failure to outsit Jordan. I mourned my failure to get through to the Council. I mourned my failure to protect my woman and our child. I mourned my failure to realize my love for her until it was too late. I mourned my lost arm.

I mourned for my father.

I mourned Wendell's unjust loss of honor and heritage, and the loss of his only friend—me. I mourned the loss of Civilization, which I had never known, and all it had promised for the future. I mourned the end of the world, which seemed to me only days or weeks away. I mourned the inability of man to rise above his own attachments and stupidity. I mourned the cussedness of fate.

Once I actually howled aloud, beating my fist against the rock floor. Alia held me and rocked me, but neither of us spoke.

Three more "days" passed in this fashion. Time did not pass; it tailgated. On the sixth day Alia and I began to see great subtle interrelations in everything we knew, began to preceive previously unseen universal patterns and cosmic knowledge which stupefied us by its sudden obviousness. It seemed that all of a sudden a switch was thrown and we understood everything that had ever puzzled us about the Universe and its workings. We babbled joyously of it for awhile, then realized the inherent folly of speech and fell silent. We achieved satori.

This did not dispel my grief. But it seemed to make it a grander, subtler thing, the awareness of Cosmic Irony. There was an Olympian detachment to my perception of the magnificent tragedy that was life.

On the seventh day we began having visions.

It was in fact while I was in the middle of a stupendous eight-color four-dimensional hallucination that the situation suddenly changed.

The hallucination in question was a breed of pageant, in which all my friends and enemies were represented. But the last one through the door was out of uniform—he'd forgotten to wear his body.

It was a Musky, and my nose said it was really there.

The rest of the procession, which had been doing a sort of zero-gravity snake dance around the cave, faded as though a heavy fog had roiled in. I rose from lotus, went to the only remaining full five-gallon bucket of the four Jordan had provided us, and plunged my head into the water. The Musky was still there when I finished spluttering, so I sat down again and reached for the undermind. It was very very near. *Four's corin' heaven years* and I was under.

I won't go into the exact conversation, as I did with the one I had with the Sirocco Name. Some of the concept-units we used can't be crammed into a single English word, so it wouldn't be accurate anyhow.

Briefly, we swapped Names, and I learned that his Name was called Zephyr. He told me that he had a message, and it took me quite a bit of time to learn the identity of the message's sender, a question that began as a conversational formality. The concept is not a simple one—to a Musky. I would, of course, have assumed the message was from Wendell, but I was groggy and got involved in the slapstick semantic business of asking the question. And so I learned that the message was not from Wendell. It was from Dr. Mike.

The message was "Come at once."

I started to explain the difficulty of this to the Zephyr spokesman, but reflected that his presence here unmolested put that difficulty in considerable doubt. Undermind perception told me that his entire Name was within the immediate vicinity. I got rustily to my feet again, discovered that I could walk if I compensated for a tendency to float, and shook Alia from a slumber that I was too dopey to perceive as ominously deep.

"Alia."

"Go away. Lemme sleep."

I pinched her in an awful place, and she yelped. "Wha . . . whassat?"

"Get your toothbrush and your comic books. We're checking out."

She blinked. "Yes, Isham." If the presence of a Musky unsettled her, she didn't show it. *Probably congratulating herself on what an imagination she's got,* I thought dizzily. *Maybe she's right.*

We were not fired on in the tunnel. It opened, after what I vaguely estimated as a quarter mile, onto a comparatively enormous cave, the size of a prosperous farmer's barn. Three male corpses and one female lay around it like sacks of grain, their faces the characteristic blue-green of someone who has breathed a Musky. The smell of death was not too bad yet. I giggled at them. The Musky led us down a much bigger tunnel to a much bigger cave. Along the way I saw occasional terrified people staring at us from side tunnels that were blocked by hovering Zephyrs. None spoke. I found none of this remarkable.

The new cave was enormous. Daylight came through a great beamed door in its far wall. There were eight corpses here, two with the front of their skulls blown away—Faceless Ones who hadn't survived the operation. The air stank of fried Musky. *I thought that last hallucination was a noisy one,* I thought, and giggled again. The giggle got louder, and kept on getting louder, and it might have gone on forever if I hadn't tripped over my feet and smacked my face on the rock floor.

That cleared my head—which was as well, as it turned out. One of the people huddling against the far wall, ringed in by Muskies, was Jordan himself. He glared at me with a ferocious bloodlust that his white mask didn't begin to hide.

"Mighty funny, ain't it?" he boomed. "Seein' my people lyin' dead at your feet. Fat city for traitors and Uncle Toms. You Musky-lovin' sonofabitch, I get loose an' you lose that other arm an' your balls. I'll eat your baby, boy!"

For a moment I marveled at his courage in the face of what must have been his most persistent and recurring nightmare—I wouldn't have believed any Faceless One could be capable of speech in the presence of so many Muskies. But my admiration was tempered by practical considerations.

"Not a chance, Jordan," I hollered back, disgusted at how thin my voice sounded beside his. "I'm just like you: a practical man. You're just too powerful to live—and too dangerous an enemy to leave behind me." I sat down and began smoothing out my conscious mind, refining my thoughts to a gestalt essence that I could carry into the undermind. It was surprisingly difficult to reach the undermind state, but I was getting close when a hand slapped me sharply in the face.

"*No,* Isham!"

I shivered hugely like a sleeper awakened with ice water and forced my eyes to track. Alia's face was before mine, a drawn, tangle-haired scarecrow face stained with anger and urgency. Muskies hovered at her shoulder like angry bees, a terrifying spoor, but she ignored them utterly. "You *can't!*" she shouted, shaking my shoulders. "Oh, you damned fool, haven't you learned anything? Are you still the same bloodthirsty shithead I turned my back on six years ago?"

And as I blinked, Jordan sprang through the cordon of Muskies around him and yanked her away from me by the hair.

I extricated myself from the full lotus and went for him low. He was big, but I was skilled.

And half-starved. Fast as he was at drawing that long knife, I'd have beat him otherwise; but instead I must pull up short and watch the shining blade caress my Alia's throat. He held her oddly, face-up across one knee, as though he were about to life his veil and kiss her. "Who the man on top now, boy?"

"You can lose the other half of that face mighty easy, ugly man."

"Sky-devil come near me, I put my nose on hers, an' you bet your ass I'll hold my breath longer'n she can. Now *call your dogs off,* or I cut the roast."

I cudgeled my brains, trying desperately to think, to function, to pull a scheme or trick or double-cross from my terrific combat computer. I came up dry, utterly at a loss. *Collaci'd have my ass. Hot-shot hero.*

End of the road.

"All right, Jordan. God knows your word is worthless, but guess I haven't got any choice. You win."

"I'll let her live, boy. You too. Hope for you both yet."

161

I didn't bother answering that one. I sank back into lotus, and began again the extended mantra that led me into the undermind state. It was easier this time, but I was too heart-sick to wonder at that.

I felt the cave vanish, and then my body, and then my thoughts themselves. My identity refined itself to a kernel, in a place unrelated to space and time. Scattered about me in that place were the Zephyr Muskies, all pulsing in an identical sequence that was, somehow, the name of their Name. The "color" of the pulsing was the "feelings" that were going through their "mind," a clumsy analogy-series that is the best English has to offer.

The emotional sum conveyed was extreme confusion, with an undertone I could not identify. In effect, they were puzzled by the inexplicable delay, by this odd detour I was taking on the way to New York. The emotions produced were clearly unpleasant—why didn't I get on with it?

I informed them that the trip was off. *Sorry, fellas. Something came up—you go ahead without me. I'll be along when I can.*

They rejected this flatly.

I attempted to explain that I was not unwilling but unable. The reply was oddly like an echo—my projection seemed to bounce off them and return. Were they refusing communication? Why?

I tried again, and then again. The Zephyr Name would simply not hear of delay. The journey was to be made, at once. I was baffled by their intransigence—this was not the lack of understanding I had encountered so many times before with Muskies, but a willful refusal to understand.

I gave up. I could not command them to go, and I dared not bid them attack Jordan. So I had to ignore them. I figuratively jettisoned my weight-belt and kicked for the surface.

Random dots resolved into a picture again, the weight of air pressed reborn flesh, distant roaring became local sound and the stench of fear, hate and death was everywhere. Jordan was glaring at me with expectant triumph, that cut off as he saw my expression.

"No good, Jordan. They won't listen. They don't care about Alia—but they want me to go with them, now, and they won't take no for an answer."

162

He growled. "Lyin' motherfucker, I told you what'd happen! Watch your woman die." Alia's eyes were wide, but she made no sound.

"Kill her if you have to. Then you'll be twice my size with a full belly and a knife in your hand, and I'll pull your brains out through your eyesockets. Either way, these damfool Muskies won't leave until I do." My voice was flat and dead, and his forehead wrinkled as he read my sincerity. I think he was recalling that I was Collaci's star pupil.

"You too far gone to bluff," he said at last. "I guess the sky-devils don't do what you say at that. What happen now?"

"Beats the piss out of me. As soon as they figure out that you're what's holding me up, you and Alia will die. I guess I walk."

He turned it over in his mind. "I guess you do."

"I'll be back, Jordan. She'd better be alive—and un-harmed—when I do."

"Don't worry, boy. I got plans for this here lady. Be seein' you."

Muskies were swarming angrily, projecting for the first time a concerted mood-pattern that impinged on conscious thought. It was impatience, with an overtone of menace. I understood why ghosts had so terrified mankind for centuries—sweat broke out all over me, coldest in armpits and groin. "Maybe not," I answered cheerily, "but we'll meet again. Bye-bye, Alia. I'll be back for you when I can."

"I know," she said quietly, smiling at me from her awkward position across Jordan's thigh. "Take care."

I nodded, got to my feet and walked from the cave into daylight, followed by a phalanx of Muskies.

It was a chilly day, clouds moving south overhead. The trees were achingly green, and the purple of lupines around the mine entrance stabbed at eyes that had seen only black for a long week. The world was so intolerable beautiful that I spared it a full two seconds as I turned from the road that led into the cave-mine, and headed for the nearby forest. By the time I reached its cover I had finalized my plans as well as I could. Speed was essential—the only possible assets I had or was likely to get were surprise and audacity. A quick smash-

163

and-grab had at least a slim chance of success. I began circling north so as to hit them from an unexpected direction.

And ran into a wall of Muskies.

The damned things would not let me by. Intangible individually, in the mass they formed something through which I could not pass, cohering by a means I didn't understand. Whether the constraint was physical or psychic I don't know—but in my weakened condition I lacked whatever kind of strength it took to push my way through. I battered at them with my body and my mind, raving and cursing in English and Swahili, but it was useless. They were gentle, but insistent—I was to go south or not at all. No more detours.

After ten minutes of concentrated effort that left me aching in every cell I gave up and staggered, sobbing with frustration and rage, through the forest, heading for the Big Apple.

Chapter Fourteen

As I trudged, showered with coins of sunlight, through mounds of new-fallen leaves, my thoughts kept returning to that last confrontation with Jordan. I couldn't understand why Alia had prevented me from asking the Zephyrs to kill him. It didn't make sense. She had suffered as much at his hands as I had, could envisage just as clearly the untold damage he could cause to the world with the ammunition I had given him. Didn't she understand that he was in his own way as dangerous to the world as Hitler or Rockefeller had been? Why, his death was *imperative*, as necessary as had been . . . . . . Dad's?

"Haven't you learned anything?" she asked. *Well, have you?*

I had regretted having killed my father at least a dozen times, one way or another, ever since I heard the flushing of the booby-trapped toilet. In a hundred ways it had been brought home to me that the hasty killing of anyone (let alone anyone possessing as much stature and power as Dad or Jordan) could only bring chaos and sorrow, no matter how apparently evil the victim or heinous his crime. Every evil action can be redeemed—if its perpetrator lives long enough. Hadn't Dad dedicated himself to the most spectacular life of reparation since St. Augustine?

Even if Jordan were that favorite construct of adventure fiction, The Man Too Dangerous to Live, even if he represented as much potential harm as a Hitler (which I felt he did), I could not kid myself that that had had anything to do with my wish to kill him. I had thirsted for his blood because he had harmed my woman, my child, and myself, and because I hated him for the ease with which he had peeled secrets out of me. I had tried to kill him for ego reasons.

Just as I had killed Dad.

Just as the Council had condemned me.

Was passing that sort of moral irresponsibility back and forth the best thing to do with it? Wendell was the only man I knew who had refused to return evil for evil, and could that be why I respected him so much? If killing were ever truly necessary, it ought to be approached dispassionately, even compassionately, after due deliberation. I hadn't wanted Jordan to not-be; I had wanted him to suffer. Now, I was not certain either alternative was desirable.

This notwithstanding the fact that a portion of my hindbrain, knowing Jordan held my Alia hostage, wanted to rip out his entrails. No doubt close friends of his had died in the first wave of the Zephyr assault—Jordan probably wished at least as earnestly to see my own bones bleaching in the sun. Upon which of us, then, did the homicidal impulse confer moral superiority?

It's wrong but it seems necessary. It's necessary but it seems wrong, but it seems necessary but it seems . . .

With a flash of pain I recalled one of the sporadic, terse conversations Alia and I had attempted during the last day of our fast. We had reached that point of hunger when brain cells begin to die, producing a natural state of stonedness far beyond pot-high, something like what I imagine the Hippie old-timers must experience when they eat amanita muscaria and psilocybin mushrooms. We had both simultaneously experienced the cosmic revelation that we were unique, an insight so stupendous that we accorded it a half hour's awed contemplation. One of those conversations.

"I mean," Alia said at last, "everyone needs to feel unique'. . . but it's okay, because they are. Look at me: I'm the best blacksmith in the known world."

"*I'm* unique," I heard myself say. "I am the second-best killer in the world."

And the expression that passed over Alia's face sent me careening into a safe haven of visual hallucinations and metaphysical speculations of an abstract nature.

Isham Stone, by any other name, would smell a damn sight better. Was this the identity I had chosen for myself? Or had I

166

myself be driven, like a child star thrust out onto a stage, ready to spend the rest of my days in the tortured belief that what I had been made was what I wanted to become?

With a flash of empathy/sympathy I recognized the previously inexplicable aspect of the Zephyr tribe's collective demeanor which had so puzzled and frustrated me. The poor bastards were *under compulsion,* from one they regarded as superior . . . and they didn't like it a damn bit. Perhaps they had doubts about what they were doing—but they were somehow forbidden to entertain doubt. I wondered how Dr. Mike could pull off a tall order like that, but it felt too *right* to be wrong.

All of a sudden, I understood them a bit better. Maybe.

I came to a clearing in the woods.

The forest fell away from the spot where I sat: between balding treetops the sunset lingered, a sunset so muted I could not say just where grey became pink. The undersides of the two rain clouds visible were a pink-related color I could not name—but only when I didn't look directly at them. Winged things flew widening arcs, some silently, some not. Some thirsted for my blood; some did not.

I smelled sweet cloves, smelled wild raspberries somewhere nearby, smelled a rich stew of spruce and pine and acres of ferns, spiced with traces of yarrow and Queen Anne's lace and distant deer-berries. There was a deer to the northeast—a doe—but she would not come close enough to be seen. Brilliant orange butterflies flew broken-field through swaying ferns at ground level; branch-bound leaves fluttered in pale imitation above.

Someone had lived here once, not too many years ago. Bleached, fire-charred eight-by-eight beams lay strewn about the clearing, barely visible in thigh-high grass. Here and there a baby spruce rose six or eight feet from the lighter green of weeds and wildflowers, first footholds of a forest reclaiming its territory. In twenty years there would be no way to tell that there had ever been a clearing here, let alone a dwelling, a structure within which humans had lived and laughed and loved and cried and hated and died. *The forest always wins in the end,* I thought, and suddenly I understood for the first time a thing which had always puzzled me: why men would want to build cities.

Until the coming of concrete, a man battled nature for land, cleared a piece of forest with ax and shovel and held that piece by main strength, fighting primeval forces like weed, weather, and wild animal. If a man died without issue, nature would destroy his works and reclaim his fields within the space of a generation or two. Nature was mysterious, ubiquitous, powered by forces so diverse and tenacious that they dwarfed and terrified man. *Naturam expelles furca tamen usque recurret,* said the Romans: you may drive nature out with a pitchfork, but it will return.

Well then: rip it up. Tear it asunder with great machines and seal the earth against reseeding with an impenetrable shell of stone. Make the city man's forever, his its only lifeforce. Kill the trees and flowers and grasses and brush, drive out the animals and insects, sterilize the region and roof it over. Keep on a few pigeons and dogs, reluctantly, as pensioners. Retain a few tamed bits of nature on exhibit, but thinned, gelded, dependent on man.

Then discover that there is something more terrible than nature to be locked in with: yourself.

Where once men linked arms in common cause to withstand a mystifying and hostile nature, they built a place so safe, so secure that they had nothing against which to strive, save each other. No wonder they built their cities. And no wonder they left them.

I stopped in my tracks, sat down on crackly autumn leaves and rolled my eyes upward. Almost before I began the mantra, I was in that sidewise plane of being Wendell had named the undermind, and this time a visual analogy was by far the strongest perception I had of the Zephyrs: I "saw" them as points in a lattice, a three-dimensional and not at all symmetrical network of amber fireflies against a field azure, all this with a clarity I had never before experienced.

I assembled my thought into a gestalt, refined it to its essence. *(Pawns?)* is about as close as I can render it in English.

The response was a joyous blast combining elements of

168

agreement, delight in our mutual discovery, and respect; all somehow compressed into one concept-unit.

(Me too) I sent back, connoting *don't feel so bad: I walk the same road. (All/one?) Are we not all part of the same thing?*

Their reply translated best as a maxim I have heard attributed to the Vikings: *no man escapes his weird.* It contained neither despair nor resignation, but calm acceptance. As stated, it did not seem to conflict with free will.

I made a final sending approximating *(Q.E.D.)* or *(There you go.)* We exchanged the extrasensory equivalent of a smile, and broke contact.

But it seemed to me, as the next few miles put themselves behind me, that I had not entirely left the undermind, and that from that day forth, a part of me never would.

Five days' travel had brought us to New York. It didn't seem to smell as bad as I remembered. My Musky honor guard left me at the Broadway entrance to Columbia and vanished among the rooftops, all thirty-four of them, each in a different direction. Before I was halfway to Butler, Gowan and Wendell came running to meet me, both obviously excited and elated. We embraced. It was a moment of strong emotion, but of course I had to try and ground it out.

"You," I growled at Gowan, the moment we untangled ourselves. "Was it you sicked those animated farts on me?"

"Eh?" He blinked. "Well, yes. I asked the Zephyr Name to find you and bring you back at all costs—when you didn't arrive back here soon after I did I thought your escape had gone sour. I was half-afraid you were dead. Did I do wrong?"

"The damned things wouldn't let me hang around long enough to spring Alia. Jordan snatched us both from Fresh Start."

"Oh, *no!*" We took turns explaining to Wendell who Alia was, and his face too became sad. I brought them both up to date.

"Well, what's done is done," I told Gowan at last. "You probably saved my life. While I'm here I can pick up some things I need to spring Alia from that hole in the ground. Hell, there's even a chance that pucker-faced clown actually

169

let her go. He did promise, once—maybe he stood in a draft and caught a bad case of honor."

Gowan made the terrible face that meant he had something unpleasant to say. "Isham—I hope so."

"Huh? What do you mean?"

"I hope Alia is all right where she is—because you must not leave. Not soon, at any rate. There is work for you here."

"Now, listen . . . "

"Hear me out. Or better yet, hear me in—it's chilly out." He turned and headed for Butler. I followed, in angry confusion. Didn't he understand that *Alia* was in danger? By damn, if he tried to stop me with those Zephyrs again, I'd load up with Musky-shot and . . .

Fight my way through my brothers? *Shut up, old son—your stupidity is showing.*

We entered Butler. A large piece of equipment stood in the lobby—the alpha-feedback amplifier and transmitter that Wendell and I had used both to train our undermind and to broadcast it like a beacon. But it was changed almost beyond recognition. It had been built onto, to such an enormous extent that its own four wheels were no longer adequate to support it. It rested now on a large pallet with two fixed and two free wheels, surrounded by auxiliary devices bound to it with a forest of cables. Its omnidirectional antenna had been replaced by a tweeterlike horn, and there were other changes I vaguely perceived but was not equipped to recognize. In all it only slightly resembled the machine I had first seen Wendell using to communicate with Muskies, from my sickroom window, about a thousand years earlier.

"I bet it gets FM and police band now, huh, doc?" I said, examining it and feeling my composure return.

"Don't make light of it, Isham," Wendell said almost paternally. "Michael has improved immeasurably on my work, and in a very short time."

"I wasn't making light," I protested. "I'm really impressed."

"Exactly what you are, my boy," Gowan said jovially. "Impressed—in the old sense of the word. 'Drafted,' as it was described more recently."

"What for?"

"To use this Frankensteinian gizmo that Wendell and I have made to talk with the High Muskies."

"*Huh?* You mean you can get through to them with that contraption?"

"No, I mean we can reach them with that contraption. We can knock on their figurative door. It is my devout hope that *you* can 'get through to' them."

"Why me? What makes you think I can do it if you can't?"

"Because you're unique, Isham." Wendell put in excitedly.

"I know that—but I don't see how it'll help in this case."

"Eh?"

"Skip it—I want to know what *you* mean."

"What Wendell means, Isham," Gowan said cheerfully, "is that you are, so far as is known, humanity's best telepath."

"*What?*"

"Yep. Oh, you're only an apprentice yet. But I believe training and practice will make you the world's most efficient communicator—at least on the psychic band."

Inside me, something was careening and shifting like unstowed cargo in a storm-tossed vessel; yet I hadn't moved a muscle. "What the hell gives you that idea?" I asked almost angrily.

"The EEG built into that alpha-feedback machine of Wendell's," Gowan returned calmly. "The two of you were using a device you had found, not made, and you never fully explored its potential. It monitored your brainwave patterns and fed you a visual cue—soft light—when you attained a consistent state of alpha wave production—the doorway to the undermind. But at the same time the machine was *recording* your brainwaves—and you never thought to examine the EEG tapes."

"I don't get it."

"Okay. Pardon me if I get pedantic—the lecture habit is hard to break. Alpha waves are one kind or pattern of electrical activity produced by the human brain, lying between either eight and twelve or seven and thirteen cycles per second depending on which authority you subscribe to. It's a subtle energy, measured in microvolts. It wasn't discovered until 1929, and very little was done with it until the seventies and eighties, when the spiritual renaissance hit the Pre-Exodus world. Virtually everyone produces alpha naturally: Rosenberg's researches indicated that only about eight percent of people produced no alpha in normal waking state. The key, however, is in amplitude.

"The average untrained human's alpha production measures about ten or fifteen microvolts. With careful and intensive training, it can peak as high as sixty microvolts. In the late seventies, recordings were made of Zen masters who registered as high as a hundred microvolts, though only in surges, and only in near-cataleptic meditative trance.

"I can show you recordings of your own alpha, made by you on that infernal machine there, that peak at a hundred and twenty-seven microvolts, and average ninety-eight."

From assassin to Zen master in one easy lesson. There you go.

"That's nice," I said weakly.

"Nice? It's essential!" Wendell burst out. "Thanks to Michael's timely arrival and unceasing labor, we now have a functioning EM carrier wave which a High Musky could follow down to us, hand over hand as it were."

"Ordinary Muskies come down the thing like a homesick water buffalo down a viaduct," Gowan put in.

"But we have been unable to contact a High Musky, or induce one to follow the carrier wave to us," Wendell went on. "The lesser Muskies seem to assure us that it can be done, that a High Musky could reach us by such means—but none have."

"There's a bunch of folks we *need* to speak with, ten stories up," Gowan interrupted again, "and so we keep slapping a ladder against the side of the building. What we need is somebody with enough lungpower to shout 'Hey! Come on down!'—and be heard. I haven't got the psychic lungs for it, and neither does Wendell."

"That's why you must stay," Wendell continued. "It's essential that . . . "

"Whoa!" I said, "Hold off the vaudeville cross-talk act for a minute and let me get a word in edgewise. Why me? Why can't the lower Muskies pass along a message by riding our EM wave *up?*"

"Beats me," Gowan said cheerfully, "but they refuse. Maybe they're reluctant to disturb the boss. Maybe their language lacks the necessary concepts. Maybe there's some sort of taboo involved. All I know is, they can't or won't extend a dinner invitation upstairs for us. We've been trying for days."

"What makes you think *I* could?"

"You're the only one we have left. What you've told me about the political situation up north makes it even more imperative that we *end the damned war now!* Before the last two factions left in the nation destroy each other in a stupid, useless ideological wrangle.

"If we can get through to the High Muskies we can offer them the deal you failed to sell to the Council—and if they buy it, you and I *can* sell it to Krishnamurti—because I'll stuff it down his throat with a history text. We're gambling that the High Muskies can talk with one another—because we haven't the time to wait for a worldwide congress—and we're gambling that they're psychologically equipped to make racial policy in agreement, and we're gambling that their social structure allows them to put it across. Not to mention the gamble that the idea of peaceful coexistence will appeal to them.

"But most of all we're gambling on you."

"But why?" I cried for what seemed the thousandth time. "Because I have a gift for relaxed thinking? That's all alpha *is,* you know—the characteristic pattern of meditative thought. It's not telepathy, any more than closing your eyes is sleeping."

"Yes, but that's a good analogy," Gowan insisted, "—because closing your eyes, while not essential, is a big help. I cite studies by Krippner and Ullman, Stanford and Levin, the Dream Laboratories at Maimonides in Brooklyn and the Paranormal Activities Department of Columbia, all of which indicated a close connection between alpha production and paranormal sensitivity. None but the last of these studies dealt with telepathy as such—Rhine-card guessing was their main focus—but even earlier studies by Kamiya and by Budzynski and Stoyva showed that alpha production, and particularly alpha training by feedback, caused subjects to experi-

173

ence marked increases in empathy. And you know perhaps better than I, Isham, that what Muskies do is closer to empathy than it is to telepathy."

"About sixty-forty," I corrected absently. My mind was humming like a cable under strain.

"Wendell tells me you've had infinitely more success with undermind communication than he has . . . "

"More depth," Wendell interrupted.

" . . . despite the fact that he's had a twenty-year head start and a damned sight more motivation. Hadn't the significance of that struck you?"

"I guess I just thought I smoked more dope," I mumbled without thinking. The notion had been largely subconscious.

"Don't forget that idea," Gowan suggested. "Someday the researchers picking over your brain may get five hundred pages of speculation out of it. The correlation between use of mild psychedelics and alpha-proficiency is one of the things that was under study at Columbia when the Exodus intervened—but I suspect that in future days our best ambassadors will be those offspring of old hippie stock who haven't rebelled against their parents' life-styles. God knows not many kids at Fresh Start smoke the stuff, the way Krishnamurti discourages it . . . you being of course exempt by virtue of parentage. However, Isham, I'd also credit the fact that you're trained in Eastern philosophy, in meditative disciplines—thanks to me—and I'll mention it to any researchers I meet.

"All this, of course, assumes that the human race will survive long enough to produce either researchers or ambassadors, which is by no means certain. But if you feel you *must* go back north to pull Alia out of the hole, it *will* be certain, in my mind . . . that we are, god forgive the cliché, doomed."

"Something I forgot to tell you, Dr. Mike."

"Please, Isham—you're a grownup now. Michael, or Mike. What's the forgot?"

"Alia's pregnant, Mike."

His face went expressionless. "Oh my god. Yours, of course? Of course. Well, I suppose we can get along without you after all—there's a trick with hypothalamus-induced feedback training I've been meaning to try . . . " His thoughts were already leaving the here and now.

174

"You misunderstand me. I want my baby to grow up. When do we start?"

He grinned. "Five minutes ago." Something about the grin said he was proud of me. Well, so was I—but there was a terrible knot in my heart that seemed to be seriously interfering with its function.

I'm sorry, my beloved—no man can escape his weird.

Four hours later we were outside, under a starry sky, gathered near a fire that leaped and crackled.

"Well," I said, breaking a long silence, "I wonder if the folks back home miss the truck, Mike."

"Your father insisted we have no more than one internal combustion vehicle running specifically so we wouldn't get dependent on them. I'm sure the fuel will be put to good use."

"Cut with lemon juice and sugar," I guessed wistfully.

Wendell reached into a brand-new (from his point of view) U.S. Army field jacket and produced a long green bottle. It bore a handmade white label whose only legend was four crude Xs—a classical touch I admired. It gurgled pleasantly.

"I have a little tonic of my own, here," he said diffidently, "which you gentlemen might find tolerable. It's an excellent vintage: two weeks old."

"I'll drink to that," Gowan and I simultaneously said, and we did. I don't want to use a lot of clichés about the potency of Carlson's moonshine—I won't claim smoke came out of our ears, or that our fillings melted, or any of that. But I will say that if you poured some across an itching back, the stuff would scratch it. I must admit that Gowan outdid me. His eyes watered too, but his nose didn't run and he was able to talk in almost no time. "Smooth," he croaked. "What do you call this stuff?"

Wendell recovered the bottle, took a staggering long swallow, and smiled like an angel.

"Boozo," he said placidly.

Before long we were agreeing, just like they all do, that the stuff grew on you once the scar tissue had formed on your tongue, and not long after that I discovered I was feeling better. Alcohol is a drug I use only seldom; in consequence I appreciate it. Alcoholism, Shorty always used to say, is what happens when good liquor falls into the hands of amateurs.

But it came to me, while I scratched some overlooked electrode-paste from my arm, that the peace I was feeling was only partly drug-induced. It occurred to me that although I had scavenged marijuana as well as food on the way to New York, I hadn't felt the need to smoke any lately. I spoke of this to Wendell and Mike. "Right now my woman and unborn child are in Jordan's hands, Fresh Start is in danger of mob violence, and I can't seem to get a High Musky on the phone. And yet I'm sitting here in relative tranquillity, and my fingernails are long enough to need clipping. Where's that at?"

"A number of possible explanations," Gowan said. His lean features took well to firelight; it struck gold from his Van Dyke, and made his nose lordly. "For one thing, alpha-feedback training is said to reduce anxiety, to allow you to adapt to and tolerate anxiety-producing situations. Your unique talent for communication is more than a parlor trick, you know. It carries over into your life, one influencing the other. To me your calm is a sure sign that we *will* succeed tomorrow. This afternoon was only the first try—you can't expect instant success.

"Another possibility is that you've burned out your adrenals. So much has happened to you lately that by now you must have learned that anxiety is pragmatically unsound." That rang a bell. "Or it could be that you're too fatigued to worry."

"I favor another possibility," Wendell put in. "It involves the ability to appreciate the inevitable. You know in your heart that you're doing the best you can for Alia, Fresh Start, *and* the High Muskies—so you've put away fear and uncertainty."

"'There was nothing more I could do, so I took a nap,'" Gowan quoted thoughtfully. "I believe you've hit it, Wendell. He's grown up."

"Thanks, fellas," I said dryly, but I confess I was proud. "If I'm so smart why won't a High Musky talk to me?"

"Now don't go spoiling your tranquillity," Gowan mocked, and then paused. "Isham . . . I've got only one suggestion. There was a man called Stephen Gaskin, once—for all I

176

know he's still alive in Tennessee—who wrote a mighty book called *Monday Night Class*. I haven't read it in over twenty years, but one part comes back to me now."

"Yeah?"

"Stephen suggested that if telepathy ever got to be popular, people were going to find out that they had to shovel out the Communications Room before they could get anywhere."

"I don't get you."

"The Communications Room, he said, was the subconscious."

"Oh."

Wendell got warily to his feet and tossed another few pieces of chair on the fire. "In twenty years of cold winters I haven't made a dent in the supply of chairs Columbia has to offer," he said reflectively. "I imagine I never will. I'm going to bed, gentlemen."

"Good night."

"Good night, Wendell."

He left, whistling a tune I didn't recognize. A silence ensued.

"How do you shovel out your subconscious, Doct . . . Mike?"

"Well, actually, it's more a matter of opening it up than anything else. Shit decomposes in the presence of air and sunlight. The Catholics used to have a very effective custom called confession."

I thought about it. "I still feel confusion about Dad," I said at last. "No—about the idea of killing in general. I know I tried to kill Jordan for what seemed to me to be totally righteous reasons—and yet Alia made me realize, hours later, that it was just that killer ape that lives in the back of my brain. Hey, I'll bet that's why I had so much trouble getting to the undermind, that one time I tried to get the Zephyrs to kill Jordan for me. I never thought of that."

"It's hard to be relaxed when you're thinking of murder," Gowan agreed.

"Dammit, Mike, I made a conscious decision, a few years back, to let you drift out of my life and let Collaci drift in. He taught me everything there is to know about killing—and it's about everything I know. I think I made a bum decision. Thanks for giving me a line on a new profession."

"Perfectly all right," he said lightly. "Vocational counseling is a hobby of mine."

And he left, and I sat by a waning fire and thought until I had killed the Boozo and worked it out for myself. Then I kicked earth over the coals and went to bed.

Communication, I thought as I drifted off to sleep on the first mattress I had known in weeks, *what a lovely thing to be unique at. What an altogether fine thing.*

Chapter Fifteen

Gowan didn't appear at breakfast the next morning. Wendell and I managed to find a use for his share of the oatmeal but it took us a while, and we spent another half an hour in sitting around and belching. As we seemed to be out of conversation, this made for a lot of silence. After a time I couldn't stand it any more.

"Why don't you ask me how I made out shoveling out my subconscious last night, Wendell?"

He made no answer. His hand crept up to his beard and stroked it nervously.

"Why is there this unease between us?"

He made an abortive effort at piling up the dishes for washing, and gave it up half-done. He sat back and sighed, looking around the kitchen he had made out of an office. "I don't know," he said at last.

"This father-son thing between us," I said softly. "It isn't working out, is it?"

He tried to look startled and failed. "I suppose not."

"Is it because of the closer rapport that Mike and I already have?"

I could not interpret his silence.

"Is it because of my father?"

No answer.

"Is it because I'm black?"

"Damnation!" he burst out, eyes flashing in aged sockets. "All of those things and none of them! Devil take it, why do you *tug* so hard? Isham, I am too *old* to be a father. And you are too old to be a son. A man my age isn't prepared to undertake as intense and involved a relationship as parenthood—that's why my prime child-siring years passed decades ago. And if that weren't enough, I've spent twenty years in

179

utter isolation from my own kind, relating only to myself. I expect to be emotionally and socially crippled for the rest of my life, and I must tell you that at times I find the simple presence of another human irritating beyond belief. I don't *want* to leave New York—and you can't stay. When you came here I did my best to meet your needs, physical and emotional—but frankly, I made a rotten father, and I believe you know it. I sensed violences in your soul, terrible twistings in your heart. But I never spoke of them, never tried to ease them, because after so many years, emotion of that intensity terrified me. I hadn't the courage to be frank with you, as a father must, and so there is a last death on my conscience.

"Damn you, take your emotions and your emotional needs and your aching guilts and get away from me. At this time in my life I need friends, not children!" And he fled weeping.

The man speaks truth, old son. You are an awful old son, at that. You can scrap your father, but you can't start over. Wendell saved your life—he didn't offer you his.

Gowan came in the door with an armload of electronic hardware. I snapped out of my trance.

"I just passed Wendell on the quadrangle," he said. "What are his tears for?"

"Those aren't his tears he's crying," I said bitterly. "They're mine."

"Oh." He placed his foraged swag on the breakfast table, and ran a hand through his tangled yellow mane. "Want some pearls of wisdom?"

"Sure," I said resignedly, and then I said "Sure," in a completely different way.

"When you do someone a disservice, you can brood on it, thereby doubling its ill effect on the world in general. Or you can go do them a service."

I thought awhile. "Well," I said finally, "I know the choice that Dad made." I got up and brushed past him.

"Isham . . . " he called out as I went out the door.

I turned back. "Yeah?"

"Be easy on yourself. You've been doing your level best all along. You've just got to keep growing all the time to stay alive."

I thought that over. "Thanks, Mike. See you at the perpetual emotion machine."

180

"I'll have some surprises for you."

I found Wendell behind Low, sitting at the base of a broad tree, gazing up at Low's great vaulting dome. It was a chilly morning, and of course he had forgotten his jacket, so I gave him the spare I'd fetched. He put it on gratefully, and the locking of our eyes for the next minute may have been the bravest thing either of us has ever done. I knew that if I apologized I would only make him feel worse, but I didn't know what else to say.

In the end I stuck out my hand. "Dr. Carlson," I said formally, "I'd like to introduce myself. My name is Isham Stone. I believe you knew my father Jacob."

His face lit up with a smile that dislodged dust from his beard. "Louie," he said, appearing to be quoting something, "something tells me this is the start of a beautiful friendship." He took my hand and shook it for a long time.

When we got back to Butler, Gowan was making final adjustments on his new mad scientists' components, which he had set up near the modified alpha machine/EM transmitter and connected to its power source. He looked up, assessed our expressions and smiled, scratching his thigh with a screwdriver. "Should have thought of this days ago," he greeted us.

"Thought of what?"

"Come here."

He had placed an improvised za-zen cushion on the ground between the machines for me to sit on. I put it under my tailbone, where it would help keep my spine straight, and let him put the helmet on me and fasten the electrode tendrils to all my strategic points with paste. With the new machine there were almost twice as many, in different places, and I began to feel like an overloaded fuse box. "What's the new gadget?"

"The surprise I promised you," Gowan said, continuing to work. "I had a genuine, certified Inspiration, and I found what I needed in the Psych Department. There—you're connected. Now I want you to drop into undermind—but don't bother chatting with the locals, and *don't* reach for the sky. Not yet."

"Okay, Mike. Setting up exercises it is."

The neighborhood undermind was not crowded at this time of day. I sensed a few windriders beyond Low, but they were headed for the Hudson with a strong tail wind. I hung around for awhile in what seemed like a sea of purple velvet, thinking no thoughts at all. Then I made the hand-over-hand climb back to consciousness.

" . . .st as I thought," Gowan was saying. "Look there, Wendell." They were peering in the opened lid of the new machine. Their eyes flickered from side to side.

"Well, doc?"

Gowan looked up, glee in his eyes. "Come look at this."

I rose and dragged my web over to him and Wendell. The thing they were watching was a strip of recording tape just like that made by the EEG. EKG? It was not recording anything at the moment; the stylus traced a straight line. "Looks like I've had a cardiac arrest."

"Idiot," Gowan said fondly. "I've shut off the inputs—or you'd have given it St. Vitus's Dance when you got up. Wait." He ran the tape back to the test section. Whatever the machine recorded had obviously been happening intensely—the peaks were high and close together.

"I give up. That sure isn't either EEG or EKG."

"It's EMG, Isham."

"I *said* I give up."

"An electromyograph. It measures electrical activity of the muscles. This particular model is hypersensitive, designed to detect muscle tension in 'motionless' subjects. And it confirms what I suspected: that while you're in the undermind state your muscles tense up to a significant degree."

"Why?"

"Beats me." He shrugged. "Maybe just some kind of subconscious sentry system . . . did I say something wrong?"

"*Au contraire*," I said weakly. "Okay, so I'm tensed up some. So?"

"So alpha is the pattern of relaxed thought. If you're tensing up your muscles, it cuts down on your alpha performance."

"You mean I've been making Zen masters look like twitches and *I wasn't even at peak efficiency?*"

"Just what I mean."

"Hmmm." I resisted the urge to scratch an electrode.

182

"Well, I don't see how I can fix it. When I'm in the under-mind, I'm *away*."

"I've got an idea," Gowan suggested. "Are you holding?"

"Eh? Yeah. Five jays in my pocket. Why?"

"Light up, lad. Light up. Cannabis sativa is an excellent muscle relaxant. I may have a toke myself."

Wendell looked scandalized, but said nothing. I took the old tobacco tin from my Agro-shirt pocket, and removed a fat joint I had rolled hash flecks into. The doobie had been in the tin long enough to smell like the twenty-year-old Erin-more Flake it had formerly contained, a not unpleasant mix-ture with the scent of the grass itself. Gowan produced a light, and we passed the blast back and forth for a few min-utes, while Wendell studied the ground. "Ever go under-mind stoned?" Gowan squeaked, holding down his last toke. The world had begun to sparkle while I wasn't looking.

"I'll be damned," I decided. "No." I took my own last hit and ate the roach. "I guess," I said and sucked air, "I want-ed," sucked air, "to have my head," sucked air, "clear," ex-haled. "Or something."

Gowan let his out too. "Maybe you just didn't want to put those sentries to sleep."

"Past their bedtime," I said. "Want to try the EMG again?"

"Let it take hold first," he suggested. "Relax."

"Fine. Hey, Mike! I've got an Inspiration of my own. How about if we wait for some Muskies to come along, then have them cluster around me while I transmit?"

"Why?"

"I dunno. It *feels* like a good idea."

"We'll try it, then," he said at once. "Maybe their presence will help make your gestalt sendings more recognizable to a High Musky. Or something. How the hell do I know?"

"Okay, then. I'll wait in the undermind, if it's all the same to you guys, but don't expect anything until you smell a bunch of Muskies gathering 'round. Then start praying."

"We will, brother," Wendell said.

I had hardly got seated properly when the undermind came on, and this time it was not something I entered but something that washed over me like a tidal wave.

I can't describe the difference adequately—it was something like the difference between kissing and making love. Instead of being immersed in purple velvety Jell-O, I *was* purple velvety Jell-O. I seemed to have more than six senses. The ninth—or was it the tenth?—sense perceived a kind of ongoing phenomenon that reminded me startlingly of Miles Davis's later work, although it was more analagous to light than to sound.

The other senses I can't even describe by analogy. Nor even number—my memory banks simply weren't geared up to accept them, and they rejected all but a few.

But one thing I retain. I realized with a shocking suddenness that I was *moving*, that I had left my physical body. It was a feeling very like losing your steering box halfway down the mountain—all at once you're in uncontrolled motion. I was not *falling*—the motion was multidirectional, simultaneous and quite violent. I was an immense inertialess bullet caroming off the walls of the Universe at translight velocities. I reached for the brakes, and they weren't there.

Fear tugged at me, a fear I'm sure my six familiar senses would never have consciously perceived. With all the force of my will I struck at the fear, smothering it with all the wisdom I had gleaned from my life, choking it with the conviction that only the mind at peace can accomplish anything useful. Hours passed while I strove.

It was a terrific struggle.

The fear died.

I monitored the old six senses of the body I had left behind—a thing I had never been capable of in the undermind before—along some inexplicable but invulnerable conduit, and learned that my body was utterly relaxed, all muscles limp, eyeballs rolled up. I had been away for a long time—the sun was setting.

("A hundred and forty-four microvolts!" Mike was breathing, but I ignored it.)

I cast my *self* back outward and rode the multidirectional psychic "wave" like a surfer, like a pinball, like . . .

Like a Musky.

Oh, yeah—you're working.

I realized that I had been for some time aware of hundreds of other hurtling *selves*, in swarms like psychedelic

184

sparks from the Universal Fire, and knew that they were Muskies. Conscious translation into terms acceptable to my "old," six-senses orientation told me that they were all the Muskies within a hundred mile radius. I would later find this considerably impressive, but at the time I only ascertained the geographically closest Name and forced myself (by a means indescribable that simply occurred to me as I needed it) into a matching course with them.

(*Attend me*), I commanded.

Profoundly startled, they did so.

Their Name was Mistral. At my direction, they ranged their physical selves around my own. Dimly, I sensed the nearby sparks that were Wendell and Mike. I was becoming more accustomed to the wild motion of my psychic *self*, noticing correlations between it and the physical universe with which I was familiar. I took a sight from that universe-plane and analogized it into the "direction" (slightly more accurately, the "pattern") I wanted to "face" ("assume"). I allowed myself to meld identities with the Muskies, to blend my *self* with theirs until it seemed that I rode the swirling breezes of the campus about my own body. A hippie would say that I "cut loose of my ego."

I married them.

The thing I waited for came.

It was blue, and it was vaguely warm, and it was metallic, and it was none of these things. It sounded like an oboe, and it felt like an angora, and it tasted like aspirin, and it looked like ball lightning, and it did none of these things. It projected love and concern and suspicion and curiosity, and it felt none of these things.

It was a High Musky, and its name and its Name, I knew, were Mistral. High Mistral.

(THANK BEING,) it "said." (WE HAVE WAITED FOR SO LONG!)

" . . . so they did the only thing they could do," I said, and gulped more coffee. "Kept sending the lower Muskies into contact with us, in the faint hope of reaching a human mind for long enough to teach it telepathy." My body was shivering, but I felt okay.

185

"Even though they knew our own subconscious hate and fear would probably drive the Muskies kill-crazy," Mike said wonderingly, and sighed through his teeth. "I often wondered why the war went on and on, even though possession of territory didn't seem to be an issue. Why fight a human when you can catch the next breeze and be miles away in seconds? Answer: because your elders insist you try and teach him how to talk, even if he does shoot you on smell."

"God, how patient and forgiving the High Muskies must be!" Wendell burst out.

"No," I corrected. "Any attempt you make at attributing human thoughts, concepts or emotional patterns to High Muskies will inevitably be incorrect, crude analogy *at best.* You can not attempt to make their motivations fit any scheme you can comprehend. They're *different.* By their lights they've only been doing what was the next thing to do."

"What have *we* done by *our* lights, then," Wendell cried, "if that's all we can evaluate? For centuries we've perverted their children, turned them into werewolves and demons and ghosts with our twisted hates and fears and needs—and then we remove their food supply and offer them waves of hate to empathize with."

"I'm afraid so," I agreed sourly. "Because of the nature of a Name, Muskies can't *help* empathizing—it's what keeps them together and in contact with the High Muskies. And it also makes them vulnerable to human minds—in shifting psychic orientation enough to project emotions and moods at us, they necessarily take on enough of our way of thinking to become emotionally disturbed."

"Hence the long-noted perversity and sadism of ghosts," Mike said sadly. "Man literally fashioned his own bogey-men."

"And his own enemies."

"And his own friends, brother. How much of a friend is High Mistral?"

"I don't know how to answer that, in human terms. He was in contact with all the other High Muskies now living, somehow, but he wouldn't let me perceive any but him—he said it would 'derange' me. In effect I guess he was the Ambassador for the Stratosphere. There was a general awareness that we wanted the War ended, but we didn't think a lot about it. If

186

you want to know the truth, we spent most of the conversation examining a sequence of . . . phenomena that haven't got words, trying to decide whether or not it was beautiful."

"You did propose the treaty?"

I guess I looked sheepish. "It never entered my mind."

"Suffering Jesus, Isham!"

"Mike—*you had to be there.*"

He started to speak, then shut up. "I guess so," he said softly. "I guess so." Wendell looked thoughtful—almost wistful.

"Mostly he 'talked' and I 'listened.' I absorbed a lot of information from him that he wasn't actually sending, and for all I know he read the treaty in my mind. But it never became a topic of discussion. What we were trying to accomplish seemed to be perfecting the empathy between us, learning to think and feel in a sort of third language acceptable to us both. And so we spoke of beauty, rather than politics."

"You don't sound a lot like you, Isham," Mike said curiously.

"Maybe I'm not," I grinned, "but I feel just fine. We'll get around to the treaty, Mike, and damned soon. Don't worry."

"I'm not worried about a single thing, Isham. You've done magnificently."

"You have indeed," Wendell said gravely, and I felt a wave of warmth from both of them. It pleased me in a way I had never known before.

"I just had to learn one thing," I said, "and the lesson was given me *months* ago. Just before I came up to your front door with guns blazing, Wendell, I massacred a cat that leaped out in front of me on the street. Just pulverized it before I even saw it.

"I shot without thinking because I was in New York, and I was afraid.

"Again and again since that time, I've lashed out, for the most logical- and noble-sounding reasons—because I was afraid. It's an entirely human reflex, and one that probably was of great use to the Neanderthal. But Cro-Magnon began suppressing it, and we've got to complete the job if we're ever going to live in peace with the Muskies. I had to defeat my fear before High Mistral would *let me* perceive him—I think by sheer force of will he could have held me at a lower plane of awareness, and I think he would have. I had to grow up, as you gentlemen put it.

"Muskies occupy a peculiar ecological niche. They're perpetually being whirled into the unexpected, and have little to fear in the way of natural enemies. That's not to say that they don't know fear—but when they do feel it, their impulse is to catch a stiff wind to elsewhere and think about it. From the High Musky point of view, our panic response to the unknown made us dangerously insane. Contagiously so. They decided to remain aloof and contact us only through the lower Muskies."

"The Muskies told me I had to 'go higher' to reach the High Muskies," Wendell said, shaking his head, "and for ten years I thought they meant physically."

"High Mistral could have come down and sat in my lap," I told him dryly, "if there'd been any reason to. High Muskies keep their bodies parked in the stratosphere, not because age has diminished their mass—although it has, considerably— but because it's a better neighborhood up there. To hang out down here they'd have to develop the same sort of subconscious sentries I used to have—and as we all learned, that sort of thing is alien to their whole being."

"One thing puzzles me," Wendell spoke up. "This emotional contagion business—do you mean to say that the Muskies who attacked you so savagely when you came here—?"

" . . . were my own kill-frenzy, all the poison in my skull embodied in the temporary insanity of a few passing empaths."

"Then how did you manage to communicate with the Zephyrs at Jordan's Cave? Why didn't they sense the murder in your heart and become deranged?"

"They might have—if they had only come by in response to Mike's request. But High Zephyr apparently followed enough of the conversation to become interested, and 'seconded the motion' with some kind of dire compulsion. The Zephyrs were insulated from my rage, partly because it was not directed at them, and partly because they were fixated on the accomplishment of an utterly imperative task: to wit, fetching me back to your EEG/EMG/PDQ, Mike."

He was lounging in the doorway, hands in his coveralls. "I

188

thought it was snappy service I was getting," he said, and smiled. "Good night, you two."

"Good night, Michael."

"Dream good dreams, Mike."

Wendell looked a bit awkward when Mike was gone, and I remembered a thing I had nearly forgotten. "Wendell?"

"Yes, Isham?"

"When I wanted to get the Zephyrs to off Jordan for me, I had great difficulty reaching the undermind. Then when I cut loose of killing him, I was able to achieve rapport to a degree. Do you know why?

"Because when I made that decision, I figured I was completely licked, just finally and forever fucked. Jordan had Alia and the jig was up. And so they were able to 'let me in' for the same reason you've gotten along so peacefully with Muskies for twenty years—which is the same reason you've never gotten any farther with them than you have."

He looked puzzled and a bit hurt, but I plunged on.

"I despaired, Wendell. I despaired, and instead of disturbing them, it rolled right off their backs. Despair isn't an emotion they find dangerous or threatening.

"To them it's just utterly incomprehensible."

His face became very old for a long time. And then gradually years seemed to melt from it, and its deep lines became only a record of history. He smiled, a much softer and younger smile than the one I'd seen that morning.

"Isham," he said wistfully, "do you think perhaps some day somehow you and your hundred and forty-four microvolts could take along a hitchiker?"

"Wendell," I said, grinning fiercely, "I purely hope so."

After he had gone I lay back on the familiar bed and looked around the room I remembered so well. In days and nights past it had been a battleground, the scene of huge warring emotions and bitter interior dialogues, a place where my subconscious fomented bloody conflict.

Right at the moment it seemed like a very peaceful place.

I awoke to find myself running full-tilt down the hallway.

"MIKE!" I roared. "WENDELL! Up and at 'em—scramble. *Red alert.*" I tore past their rooms without waiting for reply. I noted that I was carrying my old one-heeled pair of shoes in my hand, the rest of my clothes pinned against my chest by my arm. Then I was tearing around a corner, bare feet giving excellent traction.

I didn't take time to dress until I had the truck started and backed around to the front doors of Butler. It was a rosy dawn. By the time I zipped up my shirt, Mike and Wendell had arrived. Neither was the least bit bleary-eyed or befuddled, for which I was briefly grateful. "Mike," I ordered. "go scrounge food and water for a day or two, and a couple of blankets, and coats for all of us. Wendell, get aboard and direct me to the Organic Chem building—I want to fuel up."

"There's gasoline here," he began.

"Too inefficient—I want all the horsepower and mileage I can get, and that means pure grain alcohol."

He shut up and climbed into the truck with a limberness that belied his years. We sped across the campus through tall grasses, and I prayed for an absence of broken beer bottles. There were two spare tires in the bed of the truck, World War II unstoppables on modified rims, but I figured to need them both: Mike had left Fresh Start with six. We crashed up a flight of steps and onto College Walk, and now I know what a milkshake feels like.

"Doesn't burning alcohol affect your carburetor?" was all Wendell asked.

"Sure—cleans it out and keeps it that way. Only reason they ever started using petrol was that it used to be the cheapest thing imaginable. Waste product of kerosene production."

We alkied up and stowed a number of drums of the stuff in silent haste, then sped back to Butler. Mike was waiting with a two-day-on-the-road survival kit that showed rapid, careful thought, and he had it aboard almost before we stopped. He vaulted over the tailgate, blond mane flying, and waved wagons-ho. With a screech of tires and the roar of an indignant transmission, we tore around Butler and onto the street. It was tricky having to let go of the wheel to shift gears, so I left her in second.

Mike climbed in the window as we sailed down Amsterdam Avenue, swerving around obstacles, on and off the sidewalk averaging forty per. He slid next to Wendell and ran a hand through his blond hair.

"Lot of Muskies following us," he said conversationally.

"I know."

They both waited patiently until I had a clear stretch which allowed me to give driving less than total attention, which pleased me deeply. "Got a visitation," I said then, "in the nature of a news bulletin, from High Mistral. He preempted a dream to tell me that a large army is massing at Jordan's Cave. They keep looking to the west and rattling their sabers."

"How many?" from Mike. (I was twiced as pleased—that no one had asked if it couldn't have been only a continuation of my dream. *It's nice to be respected by men like these.*)

"'Names of Names,' was the phrase he used—analogously speaking, of course. He said their vibes stank."

"Why the hell are we heading south? The tunnels must be . . . "

"Small detour. The armory. I want to pick up some firepower."

Wendell looked startled. "I thought you'd given up the sword, Isham."

"Sure. But if I go to dicker with a man who wears one, I will, too. It keeps him from slaying you out of hand, and it's peachy for misdirection. Or self-defense."

"Oh," he said, and Mike nodded.

The truck raced downtown, paced by a five-Name battalion of Muskies.

Chapter Sixteen

We left New York through Harlem, the only route we knew for sure was clear. Only it wasn't, entirely. A panel truck that Mike had jacked up out of the way had fallen over again, blocking access to the bridge. Wendell remained in the truck while Mike and I jumped out to fix things. It was while we were setting the jack that I smelled them.

I straightened quickly, and Mike looked up in surprise. "Grey brother," I whispered, and by then he could hear them.

There were hundreds of them, a vast army that chittered and scurried. They came from the river banks and from the deserted ghetto itself, around smashed autos and through mounds of bones. We had seen occasional packs on our way through Harlem, but nothing approaching this number. Some were the size of tomcats. They were like a great grey carpet of death.

A flamethrower was beside me in the truckbed. It might even be operable. There were incendiary grenades, and a comparatively inefficient but psychologically-appealing Browning spray-gun. I kept my hand at my side, palm open, and faced the army of rats.

(Ho, grey brother,) I something-more-than-thought. *(I am returned. You cost me an arm, some days past.*

(Let there be peace among us.)

There was no response that I could detect. But they watched in silent stillness as we completed the removal of the wreck, climbed into the ancient cab and drove north. Mike was white and sweating as we pulled away, and Wendell's face was ashen.

"What did you say to them?" Mike asked a few miles later.

"'Hello,'" I replied. "About all I could get across, I think. They're even farther behind us than we are behind the High Muskies. But I touched them."

"Good lord," Wendell breathed. "Can even *that* war be ended someday?"

I made the best time I could, but after the second spare blew out it took me twelve swearing hours to locate a usable tire in Kingston. It was damn near twenty-four hours after we left Columbia that I halted for the last time on the Interstate, five miles from Fresh Start. I killed the headlights, left her idling, got out of the cab and fell flat on my ass. I had been sitting in one position for a *long* time.

Consequently, of course, the injured part was anesthetized, so I felt little pain. I saw stars—but then, it was five A.M. under a cloudless sky. After a long while I managed to get back up on my stilts, and swayed like a half-sawn tree. It was difficult walking with my knee-joints locked, but I managed it until I felt I could stay upright unbraced. The two older men meanwhile followed my example with much more circumspection, and made a much better job of it.

"The equipment's back home," Wendell said, limping up to join me.

"Don't need none o' them fancy doodads," I drawled. "Do all right in muh own haid. Oh, High Mistral could get his body here quicker if there was an EM carrier for him to come on—but I want to know what he sees from *up there*."

He nodded. I pulled out a joint and lit it. Mike came up in time to take the next toke, and as he passed it back to me Wendell intercepted it and took a hit himself. We made no comment; and the three of us smoked in silence for a few minutes. Then I sat down and hurled my *self* skyward.

I was a Pre-Exodus airline pilot, looking down at a living city by night. Below, against utter blackness, a million pinpoints of light shone like reflections of the stars on some vast

193

puddle, but grouped in patterns that showed human pur
pose. The lights were human minds, *selves*. There were two
groups: one that represented the sleeping population o
Northtown, and a much larger, more closely bunched nebul.
that was the Agro Army.

It lay immediately to the east, moving slowly over the to
of the East Mountain toward the Nose. I watched it for
timeless while, understanding it as an entity, empathizing t
the point where I felt I could predict its course and purpose
It tasted vaguely like Jordan.

I studied the whole double-cluster, made extrapolation.
They were bad. I stepped up the magnification and trie
tasting individual *selves*. It was oddly difficult—so much c
me was mingled with High Mistral that the *selves* I perceive
were weirdly out of focus—like trying to recognize a favori
poem from a translation into a strange language. It ha
nothing to do with the fact that the minds I touched wer
mostly asleep—that should have made the subconsciou
clearer than ever. Was that Krishnamurti? Yes, it seemed s
He was awake, quite excited, and deeply angry. That on
there was Jordan for sure, and that one was Helen Phinne
sleeping fitfully.

There were three that startled me for a moment—the
consisted, in part, of slightly distorted reflections of my ow
self. One was Alia, of course. But who were the others? Wh
in Fresh Start loved me that much? I put it aside; the sum t
tal of several dozen tastings suddenly tabulated itself an
shrieked for my attention. Technos were waking up by th
dozens, spraying feverish clouds of emotion, and the Agro
too reached a peak of excitement.

The battle of Fresh Start was nigh.

Leaving a thought-flash for High Mistral that might hav
taken a day to write out, I wrenched myself from my exalte
plane and dove headlong back into my skull.

The shock of returning to my body was much less sever
this time. I leaped to my feet and began running in circl
around the truck. Wendell and Mike stared at me, half-co
vinced I'd gone round the bend.

"Get your legs back in shape," I hollered. "We'll need to be spry pretty soon."

We jogged until we felt the blood pounding in our calves and thighs, then clambered aboard the truck again. It was coming dawn. "They're going to take the Nose," I explained as we got under way. "It's sound tactics—they can command both sides of the tracks, and just throw mud downhill until there ain't no more Fresh Start. Jordan's a *good* general."

"Collaci is too," Mike said over the roar of the abused engine. "Isn't he prepared for such an obvious move?"

"In a general way, yes—but these boys came along quick and quiet, and somehow or other none of our friendly neighbors tipped us off. Teach' just found out they're coming, and it's too late to stop 'em now."

"Oh, boy!"

"Yep. Be a bloodbath, one way or another, unless we can head it off. Christ, some of those poor stupid bastards are armed with pitchforks. Here's my notion." I explained what I had worked out with High Mistral on one plane of awareness while I had been reconnoitering on another.

"But surely Jordan has the Gate blocked," Mike objected, "if only from the other direction."

"Hell, no," I disagreed. "Now that Dad's dead, he's not especially interested in harming any people—he just wants to burn Fresh Start to the ground. He'd be just as happy if the folks all scampered out the Gate and into the woods. But they won't," I added grimly.

Sure enough, there was no one near the Gate. The building itself wasn't there—apparently it had been the loud noise I'd heard from my jail cell a few weeks back. There were Guards around, but when they saw us and smelled the incredible number of Muskies they dove for cover. We smashed through the actual gate without slowing, and turned neither right nor left, plunging off the road and onto the field behind the school building, on a direct beeline for Security HQ.

It was a helluva ride. The ground was uneven, and the shocks on the truck were purely decorative. The gravel around the pond nearly killed us and three Technos on foot,

195

but I managed a four-wheel float that carried us past them and between two massive willow trunks. Bark kissed both door handles.

Six Names of Muskies entered and left my mind so quickly as to not interfere with my driving. *(Awaiting your orders)* was all they said, and I gave some to four Names.

There was a milling crowd of armed men and women clustered around behind the security and administration buildings. Crude breastworks joining all the buildings that fronted on the Nose had been recently erected, and trained troops huddled behind them, nervously fingering their weapons. I could see a flanking team trotting cross town, hoping to sneak into the West Forest and make a surprise attack up the bridge of the Nose, but I didn't think much of their chances. Fighting uphill sucks.

The top of the Nose was crawling with Agros, outlined against the dawn sky.

Collaci didn't think much of the flank attack either. As we arrived he was putting his own energy into setting up mortar emplacements behind Security HQ. He looked up to see us coming to a screeching halt, watched the left front tire explode the moment we stopped, grinned briefly and ran toward us.

From around in front of the building came the sound of megaphoned voices being hurled up and down the mountainside.

"Teach'," I cried, jumping from the truck, "let me parley."

"What the hell are all those Muskies doing up there?" he asked suspiciously, eyes and nose on the skies.

"Remember the last time I parleyed for you?" I shot back.

His eyes came back to me at once. They recognized Wendell, and widened. "Let's go talk to Krish," he said, and spun on his heel.

Krishnamurti was kneeling behind the meager shelter of a pile of packing crates in front of the jail, a battery-powered megaphone in his hand. We ran broken-field to join him, but were not fired on. I saw George's face at the barred side window as I passed, and ignored him.

" . . . WAY I SEE IT," Jordan was bellowing through an old-fashioned acoustic megaphone, "SO WHY DON'T WH

TALK THIS OVER? WE BOTH REASONABLE MEN; I DON'T WANNA HURT YO' LITTLE GIRL. WHITE FLAG MEETIN', JUS' YOU AN' ME. WHAT YOU SAY?"

Krishnamurti looked over his shoulder, did a triple-take when he saw me and Wendell, then went inscrutable. "He knows something," Collaci told him, jabbing a finger at me. "I think you should give him the squawkbox."

"Him?"

"He won't sell us out, Sarwar," Collaci said simply. "I trust him."

Krishnamurti started, his jaw dropping. Without a word, he handed me the megaphone. He smelled terrible.

I threw them both a grateful look. "I won't betray you," I lied with great sincerity, and turned to face the Nose. *First time in human memory Teach' ever trusted someone,* I thought wryly, *and of course he's dead wrong.*

"WHAT'S YO' ANSWER, TECHNO?"

"THIS IS ISHAM STONE, JORDAN. THERE'LL BE THREE IN OUR PARTY." I wondered if Teach' had noticed Mike's absence.

"SAID I'D SEE YOU AGAIN SOMEDAY, BOY. WHERE WE TALK?"

"HALFWAY UP THE MOUNTAIN. BOTH SIDES STEP INTO VIEW AT A GIVEN SIGNAL. BY THE TIME YOU REACH DECENT COVER YOU'LL BE IN GRENADE RANGE, SO I GUESS I CAN TRUST YOU. BRING NO WEAPONS."

"I GOT YO' LADY, SO I GUESS I CAN TRUS' YOU. NO WEAPONS IT IS." He said something off-mike, then, "OKAY. SAY WHEN."

"Keep your head down, Wendell," I ordered. "Anybody from *either* side who recognizes you is liable to shoot." I hoped I was giving Mike enough time. "NOW."

Krishnamurti, Collaci and I stepped from shelter. I threw down three weapons, Krish dropped one, and Collaci dropped five. It was a tense moment, and excellent time for a doublecross. We were upwind, so Jordan knew almost at once who we were, whereas he could send four expendable ringers and start blasting at once.

But my eyes and Collaci's immediately confirmed that Jor-

197

dan was indeed among the four who came into view at the top of the Nose. So was Alia.

I watched her carefully as she descended. Her arms were bound behind her back, and Jordan held the bight of a slender wire that ended in a noose around her throat. I saw no obvious signs of ill-treatment or starvation, and relaxed a bit.

That reminded me to relax a bit more, so I began regularizing my breathing. A calm came over me, and I seemed to see myself as from a great height, one of a number of ants scurrying up and down a rock for unimaginable ant-reasons. To be sure, I was about to literally help decide the fate of a planet. But what of that? *What is man—or Musky—that thou art mindful of them?*

I was ready to dicker.

The climb took awhile.

We reached a place where slab boulders afforded cover from both sides, and waited there. Jordan's party arrived almost at once. Alia preceded him, and behind him followed the regulation two thugs, one thin and middle-aged, one surly and young. They both smelled dirty. Jordan loomed above us all.

He was dressed in the same clothes he had worn when I first met him, but the long knife was conspicuously absent. But it was obvious that a sharp yank from that powerful left arm would tighten the wire noose right through Alia's jugular and carotids. He appeared and smelled supremely calm and confident, which was just the way I was feeling. I winked at Alia, and she smiled serenely in reply.

"Figured you was around when I smelled all them sky devils," Jordan said to me. "Seem like they listen to you now."

"Well, Jordan," Krishnamurti rasped, out of breath from the long climb, "what's your offer?"

"Real simple, my man, real simple. You an' all yo' progress-lovers get an hour to clear out. Then I burn the place. After we finish toastin' marshmallows, you get yo' daughter back alive."

I've got to hand it to Krish. He stood right up to the giant. "Don't be a jackass, Jordan. I can't possibly agree to that, daughter or no daughter. Alia knows better and so should you."

"I told him," she said quietly, and Jordan yanked at her ̶ash. I took a firm hold on my own.

"You've got the advantage of position," Collaci pointed ̶ut, inserting a toothpick lazily into his mouth, "but we've got ̶ts more firepower. You can pour troops down into South-̶̶wn without our even being aware of it—but then we've ̶een mining it and booby-trapping it pretty heavily in the ̶st week, and the only map is in my head."

"Yes," I put in, "but he has a fuel train of many, many, ̶any gallons stashed about five thousand yards east of here, ̶ell-shielded, and enough covering fire to get most of it ̶rung out along the whole length of the Nose." Collaci and ̶rdan stared at me, no doubt deducing the source of my in-̶̶rmation. "The fire of God could rain down on us from the ̶eavens without an Agro leaving the mountain. Of course, ̶ur mortars could give Jordan some trouble. The point is, ̶ntlemen, that if it *is* battle you want, it looks like being a ̶̶ody one. A Pyrrhic victory for whoever's left at the end."

"I don't want no battle," Jordan growled. "I don't even ̶ant to harm one soul. But if you gentlemen can't see your ̶ay clear to takin' my offer, I'll jus' naturally cut this lady's ̶roat an' get on with the battlin'."

"You continue to put too much store in the tradition of ̶̶stage holding," Collaci answered calmly. "This time Krish ̶re understands that the stakes are just too high."

"You both put too much store in violent solutions," I cut ̶. "I believe it's time to announce my mutual disarmament ̶oposal."

I stood on one foot, twisted my right heel ninety degrees ̶̶ckwise and brought it down hard before anyone could ̶p me. Behind me to the northwest, there was a sound like ̶ dragon coughing. I hoped Mike had been able to clear ̶lks away from the Tool Shed.

"What the hell was that?" everyone asked at once.

"Excuse me," I said, and rolled up my eyes.

(Now, my brothers!)

Excited shouts came distantly from two directions.

"What kind of shit is this?" Jordan snapped. *"What'd you ̶?"*

I unrolled my eyes and opened them slowly. I showed Jor-̶n my back teeth. "Defanged both sides," I said cheerfully.

199

"Explain!" Collaci rapped.

"That noise was a shaped charge I palmed on you, Teach'. It blew the loading dock off the Tool Shed, which sort o' opens it to the general public." Teach' swore, explosively and filthily. Krish glared at Teach'. "Jordan's fuel train was already kind of open-air. Right now partisans of both sides are being dismayed and consternated to discover that their most essential assets are crawling with about sixty or seventy Muskies apiece. Those Muskies can stay there forever, if need be—and if anybody's stupid enough to fire on them, or if I tell them to suicide, the resulting explosion'll wreck the eggs."

"Double cross," Jordan snarled.

"What it is, folks, is the first sit-in since the Exodus. An' I'm happy to say I've got the drop on all of you. Better stop the fight."

There was a shocked pause, in which the sound of distant shouting was clearly audible again. We heard no gunshots but someone could lose his nerve at any moment.

"HOLD YOUR FIRE," Jordan and Collaci bellowed together, and the shouting stopped.

"My god," Krishnamurti cried, "are you *mad*? Don't you know the equipment in that Tool Shed is *vital*?"

"To what? The lives of men and women? That's what you're proposing to *spend* on them."

Krish fumed on almost incoherently, but I was watching Jordan.

He must have been just as shaken as Krish by the sudden disappearance of his only chance to destroy Fresh Start without a protracted struggle that would cost Pan most of his congregation. But he wasn't showing a thing.

"Where you at, boy?" he rumbled, cutting Krish off. "I don't figure yo' action. What *you* sellin'?"

"Peace," I said earnestly. "Peace and the notion that we can work out literally any dispute if we can all manage to keep from killing each other while we're doing it. We're repeating a pattern of madness that lay upon the world for countless centuries before the Exodus—and *we can break that pattern now*."

"What you mean?" Jordan.

"You and my father disagreed on how the world should be rebuilt. So you set up two political parties and agreed to be lifelong enemies. Along the fringes of both camps, some communication took place—but I'm the first hard-core Techno you've spoken to since you left Fresh Start, and you're the first hard-core Agro I've ever spoken with in my life.

"Can we say that our differences can never be resolved? *Can we say we have even tried?*"

Jordan blinked.

"What are you proposing?" Collaci asked.

"A chance for all the fights to stop 'keepin' on a-comin','' Teach'. All of you must have guessed by now that I'm in contact with the High Muskies. With their aid, we can make what Jordan calls 'the smelly place'—this hunk of real estate we're standing on—a very unsmelly place. Safe, from a medical rather than military standpoint. Clean, the way technology always should have been.

"It will then become essential that we have the wisdom and influence of a pantheist like Jordan."

"What?" chorused Collaci, Jordan, Krish and Alia, each in a different tone of voice.

"With air pollution gone—and by the way, quite a lot of what is now water pollution could be turned into Musky-food at very low cost—one of the few natural controls on technological progress will go. It won't be such an obvious physical nuisance anymore, and so we may take even longer than ever to perceive its psychological and psychic nuisance effect." Krish and Collaci looked blank. "Have you gentlemen actually forgotten what the world was like just before Exodus? I didn't live through those years, but I sure heard about 'em. They were a time of mass insanity, of social institutions and human values shoveled like coal into the boiler of progress with a capital P. Every human furthered his or her own self-interest—even, toward the end, to the exclusion of mate and children—and became bitter and frustrated when he learned that the best this cultural imperative could give him was more than he wanted, needed, or could cope with.

"We tried to grow too fast, and in any direction at all. We don't dare recreate the world we once had, lest we drive

201

another good man to madness. It was not my father's nose that made him visit the Hyperosmic Plague on the world. It was his soul. It cried within him at a whole world growing too fast for itself to bear, in order to stoke an immense and complex machine that fed a few at the expense of many. Why, do you know what Dad's last job was? *Biological warfare.* Making people sick as a strategic policy. No wonder he destroyed his world.

"Jordan can provide the necessary counterpressure to keep us in balance with the planet we're living on, to remind us that we belong in harmony with our world. Just cleaning up the gases we breathe won't do that. He can help us redesign Fresh Start to put it more in harmony with the world we're trying to save—you must admit that the presence of so many dissatisfied customers here today is a hard lesson to overlook. I know you feel a need to expand—there's things we *need* yet that we haven't got. But I tell you there will come a day when we have expanded enough, when we have Progressed as far as we should for the times. And I have a hunch that day might come about midway between when you think it is and when Jordan thinks it is.

"You know steel and glass; Jordan knows earth and water. We must all know *both* sides, if we are to rebuild a world worth living in.

"And you, Jordan," I went on steadily. "You speak of steel and glass as the crutch used by 'weak life-stuff,' that 'Pan woulda scrapped an' started over.' Don't you see that those are fair weapons for life to use in struggling for survival? A man whose body grew too infirm for him to continue as a warrior once wrote a book that turned literally thousands of people on to Pan. He called it 'grokking.' Don't you see that in the kind of world you say you want, most people would be working too hard and suffering too much to grok a damned thing, let alone teach each other how? Don't hate us for what we don't know—*teach* us.

"We can strike a balance, and we can make it work. Or you folks can have your battle if you really feel you must—but if *I* hear any shooting today, my Muskies will self-destruct. You pays the lives of your people and you takes your choice.

"Now, why don't we all go home to my place and have scrambled eggs?"

There was a long silence. I scratched my stump, which was aching for some reason, and caught my breath while I watched them all think. Krish looked highly skeptical, but he was thinking about it.

It was Jordan who broke the silence. "Well, you double-crossed me good, boy, in a way I wasn't expecting . . . but I guess my triple cross still works. *Slim! Eddie!*"

Skinny and Surly reached over their shoulders, and their hands came down with knives in them.

Collaci and I might have been mirror images. Our right arms blurred and two knives whipped across the intervening distance, turned over a careful one and a half times and struck the two Agros hilt-first in the forehead. The Armory commando knife got Surly, and the older Marine issue got Skinny. Both dropped in their tracks.

Collaci and I glanced at each other briefly, a flicker-glance in which a lifetime spiritual agreement was made between us. "'The serene mind avoids killing,'" he quoted briefly, and then we were confronting Jordan.

"Quadruple cross, and we're even," I announced.

"Shit we are," Jordan barked. His right hand came around from his back pocket with a crude pistol, a private-enterprise Musky-gun. "Brought this in case some o' yo' damn sky-devils come along, Stone boy," he said with satisfaction, "but they ain't any in smell. I reckon it'll put a hole in any o' you that come close. Now you call off yo' friggin' sit-in right quick, or I cut yo' lady's throat."

"No!" Krish cried in spite of himself.

"I mean it," the big man yelled, his voice rising. "Worst that happen, I lose my fuel train, but you Technos lose half o' tek-knowledge-y—then I clean up the rest."

My heart turned to ice within me. I *could not* give him what he demanded—and I knew from his eyes that he was mad enough to kill Alia and the rest of us and take his chances on bloody battle.

I stamped my foot on the ground hard and leaned on it, rolling my eyes heavenward.

(Please.)

And High Mistral was at Jordan's face before he could move. The sky-rider was too thin and insubstantial to smell until he had plunged into our midst, but his psychic aura had the impact of a bass chord from some shatteringly vast pipe organ. It shook me, and I was not the focus of its aim. The aged Musky struck at Jordan with the multilevel awareness that was his alien mind, conveying on a hundred levels one overriding, undeniable emotion.

Love.

Jordan shrieked, wasting the air in his lungs, and flung gun and wire rope blindly from him. At once High Mistral retreated to a distance, ignoring the strong north wind. The big Agro sobbed and fell to his knees.

"I'm sorry, Lord Pan," he gasped as he wept. "I didn't know . . . they was . . . your creatures too."

(ALL VIOLENCE) I "heard," (CAN BE AVOIDED BY THE TRULY SERENE MIND.)

(If it's got a right heel to home in on,) I sent back dazedly (Thank you, elder brother.)

And then I ran to my woman.

We were embracing and saying inane things when my subconscious identified some small sounds they'd been picking up from behind me. Someone was coming slowly up the mountain toward us. I turned, expecting to see Wendell, and for one awful second I knew for certain that I had blown every fuse. My heart literally faltered, and there was a roaring in my ears.

"Hello, Isham," my father said. "This time you have truly done well."

"Thanks," I whispered, and fainted dead away.

Chapter Seventeen

Somewhere in there my self tried to go to a place from which it would not be able to find its way back.

But a swarm of Muskies prevented it, and stayed with it until it was well.

Their name was Mistral.

I opened my eyes.

My own bedroom. Late afternoon. Lying on my own bed for the first time since forever. There was my guitar. There was my bookshelf and the twin speakers. There was my hookah.

There was Dad.

It's all been a dream, that's it . . .

Nuts.

"Hi, Dad."

"Hello, son."

Neither one of us spoke again for a long while. I was studying him, looking for something I could not name. I was a long time looking. It's curiously difficult to actually see your father's face, I found—you tend to assume it. But I made the effort, and found whatever it was I was looking for, knew all at once the identity of the last of the three selves in whom I had seen reflections of my own (Collaci, I'd learned on the mountainside, was the second).

By damn, my old man loved me very much. Why hadn't I ever seen that before?

"You're looking good, for a corpse."

"Don't try to get up. You rolled a way downhill after you fell, and gave your head a nasty crack."

"Wouldn't dream of it. I was thinking of skipping school today."

That got a quick smile, gone in an instant. It got me thinking that I'd like to see another. "Dad?"

"Yes?"

"I'm delighted to see that the reports of your death were exaggerated."

This smile was huge, but it dissolved in moments into tears, and we embraced awkwardly. "I'm sorry, Isham," he sobbed brokenly. "Oh, son, I'm sorry."

I discovered that I was weeping too, just as loud. "I felt just *shitty* without a father," I managed, and then I could not speak for crying. We held each other and bawled together for a very long time. It brought me—and him, I knew—back to the night Mama died. *The family's back together again,* I thought crazily, and wept anew.

Finally we disengaged and blew our noses. The honking produced enough comic relief to get us both grinning like idiots, and I decided to turn my mind to practical matters before it melted into mush. "Did you hear my proposal to Jordan?"

He sobered. "I heard the whole performance as I ran from Sarwar's home. He was wired for sound."

"How do you feel about my proposal?"

"Like a damned fool. If I had had your wisdom when I was your age, or even *my* age . . . yes, by all means, let there be peace. I don't want to rebuild *everything* I destroyed."

"Where's Jordan?"

"Gone. After you'd been carried back downhill, I went to him. I begged his pardon for closing my mind to him for so many years, for assuming an uneducated ex-Techno had nothing to teach me, and asked him to join the Council. He was like a man who'd been sandbagged; I wasn't sure he'd heard me. Then he looked up, and his mask was soggy, and he begged my pardon right back. He was so sincere he startled me. He offered to meet the Council over breakfast tomorrow, to 'discuss how he could best help us,' and I said that would be just fine. Your . . . your friend High Mistral . . . er . . . gave us to understand that he would also attend the conference. Then Jordan shook my hand and left, still looking sandbagged, and within ten minutes there wasn't an Agro left on the Nose. Did your Musky friend do all that to him, son?"

"No way," I said. "Jordan did it himself. All he had to do was decide to be afraid, and High Mistral couldn't have touched his mind at all. Since he's a brave man, the old plasmoid was able to get inside and give him a massive dose of the thing whose lack had twisted him, the thing he'd thought he could never have with a bad joke for a face: love. High Mistral forgave Jordan for being bitter; Jordan did the rest alone." I was suddenly very tired.

Dad shook his head. "I hope he feels the same tomorrow morning. Sarwar says I'm insane to trust him."

"He will," I said positively. "When you've waited as long as he has for hope to come back, you don't let it go. Dad?"

"Yes?"

"How's Helen?"

He smiled suddenly. "Very well indeed."

"She thought you were dead, too."

"So did everyone but Sarwar."

"A pretty dirty trick."

"I know. I can't for the life of me understand why she's agreed to marry me."

"Dad! That's *wonderful!* That's . . . sufferin' Jesus, that's terrific. Congratulations, man, congratulations." My head swam, but the fatigue that lay on me lessened some. "I hope you'll both be very happy. I've been wanting to build me a house of my own for a while now."

"You'll always be welcome here, son."

"Not with a family of my own. Alia's carrying my baby."

He blinked violently. And then he smiled again. "It looks as though the congratulations are mutual, Isham."

It was all too much. I hadn't exchanged this much juice with my father in all my twenty years, and while it felt good, the unfamiliar intensity was exhausting. There were a thousand questions I wanted to ask, and the sheer weight of them made my eyelids suddenly heavy.

"Gonna fall asleep," I said faintly. "Hey Dad. What did George say when he saw you?"

"Hollered for five minutes about how nobody tells him nothing around this goddamned place, and then he shook my hand. He said to tell you he's sorry, by the way. Er . . . Helen still bears traces of a grudge, but I'm sure she'll come around."

"I'm sure she will," I agreed groggily. "Me too."

"We all will, sooner or later," Dad said, "Now sleep."

I slept.

(High Mistral?)

(YES, ISHAM?)

(Why did it take our races so long to get together? We could have used you, the past couple thousand years.)

(AND WE YOU. A MINIMUM POPULATION IS NEEDED FOR SATISFACTORY ((untranslatable))ING. THANKS TO YOU, WE CAN NOW MAINTAIN THAT LEVEL, AND OUR ((untranslatable)) WILL BE ((untranslatable)). BOTH RACES WERE SLOW TO PERCEIVE THEIR NEED, AND NEITHER COULD HAVE KNOWN THAT THE OTHER FILLED IT.)

(What you need is always there. Just a matter of finding it.)

(SO I/WE BELIEVE.)

(Nice working with you, pal.)

(LIKEWISE.)

(See you tomorrow.)

(IT IS/WILL BE WELL.)

I was sitting in a comfortable chair by a crackling fire that warmed the autumn night. It felt inexpressibly good to be back home, to know that you Can Go Home Again, and find it a better place than you left it. Mike, Krishnamurti, Collaci and Wendell were ranged about the room in other armchairs, and Alia was at my side. Helen was at the chapel, praying, and I was sure she wasn't alone.

"So you *did* have a sense of smell all these years," I said wonderingly.

Standing by the fireplace, back to us, Dad nodded. "How else would I have detected the bomb in the bathroom? I triggered it with a broom handle and thought hard for several hours before going to see Sarwar. I had been horrified at the loss of your arm, and when I realized the only reason you could have for setting such a trap I had my nose literally rubbed in the fact that it had been my own fault.

"Then I found and played your tape recording.

"I believed that if you learned I had not been killed after all, you would return and stalk me again—no doubt with better success. And so I crept through the dark to Sarwar's home and told him to announce my successful murder." Krish shuddered at the memory. "Since Alia no longer lives at home, I was able to stay out of sight in his attic for weeks, totally alone, eating whatever he brought me. I was trying to come to terms with myself.

"In that time I finally confronted the insanity I had committed upon you.

"You see, son, I never believed for a moment in all these twenty years that Wendell was actually still alive. I had left him unconscious in his laboratory and was convinced I had killed him. I struck him quite hard.

"But I knew that the world would need a target for its horror and fury, and there was a chance that the Hyperosmic Virus could be traced to me. To protect myself, I concocted the story of the archvillain living in exile.

"It seemed only a natural extrapolation of my lie that I should raise up my only son to kill the villain I had created. May God forgive me, son, I used you as an object, a brace to shore up a topheavy lie. I suppose I expected that you would eventually return from New York with the news that Wendell was nowhere to be found. That would have allowed me to reluctantly declare him dead and lay to rest a ghost that had long outlived its usefulness."

"And instead," Wendell said gently, "Isham has raised two ghosts to life." He and Dad exchanged a glance.

"But why did Krish sic Collaci on me, and why didn't you step forward after I first talked to the Council?" I asked.

"Sarwar was trying to force me from my isolation in his attic by having you brought back. Since you had to be publicly fetched, he had to hold a Council. Although I refused to sit on it, Sarwar's plan nearly worked. I decided I would come to your cell that night at midnight. And then when Jordan attacked Fresh Start and carried off you and Alia, and Dr. Gowan disappeared with our only truck, I realized how grossly I had neglected my responsibilities while reflecting on my sins toward you, bathing in new and old guilt. I decided my best move was to make a dramatic public reappearance, with just the right timing to defuse the coming violence. For the second time, Jordan moved before I was ready."

He turned to face me, meeting my eyes squarely. "All of

which only proves that I am too damned old and stupid to keep on bossing this town by myself. Let *alone* negotiating a relationship with several thousand plasmoids. Will you help me, son? Will you help us all?"

All eyes in the room were now on me.

"I'll help you all I can, Dad," I told him. "So will Wendell. So will Jordan. We'll all help."

"Yes, we will," Wendell agreed.

The tension went out of his shoulders, and his eyes were softer than I'd ever known them. He came forward, and Wendell and I both rose to meet him. We three embraced, for a long time. When I looked around, Mike and Teach' and Alia were grinning like demented pumpkins.

I found that I was too.

"Well, people," I said happily, "we've got a treaty to work out with some plasmoids. I volunteer to be interpreter. But for ambassadors, I nominate Wendell Morgan Carlson and the elder Stone."

And a cheer went up from the other four.

An hour later the congregation had dwindled down to Dad and Alia and me, and we were getting sleepy ourselves.

"Well," Dad was asking, "what are you going to call the baby?"

"Jacob Wendell Stone," Alia said at once, "or Anne, after my mother." I nodded.

"Make it 'Wendell Jacob,'" he said, and I nodded again. After a second Alia did too.

He yawned, and the two of us of course did too. "That's the sign," he said. "Good night, you two."

I stood and hugged him again, and Alia kissed him on the cheek. "Good night, Dad," I said. "Don't worry—the world's getting steadily better. Even Teach' has achieved his lifelong ambition—he's unemployed. Why, you can even start smoking your pipe again if you want to."

"*Eh?*"

"Forgot to tell you; half of the Hyperosmic Plague is wearing off its victims. We still have supersensitive noses—but the suppressor mechanism is starting to come back."

"You're joking."

"I lived in New York for weeks without plugs. After the first few hours it was tolerable. In a day or two I began forgetting that it smelled bad at all. And that's in a city over which the High Muskies were somehow maintaining an efficient heat sink, that they'd been using for twenty years as a pollution pantry. Mike could have done it too—if he'd had to, or believed he could."

He shook his head. "Too much for one day."

"It's not important. The point is that things are getting better all the time."

"They are at that," he agreed, and started to leave. He paused and frowned. "One thing I don't look forward to is having breakfast with Jordan tomorrow morning. Will you cover for me, son?"

"Not a chance."

"Oh, I know he has a valid viewpoint, and I concede I could learn much from him. I'll make a genuine attempt to learn from him, too. But the man is such an infernal jackass."

"Dad," I said very gently, "so are you. So am I. So is every person I have ever met, seen or heard of. Only a jackass could have released the Hyperosmic Virus, and only a jackass could have spent his left arm and endless weeks of head banging to learn the simple repeated lesson that fear breeds violence, which don't breed nothing at all but bones. Everybody that ever walked or rode the wind has been a jackass, to X degree, for X periods of his life. But if there's one thing you and I are learning, it's that you've got to learn to live with all those other jackasses, somehow.

"Or else you'll have to die with them."

Epilogue

I became aware that I was lying on my left side, my head socketed in the place between Alia's neck and her firm shoulder. My right ear ached from cold, my feet and hand were numb, my side was stiff, my stump hurt abominably in its harness, and I had to piss something awful. I felt wonderful.

Alia was still in the undermind. I wouldn't have disturbed her if a snake had crawled up my pants. I lay where I was and tasted my joy, marveled at how close it was to pain, realized that in the past night I had climbed another proud and humble step up the ladder of evolution. I felt the bittersweet wistfulness that always comes after one of those exalted moments when you are granted a hazy intuition of the answers to the Big Questions, like *what is all this doing here?* and *why am I here perceiving it?* and *what will it be like to die?*—or at least the certainty that there *are* answers, that everything matters. The wistfulness always follows such moments because that's when you realize that memory banks can't retain moments like that, when you realize that you'll have to keep recreating that certainty again and again, seeking it all your life.

She stirred, and I lifted my weight off her with my new left arm. Our gazes locked for a long moment, and we didn't take the trouble to smile with our faces. Then she did, so I did too.

"I don't remember leaving the house," she said.

"Me either, but it seems we must have."

"Let's pee," she said practically, so we did. It's nice to have two hands for trouser buttons.

The morning was cold and blustery, earmuff and scarf

212

weather, and we had neither. I took off my coat and put it on Alia and we beat it for the house. We were laughing like turkeys by the time we got inside. Not only was relief from the wind welcome, we discovered that we still had a fire going in the big Ashley, and a few chunks of maple later we were entirely thawed. Alia put the triangle on the Ashley and set the coffeepot on it, and I built a fire in the kitchen stove for breakfast, humming as I chopped the kindling. We had finished a ridiculous quantity of sausage and eggs and coffee before either of us felt the need to speak a word.

Alia put down her fork and looked thoughtful. "Isham . . . that was mostly me, wasn't it?"

I nodded.

"I thought you were the family alpha-master."

I grinned and shook my head. "You've got it all wrong, Madonna. I know your alpha-rating is nothing spectacular, but it takes more than alpha to make a telempath."

"A what?"

"Telempath. That's what Mike calls me—and himself, now. A telempath is a person who approaches telepathy by way of empathy. What was once called an Enlightened Man—if only for flashes. High alpha potential *plus* a high degree of empathy *plus* the undermind *plus* a headful of reefer *plus* a serene conscience *plus* a lifelong drive to escape the boundaries of my skull combined to make me a telempath, a man a High Musky could and would talk to."

"But how did *I* . . ."

"I have just invented a new scale, whose measurements can so far only be intuited. I call it the Empathy Scale. On a scale of ten, with me at ten and a turnip at zero, you would rate . . . oh, let's see . . . about fifty."

"Oh." One of the many *little* things I love about my beloved is that she accepts a compliment well.

"I connected with you, then connected us both with High Mistral. But it was *you* who connected us all with little Wendell. Mistral and I wouldn't have known where to look. How to look. You know whatever it is I mean."

"Yes." Her eyes got a faraway look. "God, Isham. He's so little. And so . . . fierce."

213

"Ontogeny recapitulates phylogeny. At this point in his evolution, he needs to be."

She nodded slowly. "Walk me to the smithy," she asked.

"The smithy can wait. The embassy leaves today, remember?"

"Wow, I forgot. It's Monday."

"Better shake a leg or we'll miss them."

"Isham? I know it's easier to talk in the undermind without the chatter of other minds, but why go all the way to New York? They could truck that machine of Michael's closer to home."

"Whose home?"

"Eh?"

"You were there at the Pond, the day after the War ended. You heard Dad speak to upwards of four hundred people— Agros and Technos—telling them the truth, the whole truth, and nothing but the truth. You saw the crowd look at Wendell, and you've seen them looking at him for two weeks now. It doesn't matter what they know with their heads, darling. In their hearts Wendell Morgan Carlson is the lifelong symbol of evil, the ultimately hated man. You may have also seen Wendell looking back at the crowd that day, trembling. Crowds freak him out, and no wonder. New York is Wendell's home—for now, at least. He'll have to build a tolerance to this many people, and they to him."

"The poor old man."

"Poor old man, my eye. He invented the undermind. He's given the race the greatest gift it's had in a couple thousand years, and he has the satisfaction of knowing it. If he doesn't have a mind to *live* with the race, the fact that it ain't sorry to see him go is largely irrelevant. He's no Moses. He's a man who's upset by people—perhaps he's been hanging around Muskies too long. Give him time. Give Fresh Start time. They'll fall in love—if they aren't thrown at each other by their mutual friends."

She nodded. "I guess you're right."

"Can't undo eighteen years overnight. Let's go." We bundled up and left the house. We walked along the Lake shore, cut through the woods past Dad and Helen's place, which

214

was empty. Dawn was just turning the clouds purple from underneath, and the wind was mostly from the south. *Two weeks ago,* I thought, *that would have called for noseplugs. Good old Muskies. Superb janitors. And they sho' can dance.*

We strolled down Main Street, hand in hand. People were beginning to stir in the dormitories; smoke was already twisting from the chimneys as the kitchen crews made ready for breakfast. We heard a baby cry somewhere in the Statler, and grinned together. Mrs. Wilson was just opening the General Store as we went by, and gave us a cheery wave. "Lovely day," she called out happily.

We left the road at the corner of First Avenue, passing behind Security HQ, and paused for awhile at the Pond, watching ripples chase each other in the schizoid breeze. It was indeed a lovely day. I was still dazed from the shock of telempathic contact with my unborn son, but it was the sort of daze that makes you more aware of the world rather than less. I felt kinship with the big weeping willows and the Pond and the breeze itself. My consciousness was more than planetary—it seemed universal. Alia was as much a part of me as my ribcage.

We entered the Ad Building by the back entrance, stopped to listen to Dan O'Connor botch the morning news and weather, and were heading down a corridor toward the front exit when we heard voices raised in anger.

". . . can't you get that through your ugly head?" came Krishnamurti's voice from the Planning Office next to us. We stopped walking.

"Why you pigheaded Hindu!" Jordan's unmistakable baritone blazed. "Anybody but a shit-for-brains could see that gettin' our diet together is mo' important than some kinda sunpower jive. Or don't you . . ."

I knocked and entered, grinning broadly. *The Mayor tours City Hall.* "Good morning, gentlemen."

The two looked sheepish. "Morning, Isham,"

"Mornin'."

"Isn't it a little early for you two to be at it?"

They both began speaking at once, and I waved them to silence. "What's up, Jordan?"

"This fathead wants t' put our juice into more power instead o' greenhouses, an' winter roun' the corner."

"But a solar power plant would make the methane converters obsolete, you imbecile," my father-in-law snapped. "Then you'd have unlimited fertilizer for your damned greenhouses."

"Human shit gotta be composted at leas' a year, meatbrain."

"Hold it," I cut in. "You're both right. Jordan, those methane converters have *big* slop-slopes. The stuff that comes out the bottom *is* a year old or better. Krish, we *do* need greenhouses, and soon—unless you want scurvy again this winter. Rose hips won't grow in snow."

"But we can't do both," Krishnamurti complained. "We can't spare more than twenty people, and either project would take that many."

"Seems like Technos'd be the last choice to build a greenhouse program. Jordan, why don't you recruit some of your Agros? The employment rate for guerrillas is terrible these days."

"Where they gon' live? *Winter* comin' on, dammit."

"I know where you could house twenty men right now, with a day's work or so."

"Where?"

"The hot-shot factory."

"*Oh.*" Both men got thoughtful looks. After a minute they started, looked at each other and headed for the big map on the conference table. "How much prime shit can you deliver?" Jordan asked.

"Well . . ." Krishnamurti began, and I grinned. They wouldn't be at each other's throats for at least an hour now. *I'm a good mayor. Far out.*

"Father," Alia said, speaking for the first time.

"Yes, Alia?" He pulled his attention from the map.

"I've got a problem for you two Planners. You too, Isham."

"What's that?"

"Collaci."

216

No one asked what problem she meant. Within a very few days of the Battle of Fresh Start, Teach' had begun to mope. I'd gotten drunk with him once and stoned with him twice without effect, and two days ago he'd gotten up from his desk, locked the empty and obsolete Security headquarters, and taken to the woods. His house still stood empty.

"I confess I have no solution," Krishnamurti said, his eyes pained. "What use is a general in peacetime?"

"That Collaci is a lot of man," Jordan declared. "Seem like they ought to be some kinda work for him. He need to be useful."

"I love Teach'," I said sadly, "but I'm goddamned if I can see how we can use him efficiently. I offered him a job teaching philosophy while Mike's away, but he said he'd probably find himself kicking the shit out of his students out of pure reflex. He's no good at chaperoning drunks and wife beaters either—what he is, he's the best killer in the world, and we just don't need one."

"He could boss the hunting crew," Jordan suggested, rubbing a hand across his mouth. "We be needin' lotsa meat when the cold come."

"Mmmm—close. But it feels like a Band-Aid on a slashed artery, like that teaching job. Teach' needs challenge, not makework."

"Isham," Alia said suddenly, "he's not what you said."

"Eh?"

"He's not the world's best killer. That's what the times required him to be. Collaci is the world's best survivor."

I blinked.

"By God, you're right," Krishnamurti said.

"And where does Fresh Start need a survivor-type?" she went on.

"Where?" Jordan asked.

"Out there," said Krishnamurti, waving at the window, and his daughter smiled.

"Huh?"

"What do we know about the world?" Krish asked. "There's no one on the airwaves but us—all we know about anything more than a hundred miles in any direction is hearsay and rumor from occasional wandering travelers, and the

217

stories they tell are wildly inconsistent. It appears that there may be a kingdom of some sort growing in the Deep South somewhere, and we know virtually nothing about it. We need another Balboa, another Lewis and Clark, another Livingston. We need a survivor."

"That's not all we need," Alia said. "We need a missionary. Someone has to spread the news that the War is over—that men can and must live with Muskies."

"She's right," I told Krish. "It's all very well to Save Lower New York State. But sooner or later we're just going to have to up and Save the World. And we can't do that if we don't know a damned thing about it. Old Buddhist notion, *hiniyana* and *mahayana*: small boat and big boat. You either become a hermit and try to get enlightened, or you go out and try to get everybody enlightened. We've spent the eighteen years since the world sank in perfecting and tightening up our lifeboat—now it's time to look around for other lifeboats, and for drowning men in need of one."

"Of course," Krishnamurti said wonderingly. "For eighteen years I've been certain that India survived, perhaps better than we, but there never seemed to be time to . . . but there is time, now." His eyes went far away.

"China survived," Jordan asserted. "Bet they could teach us plenty."

"We don't know if California survived," I said dryly. "But it's time we found out. Teach' ain't superfluous—he's our Most Valuable Player. Okay, as Acting Mayor of Fresh Start I order myself to take a couple days off and go offer Teach' an explorer's commission, give him a . . . uh . . . missionary position. I hate like hell to start my administration by cutting school, but I don't believe anyone else could track Teach' but me. Will you two cover for me?" I put just the least shade of emphasis on the "you two."

They glared at each other like rival tomcats, and Alia and I burst out laughing. They glared at us, and then at each other again, and then they broke up too. "We try to keep it together," Jordan said, laughing, and gathered the three of us in his great arms.

"Now design me a solar power plant and a couple greenhouses," I said awhile later. "We've got to go say goodbye to the road company." We left the two Planning Chiefs bent over the map, and got as far as the hallway. I paused then, sent Alia on ahead, and went back to the Planning Office, opening the door quietly. "Jordan?"

He looked up. "Yes, brother?"

I inclined my head. He left Krishnamurti and stepped out into the corridor. "Yeah?"

I tried to say it just right. "Been meaning to ask you. What made you decide to stop wearing that mask?"

He looked startled, ran a finger across his big smashed nose.

"None of my business, of course, but . . . well, I may be stupid, but I'm just beginning to put two and two together about my woman."

He did what I know he thought was smiling, and nodded. "You got it, man. After the Muskies took you from my cave, I got into it with yo' old lady a few times. Couldn't figure why she stop' you from killing me when you had the chance. We talked some. Whoo-*ee*, she said a lot of words I didn't wanna hear. Made me some mad. I got to thinkin', after High Mistral hit me thataway, thinkin' on things she said. I figured the thing she say that make me maddest mus' be the truest." His voice deepened. "Was she say, 'You don't need to hide behind that handkerchief.' Was, 'You should be as proud of that face as you always was of the black skin that was given you by the same Lord Pan.' She got a way of humblin' you an' makin' you proud all at the same time."

"I know what you mean."

"You know, all that time we was talkin' in that cave, I never thought I knew where she was at one time. But I believe it hadn't been for her, that High Mistral never coulda got to me. You know?"

I put my meat hand on his shoulder. "I know. The same goes for me. I'm just beginning to realize what I married."

"Man, you got *lucky*. Be worthy." He squeezed my arm.

"It's a challenge, all right. Later."

"Peace."

I hurried outside. A coffee urn squatted on a folding table beside the heavily loaded truck, and Mrs. Wilson was passing out steaming cups. I traded Alia a kiss for one and turned to face Dad, Helen, Wendell and Mike. As usual, Helen looked away. "So you mugs are our ambassadors, huh?"

"So you're our mayor, huh?" Mike asked.

"I stand foursquare for chickenshit in every pot patch. Seriously, Mike, how's your undermind? You sure you and Wendell can link up with Dad?"

"Yep. High Mistral introduced me to a colleague whose name doesn't translate, and we have excellent rapport. With the aid of the Infernal Gadget, it's a sure thing."

"What's the new Musky like?"

"Reminds me of music a lot. I call him 'Gershwind'."

I winced. "High-ra Gershwind, no doubt."

Wendell spoke up diffidently. "No, actually—'George.' The Rhapsody in Blew."

"Get thee behind me," I groaned. "Alia, have you told Helen yet?"

"No. I thought perhaps you should."

I studied her a moment in admiration. "Just can't help it, can you? Pure instinct."

"I don't know what you mean," she lied.

"Nor I," Helen said. "Tell me what?"

"Well," I said, turning to face her and Dad, "first I have to tell you what Alia and I did last night."

Mike cut in. "Three to one you haven't discovered anything I hadn't tried by your age." Helen blushed.

"You're on," I said, "for an ounce of hash. We spent the night in the undermind, linked with High Mistral, and by the end of the trip it was a five-way hookup."

"I don't follow," Dad siad. "Who were the others?"

"Alia found us the first one. A little squirt named Wendell Jacob Stone." Gasps and other exclamations. "It wasn't exactly what you'd call a dialogue—he seems to be just now growing a central nervous system. But we felt him. Felt his struggle to live and grow."

"My God," Dad said. Wendell's jaw hung down.

"I'm impressed," Mike said soberly. "What was it like?"

"Like meeting High Mistral for the first time, cubed, and then cubed again. Like looking on the face of God."

"You said 'five-way,'" Helen spoke up, meeting my eyes for the first time.

"It was Isham's idea," Alia said quietly. "Since I'd brought us into that plane, he suggested we step up our reception. So we did."

"And . . . ?"

"Helen," I told her, "I'm very glad you decided to leave the sunpower specs with George and go to New York. Dad'll be a lot of comfort to you when the morning sickness starts."

"No!" She started, and then her face went so utterly smooth that fifty years' worth of wrinkles disappeared. Dad dropped his coffee on his feet, looking like a man who'd been kicked in the head by an ox. Mike had a grin a half-meter wide, and Wendell had the other half.

"Yup. There's a little blastula in your belly."

Mike caught the feminine suffix. "A girl, eh?"

"I didn't grok any Y chromosomes. Always wanted a sister."

"Isham . . . oh, Isham! I . . . " Helen was saying. She seemed to have something else to say, but she couldn't get it out. Dad was speechless. "Oh, Isham!" Alia caught my eye, gestured with hers.

"Want to step inside a minute, Helen?" I nodded toward the door of the Ad building.

She thought about it. "No." She gulped her coffee as though it were raw whiskey, and placed the cup carefully on the urn-table. "No, I want to say this in front of Jacob. He's been asking me for two weeks now why I still seem to hold a grudge against you. He says it doesn't make sense to forgive him for what he did to the world if I can't forgive you for what you tried to do to him." She took a deep breath. "He's right, Isham. I've cordially despised you for over fifteen years, now—attempted murder had nothing to do with it."

"I don't understand."

"Your wife does—don't you, dear?" Alia said nothing. "It's your face, Isham. Your face." She got stuck then.

I must have looked stupid.

You look like her, Helen cried, and Dad jumped again.

"Oh, holy shit," I breathed, and Alia smiled.

"You looked like Barbara," Helen repeated, "You reminded me of what she had had, what I thought I could never have. Even when the War ended I despised you, because I thought I could never have Jacob's child. I thought it was too

221

late." She burst into noisy tears, and Dad snapped out of his trance and took her in his arms. His eyes met mine over her shoulder, and I ran to embrace them both. "It's all right, Mother," I said gently, "It's all right. It's over now."

She pulled away from Dad and threw her arms around me, and as I hugged her back I gave Alia a thumb-and-forefinger circle.

Finally all the hugs were over with and the congratulations had all been said and the sun was climbing high in the sky. It was time, as Lightin' Sam says, to bottle it up and go. Mrs. Wilson took her coffee-urn inside. Workers began passing by on their way to Southtown, singly and in groups. Most called out cheery farewells to Dad and Helen and Mike, and Dad thanked them all by name. One or two even said good-bye to Wendell, which pleased me. Won't be such an insuperable PR problem after all. History *can* be rewritten. Wendell acknowledged the few farewells with dignity, not in the least disturbed by their rarity.

I took him by the shoulder with my meat hand, Dad with the metal one. "Okay, you two. Off you go. Listen to your teacher Docta Mike, and do your homework. I don't want to have to boss this burg forever, you know."

"This is the first vacation I've had in eighteen years," Dad said placidly, "and my first honeymoon in twenty-five. I'll be back when I'm damned good and ready." Helen and Mike guffawed.

"That's telling him," Wendell agreed. "I haven't shared a laboratory with your father in a long time, Isham. I haven't shared a lab with *anyone* in a long time. I might get to like it."

"You'd better come back with this crew when they're done," Alia threatened, "or I'll come after you. I want you at my birthing, dammit."

"That I'll return for," Wendell promised. "Isham, you listen to *your* teacher too."

"I do," I said, grinning at Alia.

"Let's *roll*," Mike said, and got into the truck. The other three walked around the front and boarded too, and the big engine roared into life. "Mighty crowded cab," I observed, and Dad, Helen, and Wendell said "No it isn't" in chorus and then laughed together.

"Give my regards to Broadway," I said, and they were gone. The commuters walking along West Avenue cheered as the truck went by. Alia and I watched until it was out of sight, and then linked arms and headed for the Linkin' Tunnel and her smithy.

"You handled that business with Helen pretty smoothly," I told her as we entered the tunnel.

"I just like to see people be happy," she said, a bit defensively.

"I'm not mocking, Madonna, I'm applauding. You can't help being an empath, and you wouldn't if you could. Hell, right now I wouldn't be surprised if you're trying to figure out a way to fix Wendell up with a girlfriend."

"What do you think of Mrs. Wilson?" she asked seriously.